The Reluctant Ascent of Nevil Warbrook in his own words

The Reluctant Ascent of

NEVIL WARBROOK

in his own words

Volume Two

Blood & Water

AVEBURY

Published by Avebury 2023

FOREWORD

Blood & Water is the second of Nevil's journals to be published by Avebury. The title was chosen in consultation with Desmond Catterick, Nevil's agent, and Bernadette Mulvey, Nevil's colleague at Creative Havens and author of 'The Blind Ermine' and 'Moonspinner Summer.'

Nevil Warbrook is best known today for the restoration of Sir Tamburlaine Bryce MacGregor's *This Iron Race.* Originally published in the 1860s, the publishers only accepted the work after substantial revision and Nevil's restored text was an attempt to recreate the work as MacGregor intended for publication by Hare & Drum of Edenborough. *Blood & Water* continues the account begun in *Intimations of Mortality* and ideally should be read alongside book one of *This Iron Race.*

Avebury wishes to express their profound gratitude to Eurydice Glendale, and to Sister Ethelnyd of the Iona Fellowship of Grace, for saving Nevil Warbrook's journals from destruction, and to Nevil's son, Gerald, for agreeing to their publication. We also extend our gratitude to Hendryk van Zelden for his advice and constant support; thank Nevil's agent, Desmond Catterick and Associates; and his friends at Avebury where he lived, and his acquaintances at Creative Havens and Belshade College for excusing the sometimes unflattering opinions expressed herein. To all others mentioned in the text we request your tolerance and understanding.

Nevil Warbrook's journals will continue in *Mésaventures Françaises.*

North Briton

6 May; North Briton Express

The pathetic fallacy is a much-abused literary device. Even MacGregor was not above employing it: consider the foggy night in Winchester when we meet Captain Wolfe, or the stormy hillside on Skye where Bheathain Somhairle rescues the lamb. In both scenes the setting reflects the character's state of mind and today, aboard the train for Edenborough, the turbulent sky reflects my own uncertain mood.

I elected to travel via Lunden. The journey is longer than through the Midlands, but once beyond Lunden (tram from Hyde Station to Jutland Street) one enjoys a better class of train with proper compartments, unlike those ghastly open carriages now in vogue, and a non-stop service to Edenborough. In contrast, the trains of the Midland and Northern stop at every nondescript town between Oxford and The Borders.

The point is this: I can expect an undisturbed journey free of company for the next five hours; I have the window seat, forward facing, and can enjoy the scenery as I write an account of Beltane Eve.

Five hundred words shouldn't be hard, but when one's heart is not in it, it might as well be the Eiger. Peter suggested during the social after Holy Communion yesterday that it might be better not to mention the disappointing collection for the bell fund. I can see his point and Paul's contribution is also best omitted.

"Find something holy in it," was Peter's final comment.

I am considering fire as a motif. Several households accepted an ember on Beltane morning and the parallels with the Paschal Fire are obvious: the fire marking an end and a new beginning. The risen son and the, um, risen sun bringing in the summer.

That marking of change is, I suppose, connected to my business in Edenborough. Shall I continue beyond *Acts of the Servant*, assuming Hare & Drum agree, or accept that restoring the text of *Works of the Master* and *Devices &*

Executions may well harm MacGregor's reputation? When I began restoring the text I only wished to expose Van Zelden's foolish allegations. Now the threat is MacGregor himself.

Time at King James University Library and a visit to Arbinger should clarify my thoughts. At least, that is the intention.

Postscriptum: weight this morning, fifteen stone, seven. I have a week of Scotch breakfasts before me.

Evening; Dudley Hotel, Edenborough

Got into Edenborough, Caldtoun, just before six with my piece for the parish magazine completed. The low afternoon sun blazed down the length of Prince George Street and I walked into a wind cold enough to draw tears, before hailing a cab for the Dudley Hotel where I have been since. It is now ten and I shall soon be abed.

For once I remembered to order an Arbroath Smokie and poached eggs for breakfast. If one forgets, the hotel assumes you want an English breakfast and why would anyone do that in Scotland? I have also requested Dundee marmalade and Haig Tea, neither of which I have found south of the border.

Dinner this evening was excellent, though I must admit to not having much of an appetite. Travel always has that effect on me. Still, the oysters—from Musselburgh, of course—were excellent and served with Italian pasta. This was followed by medallions of veal in white wine sauce, with potatoes dressed with rosemary and rock salt.

The temptation afterwards was to catch a cab to the Royal Mile or York Street, but my current abstinence takes the fun out of an evening on the tiles. Incidentally, I am almost certain my finger is free of infection, but Dr Saunders was very insistent I complete the course of tablets.

Besides, it was then eight o'clock and I had half a mind to get an early night so retired to my room and watched the news on the television. I was just thinking strange the world appears when viewed through another people's eyes when pictures of tanks and petrol bombs got my attention. It was a report from Borneo, or so I thought, but I am now horribly confused. Gerald is, or I had supposed, in Borneo but the report had an interview with an Anglian consul in somewhere completely unpronounceable but apparently the capital city of where the coup is happening. Then I recalled Gerald had given Edith and me an address for emergencies and I'd tucked it in my wallet. Anyway, it turns out the monkey sanctuary where he's working is in Northern Sumatra, which may or may not be in Borneo, but crucially the telephone number is the Anglian consulate in Jakarta.

I'm not sure whether to be confused or relieved but as I am not persuading the Dudley to let me telephone Jakarta it will have to wait until next week.

Tartan

7 May; Cavendish Rooms, Edenborough

It is unwise, and certainly un-Scottish to spend what one has yet to earn, but as I shall be handsomely paid for the canal gig at the end of this month and don't get to Edenborough as often as I would like, it is a golden opportunity to redress a sad lack in my family history and in my apparel.

My mother, as I may have mentioned, is a proud MacStrangie of the Morayshire MacStrangies. Historically, her family owed allegiance to the Innesses, but being few in number and without lands the MacStrangies have no regalia or insignia of their own. Until a few decades ago that would be that, but the passing of the Clan Registration and Provisions Act in 1977 ended the strict regulation of the clans—always intended to humiliate and impoverish them so they would be less inclined to revolt against Edenborough—and now anyone who can prove Scottish heritage can wear a tartan of their choosing, so long as it is not claimed by any other family or clan.

Beavers on Carnegie Street is the place to go. It is not as storied as Jameson's on the Royal Mile—kilt makers to royalty—nor as cut-price as Scotch Threads behind Caldtoun

Station, but does a decent job at an almost affordable price.

Of course, I am only half Scottish—Daddy was as English as toast and marmalade—but I was prepared to prove my right to wear a tartan.

Beavers is a rather small establishment when viewed from the street but, like many properties in the Old Town, what it lacks in frontage it makes up for in depth. A bell rang as I entered and a tall, distinguished gentleman in full Highland dress looked up from the counter.

Greetings were exchanged.

"I appreciate I sound as English as custard-creams," I said, "but I assure you I am Scottish on my mother's side. And I would like to honour her family with a tartan."

"Her family, sir?"

"MacStrangie. They are from Morayshire."

"I am unfamiliar with the name. Do you have any documentation proving your descent?"

I showed my mother's certificate of baptism and my own birth certificate.

"The MacStrangies swore allegiance to the Innesses," I said. "You have heard of the Innesses?"

He gave me a baleful glance.

"Of course, sir. They are a clan. Your mother's family is of the second rank."

I fancy he had not approved of the passing of the Clan Registration and Provisions Act.

"If my certificates are in order?" I ventured.

"Of course. May I take your measurements?"

He ran a tape measure around my waist and from the waist to my knees.

"Now, a few steps if you will so I may judge your stride."

I perambulated across the room and back again. More numbers were noted.

"Now, the matter of the cloth. This way, sir."

He led me to a large table covered with small rectangles of fabric and overhung with a cat's cradle of yarn in assorted colours.

I had a sinking feeling. It is unfortunate that tartan cloth is traditionally patterned red, green, blue, and yellow, and while the latter were reasonably distinct to me—one being much lighter than the other—I could not tell the reds and greens apart.

"This might be a useful reference. The Innes tartan."

He showed me a pattern that seemed to combine every colour there was in bewildering crosshatching that made my eyes swim.

"Perhaps something less eye-catching," I said. "I have difficulty with greens and reds. Wouldn't be much use as a railway signalman. Or a sailor."

"Do you have any difficulty with blue and yellow?"

"None so far as I am aware. But I think a tartan in only two colours would be a little dull."

He smiled thinly.

"This is the tartan of Clan Fraser," he said laying out a bolt of blue and bright yellow check material. "I think no one would call it *dull*."

"Your own colours?" I tentatively asked.

"They are, sir."

I did not say that in my view it was a pattern better on a table than on a gentleman but suggested it was a little too bright for me.

"The MacStrangies are more reserved," I said.

I was somewhat funking it but then it occurred to me that if red and green were the problem then all I had to do was choose one or the other and then combine it with something else. Blue and yellow were the obvious choices but there were also darker colours and bands of white.

"The green," I said. "I think that is a sober colour. And I like this patterning of darker bands running through it. Then these in yellow. And here needs to be blue."

"It has a distinct resemblance to the Gordon tartan, sir. You might like to reconsider... if I may?" Fraser swiftly arranged the colours in a new pattern. "I think that honours the Innes tartan and has the sobriety you seek."

It was a perfectly inoffensive and pleasing pattern. I asked how long they would need to complete the kilt.

"Is sir in any hurry?"

"I am only in Edenborough for a week. I would hope to try it on before leaving."

"We offer a premium service. It is a little more, but it will be ready by Friday morning."

"Excellent. I shall collect it then."

"You understand there is considerable investment in preparing a bespoke tartan. We would require a deposit."

"Of course."

I had my chequebook out. Fraser rang up the purchase on an ancient till and produced a rubber stamp with the company name.

"If you would make it out for one-hundred and fifty crowns. The balance will be due on collection."

"Balance?"

"Also, one-hundred and fifty crowns."

I swallowed hard, realising I had rather miscalculated, but it was too late now. It was precisely a quarter what I would earn on my week of canal boating, but I suppose one only buys a kilt once in a lifetime.

Fraser took my cheque and pressed a lever on the till. The drawer slammed open and swallowed my cheque. In exchange he gave me a receipt.

"We close early on Friday, sir. Be sure to arrive before four if you wish to try it on. You will want to take these."

I had almost forgotten my mother's baptism certificate and my own papers. I hastily slipped them in my jacket pocket.

"Thank you. Friday it is," I said, and escaped onto Carnegie Street.

A family of the second-rate, indeed! But at least, thanks to Fraser, I have something decent to wear. Lord knows what I might have come up with left to my own devices. I'd have been more MacPopinjay than MacStrangie.

Breakfast at The Dudley was excellent this morning but

the tea and Dundee cake at The Cavendish Rooms are disappointing. I suspect this is a place one goes to be seen rather than to eat. Now, to the university for my talk.

Afternoon, King James University refectory

That went very satisfactorily. An invited audience certainly upped the quality of questions and O'Brien was a surprise attendee. Actually, I'm not certain how he got in: he's hardly a university trustee nor a lecturer and rather old for a student. Of course, the evil rumour that MacGregor practised magick had spread even to the KJU but everyone was respectful, and I took care to remind them that books of magick were only a small proportion of MacGregor's library.

I arrived shortly before one—the talk would begin at half-past—and was met at reception by an undergraduate, name of Futers, Ian or perhaps Iain, hard to tell.

"Would you like tea?" he asked.

"Perfectly fine, thank you. Just had lunch at the Cavendish Rooms. That reminds me. I ought to give you a note of my expenses."

"Actually, sir," young Futers said, "best you take yourself to the bursar after the talk."

"Really? Oh well. Then you had better show me the lecture hall."

"This way," he said with evident relief. I assume he is not trusted with financial matters, but I had hoped the finances would be settled before my talk. One's bargaining position is so much better.

The hall was modest, though perfectly clean and tidy.

"We are a little early," Futers said. "But we have had a delivery of books."

"Ah. That's very considerate of them."

The table beside the lectern had a jug of water and a glass on a plastic tray and a large pile of *This Iron Race, book one*.

"You didn't request these?" Futers asked.

"No, not at all. But it is handy having them here."

"We're not entirely certain how they did get here," he said. "No one has signed for them, and reception have no knowledge of a delivery. I assume they are in order?"

"Order? I should think so. Let me see."

I picked one up and quickly pronounced it was exactly as I expected it to be.

"I suppose if anyone wants a signed copy it would be perfectly all right, wouldn't it?"

"Perhaps after your talk."

"Oh, oh yes. But I am only being paid expenses you know."

Futers seemed not to approve talking of money—I suspect an un-Scottish lack of entrepreneurial spirit—and wonder if he will leave university equipped for the real world. But the arrangements were entirely suitable.

The books had that lovely inky smell fresh from the printers. I suppose Hare & Drum had them delivered and if my encounters with O'Brien are anything to go by I'm not surprised no one noticed their arrival.

"If you wait in the anteroom until the audience is seated, then I can introduce you," Futers said.

"Of course, of course. Are you an enthusiast of MacGregor?"

"Not really," he said with a trace of awkwardness. "I'm reading applied maths and physics. More of a science person. Helping at events is part of my bursary."

"Making yourself useful, I approve. There isn't the divide between arts and science you might suppose."

"I play keyboards in a Gaelic new-wave metal band," he said. "A lot of maths in music. I'm just not into old books."

"Oh, I see," I said without seeing at all. I suspect Gaelic new wave whatever it is wouldn't agree with me, but young Futers had a good point about the mathematics of music. Though I think one can detect it rather better in Bach than in whatever Gaelic metal is.

The anteroom was a perfectly bland little chamber with a comfy chair and after a few moments sitting I was reminded of the immersion chamber at Summerhill. It had the same calming atmosphere, though blessedly without being up to one's neck in bathwater. I fear I may have nodded off and young Futers had to shake me awake.

"Sir. We are ready for you. I'll give a brief introduction and then welcome you on stage."

"What? Oh of course. Awfully peaceful in here."

"Used to be part of the university chapel," he said.

"Ah, something of the ambience remains. Why ever did they get rid of the chapel?"

"We have a new omni-faith room," he said. "This was too small. About five minutes?"

"Right you are. If you could just pour a glass of water for me I'll be right along."

Futers left me, leaving the door to the hall open, and after a few moments I stood and moved to the entrance where I could hear him. After the inevitable squawks and whistles from the sound system it calmed down and I waited until I heard my name and entered to polite applause.

"Thank you, thank you so much. And thank you, Ian, for the introduction."

That's always the awkward bit. I'm much happier when I get to the meat of a talk.

"My talk is on MacGregor's Library but perhaps I ought to begin by saying what that actually means."

The stage was rather well lit, but the slope of the auditorium was mostly in shadow, apart from lights above the doors marked with a luminescent figure apparently running for their life. I tried to focus on the front row who were more or less visible to me in the overspill from the stage lighting.

"MacGregor's library at Arbinger was unlike the library here. Much of the KJU's library was acquired through bequests, one being the subject of today's talk since almost all of MacGregor's library at Arbinger is now here. But a library of donated books is necessarily replete in some areas of knowledge and incomplete in others. One is likely to find rather more on grouse shooting than on, say, applied mathematics."

I intended to smile at young Futers as I said that, but I couldn't see him in the darkness of the auditorium and fear I may have just looked foolish.

"Equally, a state library has an obligation to provide books the public will find of interest or amusement, but other than a section on local interest it has no character of its own."

I got to my point, the nature of MacGregor's library.

"The subject of my talk was a very different kind of library. There is none of the arbitrariness of the library here but equally no need to serve general interests. Instead what we have, or rather had at Arbinger, was one man expressed in books. I mean that to know MacGregor's Library is to know MacGregor, and by that I think you will understand that that is not the man Hendryk van Zelden, and others wish to pretend he was, but the real man. A man, when judged by his books, rather more interested in the management of a Borders estate than in thaumaturgy."

This produced a faint stir of interest, and feet, but I held up a hand and announced I would be taking questions only at the end of my talk.

The air was dry, and stopping to wet my throat I noticed the water in the jug shaking slightly, as though disturbed by a heavy tread. I barely had time to register it before the table collapsed, taking jug, water, and about forty copies of *This Iron Race* with it. It was fortunate I had the glass in my hand or that would have gone as well.

Futers emerged from the gloom with profuse apologies. After righting the jug he picked up one of the books before the water reached it but then stopped abruptly as though stunned.

I had begun stacking books clear of the puddle.

"I say, are you all right?" I asked.

Futers shook his head and then agreed he was.

"Static electricity," he said. "Bit of a shock, that's all."

"Apologies everyone," I announced to the audience. "If you'll give us a moment."

There was a lot of coughing and shuffling of legs, suggesting quite a few were rather glad of the break, but we had the remains of the table offstage shortly and the books stacked safely on the floor. Fortunately, the water hadn't spread too far and after Futers apologised a second time, I continued outlining the various subject headings at Arbinger, all of which is far too tedious to repeat here.

The questions afterwards where mostly ones I have heard before except for one young woman—a student I suppose—asking what chance there was for a reconciliation with Van Zelden. I was taken aback and didn't reply at all well.

"I'm not certain about a reconciliation as things have never been what you would call conciliatory. We got off to a bad start, for which I blame him, and have never recovered. In fact, as you probably know, the reason I am restoring *This Iron Race* is to disprove the nonsense he's been saying about MacGregor."

I didn't admit that my reasoning was looking increasingly threadbare.

"But he did praise you, in Lunden," she said.

The lights had come up in the auditorium for the Q&A and she looked entirely personable and intelligent.

"At the theatre, you mean? Yes, he did, though the whole experience was excruciatingly embarrassing. But alas, no reconciliation is in the offing."

"But you did go to see his show."

I could see a few faces turned towards my inquisitor. She had red hair, possibly dyed rather than natural, and reminded me of Alexandria at the Glastonbury Haven. Neither Alexandria nor Glastonbury were happy memories and I felt a little bit defensive.

"I'm sorry, this is starting to feel like an interrogation. I'm sure others have questions to ask. But yes, I saw his show and was impressed, along with thousands of other people.

He is still wrong about MacGregor. Speaking of which, assuming we have saved them from the flood, I have editions of *This Iron Race* which I can sign for anyone interested."

The rest of the questions went easily and afterwards I had a healthy queue for signed copies and not a one was left.

Young Futers closed proceedings for me, then joined me in the anteroom.

"I'm so awfully sorry," he said.

"For the table? Oh, these things happen."

"No, I meant for that woman. She was so rude."

"You think so? Don't pay it any attention. Besides, who knows what the future holds, eh?"

Afterwards, as Futers was showing me to the bursar's office I became aware of a presence at my shoulder. After a moment I turned to find O'Brien a few steps behind. I had the impression he was limping.

"Ah, we meet again," I said. "Thank you for the books. Sold like hot cakes."

"I'm sorry?" Futers asked.

"My publisher, O'Brien."

"Oh. Sure. Bursar's is along this passage on the left. Got to go."

"Thank you."

Futers left. We had overrun by several minutes and he seemed happy to get away.

"As I was saying, very good move. Sorry we missed each other at Easter. Heard the meeting was cancelled."

He muttered something like an apology, but I may have misheard. It was rather hard to get a look at him as we were walking, but I almost swear someone had blacked his eye. Braver man than me, whoever it was.

He asked about the second volume, and I assured him all was well—which it isn't—and I expected to see him at Midsummer to hand over the manuscript. That seemed to satisfy him as he promptly bowed and said farewell. It was an odd gesture, and comical in one so tall, but I'm glad he didn't offer to shake hands.

Happily, the bursar's office accepted my receipts for train ticket, lunch today, and my hotel bill and I have a cheque in my wallet. My own money, of course, as it is simply reimbursing my costs, but I now have a few days in Edenborough all my own and paid for.

LETTERS

Early evening; Dudley Hotel, Edenborough

The atmosphere in the King James University Library always sets my nose twitching. I suppose it is only the dryness of the air, but I like to imagine it is suppressed excitement at the thought of a discovery among its antique tomes: a new page revealing a private letter secreted long ago as a bookmark, or the discovery of a scrawled marginale, or perhaps a secret compartment cut into the pages.

And discoveries there were today, though one doesn't expect them to be handed on a platter, so to speak, and I hadn't dressed for two hours in the 'cell' surrounded by iron bars like a caged animal. My fingers were quite blue by the time I emerged, and my feet have still not recovered.

I arrived at three. Solomon Drake, the head librarian, was not there and instead, a woman of thirty or so in a loose-fitting skirt and blouse took my name and the numbers of the boxes I wished to study.

Nothing untoward happened until she came back with five boxes and asked if I would like to see the supplement.

"Supplement? I believed these were all the Northwood material relating to the period."

"The supplement relates to these years. The material was recently donated to the library, and we have not had time to collate it or enter details in the catalogue."

"Then, yes. I should be greatly honoured. I may even be able to help with the collating. Please, bring it to me."

"I'm afraid I can't do that sir. We suspect some of the material has thaumaturgical properties and until cleared for public access it is in the..."

"RMD," I said deflatedly.

"You are familiar with it?"

"Regrettably, yes. Has anyone else looked at it? To your knowledge, that is."

"No sir. We have only held it a month."

"May I ask who the donor was? It would be intriguing to know if there is more material."

"The donor wishes to remain anonymous. Would you care to use the depository now? It is available until we close."

I could hardly say no, even though I was neither mentally nor physically prepared. I had also noticed a lapel badge on the woman. She was a Mrs Broody.

"If you wait here, Mr Warbrook, I'll arrange for someone to help you."

"Cannot you escort me?" I asked.

Mrs Broody blushed in such a way I thought she had completely misunderstood my intentions.

"I only mean it would be more convenient, surely."

"I am three months pregnant. I am forbidden to enter the RMD."

"Oh! Yes of course. Far too hazardous in your condition. I mean in your child's condition. I shall wait here."

Mrs Broody went for assistance. The only other attendant was a young chap, probably a post-grad student, checking returned books for damage before shelving them.

"Don't suppose you've seen Mr Van Zelden here recently?" I asked him.

"Is he a member, sir?"

"I believe so. Yes, he must be."

"Then I cannot reveal that, sir. The activities of members are confidential."

"Ah well. I suppose if I have to sign the book I shall see if he has attended recently."

Mrs Broody returned with an older man.

"This is Mr Valentine," she said. "He is standing in while Mr Drake is away."

"I hope he isn't unwell," I said.

"He's researching ancestral knowledge among the

Kalahari Bushmen," she said, as though this was no more extraordinary than a week in Brighton.

I couldn't quite picture Solomon in a safari suit, but Mrs Broody was plainly honest.

"I hope it does wonders for him," I said.

"If you would sign here, Mr Warbrook."

Mr Valentine produced the book from under the desk. I saw the student peer curiously at it but then glance away as the covers creaked open. I scanned the page without appearing to examine the names too closely. Van Zelden's was not among them. I entered my name and the date and time in the space provided. Valentine completed the entry with the record number of the material I wished to examine: the so-called supplement.

"And do you still require these?" Valentine asked of the five boxes.

"Please," I said. "I shall find time later."

The boxes were set aside, and Valentine led me to the door of the Reserved Manuscript Depository.

"Are you familiar with the rules for using the 'cell'?" he asked.

"Mr Drake has brought me here many times," I said.

Valentine unlocked the iron door and escorted me through before deciding that my familiarity did not count for much and repeated everything Solomon Drake had told me: keep the door of the cage closed; return the papers and manuscripts to the boxes after I had finished; only then leave the cage and ring the bell to be allowed out of the room.

My concern was temperature as the RMD is cold as a crypt and already the chill was seeping through my shoes.

"If you would wait in the cage," Valentine concluded. "I will be but a moment fetching the box from the strong room."

I took my seat inside the iron cage and as I waited I recalled that Van Zelden also suffers from colour-blindness. It is an odd coincidence given our common interest in MacGregor and visits to the Reserved Manuscript depository, but as I have the psychic perception of a gatepost one condition plainly does not determine the other.

Valentine returned with a copper-lined box which he put on the table before me. He paused a moment, as though deliberating whether to remind me of the rules a second time, but then patted the box.

"We are a little short-staffed. Mrs Broody will be unable to let you out of the room—the proximity, you understand—and it may take a few minutes for someone to respond to the bell."

I understood and said that I doubted Lady Helena's correspondence—for that is what I was certain lay in the box—could contain anything harmful.

Valentine exited the cage and closed the door. I waited—as required—until he exited the main door before opening the box.

Disappointingly, it was only half full. The most interesting artefact was a clothbound notebook with corners rather worn and frayed. Under it was a brown envelope containing several handwritten letters in an ornate hand and much older than the envelope.

I began with the notebook, immediately recognising Lady Helena's handwriting. To my disappointment it seemed to be a register of expenditures at Arbinger. After MacGregor's death Lady Helena grew increasingly cautious about money and the costs of running the home were considerable, but not finding anything of interest I turned to the letters.

Immediately there was a change, almost tangible, not least because the handwriting was tantalisingly familiar to me, even though I could not put a name to it. Unlike Lady Helena's small and precise hand, this had exaggerated descending and ascending strokes and wide spacing between the lines. There were also numerous underlinings and words interposed between words, suggesting it was written in haste by a man framing his thoughts as he went. For some reason I did not doubt the writer was male.

Dearest Lady Helena. Is it really a whole year since last we exchanged news? I am again in Italy which agrees with me in everything except satisfying my attachment to Wahnfried...

I realised with a jolt that the handwriting was indeed familiar, but for the language which had the awkward phrasing of a man trying to write exceedingly well in a language with which he was not fully conversant. There was also the mention of Wahnfried which I recognised without being able to place.

I read to the end and the mystery was solved: the signatory was Richard Wagner.

Previously I had only read his letters in translation from the German. Here Wagner was writing in rather quaint English, and it took me a moment to recall that while MacGregor spoke excellent German and the two had corresponded in German, Lady Helena only spoke English and French.

The letter mentioned Wagner's work on *Parsifal* (written as *Parzival*), his last opera, and of course the Italian connection placed it late in his life when poor health led him to escape Germany.

His health was a preoccupation in the letter, as were references to Lady Helena's relative youth—he was her senior by twenty years—but I could not determine Wagner's purpose. His letter was a reply to her but what it concerned I have no idea. Presumably, her letter to him is somewhere among his correspondence at Bayreuth, assuming it has survived at all. Wagner concluded with a curious comment that "provision will be made should you require it, but I cannot hope my legacy will long survive me, tho beit I have strived so. Therefore, regrettably I cannot promise a permanent refuge."

I confess I did not understand it at all, except that Lady Helena had asked something of him and he could not promise to assist.

There were other letters from Wagner, including several in German addressed to MacGregor, but then I found something altogether more interesting: a letter in French from Félicien Alberix to Lady Helena. Alberix had included a date and address, and we were now in 1905, only some two years before Lady Helena's death, when she was anxious to find safekeeping for MacGregor's papers—this was before King James University approached her. Given the fair copies of *This Iron Race* and its sequels were not at the KJU Library I had long held a suspicion that Alberix, who had published MacGregor's *A History of Scottish Magick* some decades before, might have taken them into safekeeping, but never found proof.

The letter began with warmth and concern, and I had to remind myself that this was from a seventy-six-year-old man to a woman in her eighties, and ended with Alberix promising to do all he could and instruction to await his arrival in Edenborough.

This, I was certain, was it. Why else would Alberix travel so far unless it was to acquire something precious?

I scribbled down the details I might need to correlate Alberix's letter with Lady Helena's diaries and replaced the letters inside the envelope. I knew I had much more still to examine (that notebook may yet yield something) but my two hours were almost up, and I was desperate to warm my hands and feet. Alas I had no time to examine the contents of the box files so they will have to wait till tomorrow.

Of course, this is only the beginning for I must follow the trail, certainly to Paris and the *Bibliothèque de la Sorbonne* which houses copies of all France's literature from the nineteenth century onward, but I have a nose for such adventures.

It is enough excitement for one day and I am determined to risk my finger dropping off and celebrate on the Royal Mile.

Nota bene: where is the thaumaturgical material that worried the library? Must ask tomorrow.

8 May; Dudley Hotel

There was still an hour of daylight remaining when I arrived on the Royal Mile last evening and the pavements were filled with tourists carrying large black cameras hugger-mugger around the obnoxiously loud tour guides.

It was like running through a cluster of auction houses, each with its auctioneer babbling hysterically. Relief to get to the Stuffed Cock even if it didn't have the comfort it has on a dark dreich night—I think I shall never get used to the extraordinary day length one experiences at latitude in summer.

"An Owl Service, make it a double," I said at the bar.

"With ice?"

"Do I sound American?" I replied.

It's not as if it's warm out. Quite chilly actually. And ice takes the taste off a good whisky.

I paid for my whisky and sat contentedly with the day's copy of *The Scotsman*. Parliament at Holyrood was as unruly as ever and the *Prìomh Mhinistearan na h-Alba* his usual ineffectual self. Someone had sighted a flying saucer over the Isle of Skye (which experts dismissed as an unusual cloud formation) and there was an admonitory article about pickpockets in Edenborough preying on tourists. I amused myself wondering what Bartholemew Crick and Jack Merkin might make of modern Edenborough. Not much I suppose, though the pickings are surely as deep and perhaps richer.

Of course, that assumes Crick and Merkin survive the restoration of *This Iron Race*. So far no significant characters have gone missing in my editorship, but it is not impossible. I believe *This Iron Race* would be poorer without them.

I ordered a second whisky, and then a third. I promised to be good thereafter and see out the rest of these blasted antibiotics. Darkness had fallen and someone lit the fire in a cheerful inglenook with granite lintel. I finished the newspaper and made notes of what I hoped to see at Arbinger on Thursday. Then it was well past ten and time to leave.

The change from earlier was remarkable. It was positively cold out on The Mile, and I wasn't dressed for it. I hurried along looking for a taxi but was distracted by a crier announcing a tour of the wynds and closes. I had seen them before, of course, but not since editing *This Iron Race, volume one* where Paavo Jukola wanders into them. Wynds, incidentally, are pronounced as in winding a clock and so named for their convoluted progress, while Closes are the small courtyards linked by the wynds.

The crier was a tall chap made taller by a stovepipe hat with the end of it knocked out like the cap of a winkle.

"Tip MacCannie's tour of Auld Reekie's ghastly ghaists," he cried. "One hour on the hour. Your safe return cannot be guaranteed."

One does foolish things at times and there may have been a lack of judgement from overindulgence at the Stuffed Cock when I joined the group gathered beneath a lamppost. Most appeared to be young French ladies, presumably attending one of the colleges or on an educational tour, and the wait was made bearable by the vent of an air-conditioning unit bellowing out warm air.

"Plenty more spaces," MacCannie cried. "That'll be ten crowns, sir. Bargain if I do say so."

I was minded to say that I would determine how much of a bargain it was, but having spent thirty crowns at the Stuffed Cock another ten made no difference and I would be back on the wagon and sobrietous tomorrow. Besides, I couldn't help liking the chap's bravado.

Eventually, the clock struck eleven and we moved off, passing down a wynd between two buildings whose upper floors leaned over the alley like furrowed brows.

Instantly we were in near darkness and forced to follow Tip MacCannie's torch as it flickered through the night. The French ladies were all cheerful and full of energy—I'm not sure what MacCannie thought of them but any ghastly ghaist would be sure to avoid them—and MacCannie himself was no slouch. In any event I was soon at the rear of the group and then trailing. Eventually I tripped over a shoelace and on retying it found I was alone.

City lights turned the crow-stepped gables a dull brown but down on the cobbles all was dark.

"Err, MacCannie? Mr MacCannie?"

My voice was muffled by the walls, and I suspected I had alerted every footpad to my presence. Every modern-day Bartholemew Crick and Jack Merkin was now primed to take my wallet and leave me, if I was lucky, my life. I walked on, groping along the wall. Glancing up as much as along, trying to find a familiar star to tell my way.

Exasperatingly, there were snatches of drunken singing which must surely have come from the Mile, but it was impossible to tell if it was before or behind me.

The clock at Tron Church chimed the half hour. If only I had thought to bring a torch. A torch is essential at home, but here in the city I thought to have no need. Then, like a moth, I gravitated to a street lamp. An old-fashioned gas-mantled affair, it hissed like an angry snake and actual moths clung to its glazed panels. An enamelled street sign declared this was Mab's Close. I had only the vaguest idea where that might be. What I did recall is that for all their convolutions, each wynd does not intermingle with any other but winds from the Royal Mile at one end to Market Street to the north or Cowgate to the south. Of course, I could not recall which side of the Mile we had left from, but I knew if I continued in one direction eventually I must reach a lighted road.

Except, that isn't what happened. Instead I became familiar with the same lamppost twice more. I knew it was the same because the advertisements of ladies of no repute pasted about its post did not change in name or promise.

A black cat wandered into the glow cast by the lamp but, despite entreaties, refused to lead me to safety. I do not believe there were any ghosts, and certainly no striped tents of the booth-scryers, but perhaps either would have been welcome company. Then, after another ten minutes of chilled wanderings I heard a familiar voice and a torch danced into view like a will o' the wisp. Tip MacCannic had returned.

He only glanced at me a moment and doffed his battered hat, but the gaggle of mademoiselles and mesdames gathered round and swept me along and with various noises claimed I was, 'ze comeecal leetle Inglishman oo vaneesh'ed' and how they were glad to have rescued me.

I did not demure. Frankly, I was grateful for the attention and more grateful still when we emerged onto the Royal Mile at the exact point we had left it.

I said my farewell to France's finest and to Mr MacCannic and added to the evening's expense with a taxi back to The Dudley Hotel.

Lunchtime; Buttery, Holyrood

A pot of tea and a scone here cost very nearly as much as an entire lunch at any other establishment in the city, but it is convenient, and I must eat something before venturing into the hills.

It's all very unexpected. I had anticipated a bit of shopping in Old Town this afternoon—I must get Mrs Pumphrey something for looking after the cats—and calling on the Scottish Records Office for a spot of genealogical research, but this morning's visit to the Reserved Manuscript Depository has been surprising.

I knew there must be more to Lady Helena's notebook than met the eye. True, I found no revelations in the notebook itself, but tucked inside the back cover was a small envelope, obviously of some age, and inside that a folded document dated 1847 from the Register of Land Holdings. I didn't need to guess what must be inside and gingerly opened up the document taking care not to crack the fold lines. It was, as I assumed, title deeds but the surprise was the location and that is why I will be dodging rain showers this afternoon.

There are three reasons why this is a surprise. The least is that I believed the last of MacGregor's landholdings in the city were sold after Lady Helena's death. The greater is that this holding is within the royal park at Holyrood. But the greatest is the back of the title deed had a runic symbol: the so-called Helm of Awe and a name, also written in runic symbols. Since such symbols are only as powerful as the skill with which they are drawn, I had few qualms about copying them into my notebook, along with the date and other details of the land holding, with a hope to get expert advice on their meaning.

One assumes King Charles must have been consulted on the sale of an acre of the royal park but why he assented is a mystery. MacGregor had been Master of The King's Revels from 1853 to shortly after Lady Madeleine's death when he resigned the post, and again a few years after that until he resigned due to ill-health. Given there was a personal bond between them, King Charles may have granted the land as a favour, but that invites one to wonder why MacGregor wanted an acre of Holyrood Park.

I shall finish the tea and go exploring.

Strange encounter

Early evening; Dudley Hotel

The bright weather did not last long—it was ever thus in Scotland—but I turned up my collar and continued on. Sensibly, I had worn my old coat and it kept out most of the wind, even if it had no real protection against the rain.

I had copied the map from the title deeds and knew it lay to the west of Hunter's Bog—the damp defile north and west of Arthur's Seat—and below Creag nam Marbh, or the Crag of the Dead, which frowns over the city like a great basalt wall. It was, I suppose, barely a half mile and ought to have taken fifteen minutes or so, but the miserable weather and the damp had a chilling effect and I seemed to be walking slower and slower. The heights were fixed in the air, even as the clouds rolled over them, and the small lochan at the centre of the bog remained lodged at the end of my elbow.

I am the least superstitious chap you can imagine but eventually, if only out of frustration, I stopped, took off my coat and turned it inside out before continuing. Admittedly,

I had not gone many yards before I turned it right-side-out again, but it seemed to do the trick and the lochan unpinned itself and I made progress beyond the water before climbing onto the rear slope of Creag nam Marbh.

The map suggested that if I kept the crags to my left and the peak of Arthur's Seat directly behind me, I should come to the mysterious acre of land, but that depended on the modern path being the same as that on the map, and there were sixteen decades intervening. It was confused by there now being two paths—one in the valley floor and the other, where I was, partway up the western slope. On the map only one was marked. Or at least I had noted only one. Stunted birches and thorn grew among the gorse but apart from the knoll of Arthur's Seat the dominant landscape was unkempt grass strewn with buttercup and purple loosestrife. On a sunny day it would have been delightful, but the grass soaked my trouser legs.

Nothing in that entire vista looked like a wall or any other feature that might indicate a boundary, though I suppose there might be something hidden under the gorse.

I was interrupted in my survey by a man walking a shaggy dog. He was tall and bearded and carried a walking stick. A hat kept the rain off his grey head and the collar of a black coat was turned up extravagantly into two peaks, like miniature black wings.

"Are you lost?" he asked.

"No, no. I know where I am."

"You appear lost."

He lifted his head into the wind and as the shadow of his hat brim fell away I saw he was blind in one eye. Not even an eyepatch, just a blank, dark socket. It gave me a turn.

"I have walked up from Holyrood," I said.

"I have walked from the Dead," he said.

"Creag nam Marbh," I said. "I know its meaning."

I decided nothing ventured nothing gained and there was a chance the chap's local knowledge might be useful, so I asked if he walked here regularly.

"My home," he said with a broad arm. "I am Merrowey."

"Nevil," I said with a pat on my chest. "Nevil Warbrook. No reason you'll have heard of me." Nor I you, I thought, but kept that to myself. "I'm trying to find a plot of land. It's supposed to belong to someone. I have seen the title deeds but can't see anything on the ground."

I didn't bother to mention MacGregor as Merrowey hardly looked like a reading man. I only hoped he might have heard a story concerning a plot of land not part of the Royal Park, It seemed such an anomaly I couldn't believe no one knew of it.

"The king's," he said, again with the same gesture.

"Yes, that's what I thought," I said. "Only this patch, an acre somewhere near here, belongs to someone else."

He turned sharply and I caught the full force of that empty eye. It seemed accusative, even more so than its alert companion.

"The king's," he said again. "As far as the eye can see."

This was hyperbole of course as the city and the rainswept firth were in sight, but I did not quibble. The dog shook itself vigorously and this seemed to bring the man to action, and he passed by me and turned from the path onto the rough ground below Arthur's Seat itself.

I took a last look round. Merrowey had vanished among the rocks and there wasn't a soul to be seen. I felt unaccountably alone and rather chill. I suppose it was just the dourness of the scene and the weather. I began walking back but shortly a distant noise, like snarling dogs, caught my attention. Moments later a pack of rough-riders appeared, and I had to step smartly from the path to avoid them. There must have been a dozen: all youths, I think; lean and grim-faced and only concerned with their race. Harum-scarum they were, sending up a shower of mud and grit. I was very nearly spattered by filth.

It was all over in far less than a minute, but I spent the rest of the walk in their tyre tracks until I reached the road.

Caught a bus back to town and returned to the hotel.

Want to dry my things as I am out again this evening. If the MacGregor Estate really does own an acre of the Royal Park I hope they have better luck finding it.

Night Fair

9 May; Caldtoun Station

The Galashiels train is delayed twenty minutes. I have telephoned Diane Dickinson to tell her I will be late arriving. The delay is annoying as I dashed through breakfast to be here on time. One should never rush an Arbroath Smokie. Better men than I have died on a fishbone.

Catch up on last evening while I am here.

I already had a mind to discuss MacGregor's depiction of Eolhwynne with someone who knows about the subject and that meant finding a booth-scryer, or the modern equivalent—preferably one with a gift for magick rather than showmanship and subterfuge.

According to Tip MacCannie's account on Tuesday evening, most of the closes are now home to artists' studios, swanky apartments, and lodging rooms for students. No longer are they the haunt of "milch cows and horses where no grass grew, loitering dogs and squealing swine, loafers, idlers, knife-sharpeners, pudding-faced drunkards, and painted whores," as MacGregor so vividly described them. Nor are they welcoming to booth-scryers.

That said, the advertisements on the lamppost suggests a few of the painted whores remain and if the closes are now upmarket I would expect better street-lighting.

Along with the detritus of society, the booth-scryers have gone, but not, happily, gone too far and the Night Fair in Nor'loch Gardens is, MacCannie told me, the place to go. I had also, after discovering the Helm of Awe, another matter to pursue.

I arrived shortly after dark. That was a little early as the fair doesn't hit its stride until midnight, but I hoped to be there only an hour before returning to The Dudley for an early night. Needless to say, that proved optimistic.

I walked down from Melville Street and entered the gardens by the steps near the statue of Dr Simpson. This was the nearest entrance to the Night Fair which occupies a shallow amphitheatre behind the churches of St John's and St Cuthbert's. The Castle Rock and castle walls loomed above eerily lit by floodlighting which slowly faded from white to dark blue and then back again. Between the Castle Rock and the gardens all was inky black so the castle appeared suspended in mid air.

I descended from Melville Street slowly, taking care to get my bearings. There were a row of stalls gathered in a wide horseshoe with the open end facing west. They seemed to be wooden as they were dark except for the entrances. Beyond them scattered among the trees were the lights of tents, the whole of them aglow from interior light. This was my first time at the fair and indeed my first time in many years in the gardens. The soft pulse of drumming floated up from the amphitheatre.

I was interrupted by a woman behind me.

"Will ye not be standing in the way," she said.

I was blocking the steps, and she was descending with a pushchair.

"Sorry. Most sorry. Taking in the view. Would you like a hand?"

"I'm fine, mister."

I stepped aside and the woman descended. The child must be out very late, assuming there was a child.

Whoever I sought would likely be in one of the tents under the trees, but it was best to begin at the stalls. They were better lit, and I could ask there and be directed. Not for the first time that evening I felt for my notebook. Tucked in my coat pocket it had the questions I wished answers for. All I needed was the right person to ask.

The drums were now a great deal louder and the beat slightly too fast for my liking, leaving me breathless and uneasy as I approached the centre of the amphitheatre. There were jugglers tossing blazing torches, stilt walkers, unicyclists, firewalkers scampering over glowing embers, the pungent smells of aromatics and acrid wood smoke. A train hooted, reminding me that between the gardens and the castle the railway lent a note of reality, even if the horn had a rather unearthly tone. Beyond the firewalkers was a tunnel of willow hoops. I had seen something like it at Avebury and heard it called a rebirthing tunnel. A stall offered oriental head massage. Another spiritual barbering, promising to exorcise the past by burning one's shorn locks—never let a witch have fingernails or hair, if you know what's good for you. What I could not see was anyone that looked like a booth-scryer.

The first stall I passed was selling gemstones and crystals. Of course, I don't take crystallomancy at all seriously. Antiquity has little to say about it and although amber and quartz were commonly used for touchpieces, their modern popularity is almost solely down to their attractiveness. A dead frog impaled on a skewer is far more potent but doesn't look good around the neck. Surprising how much knowledge of the black arts one picks up by studying Scottish literature.

The next stall, which was appreciably bigger, was selling owl-therapy. Owls, contrary to folklore, are remarkably stupid birds and quite what benefit one gets from stroking one I have no idea. I suppose people assume those wide staring eyes are benevolent.

No need to describe more. All the stalls in the centre of the amphitheatre were much the same: shallow, mindless, not offering anything of substance. That is, all except one which I very nearly missed because it wasn't a stall, as such, but a small tent unmistakeably modelled on that of the booth-scryers with a domed roof of wool and animal hide and with the entrance partly-covered by the telltale yellow curtain. Of course, I doubted the occupant was a genuine booth-scryer, but they were trying.

I waited a moment just in case someone was already in there. Then, when I had heard no sound and seen no movement, I drew the curtain aside and peered in. The proprietor was a middle-aged woman. Rather plump and with dyed black hair. She had been expecting me.

"Why did you wait?" she asked.

"I... did not know if anyone else was here?"

"I would have drawn the curtain."

"Of course. I'm unfamiliar with this. I'm hoping you can tell me something."

"That's generally how this works," she said.

"Ah. No. I don't mean my fortune. I'm afraid my diary is full. No room for surprises."

She said nothing and then it crossed my mind I should be clearer.

"I am of course happy to pay, but it's information I'm hoping for. Though it rather depends..."

Clearly, it was not going well. It did not improve when I had the sense to ask if she had read any of MacGregor's novels. Thankfully, she had, but not *Acts of the Servant* or the sequels.

"Not after they butchered them," she said.

I explained I was attempting to amend that, but as she was completely unaware of Eolhwynne there was no point asking about her portrayal.

"Do you know anyone who might help? I really would like to speak to someone who has the gift and is familiar with the novel."

"A true version?" she asked.

"I hope it will be so. That is why I wish for a practitioner's insight into the character of this woman as portrayed by MacGregor. I want to be as accurate as I can."

"You have no inkling of your own?" she asked.

"Why ever would I? Afraid I have the sensitivity of wood."

I tapped the wooden pole supporting the roof and the edifice shook alarmingly.

"Perhaps what you believe is not how it is," she said cryptically. "But it's not for me to tell. There's a bookmaker on Salamander Street in Leith. Name of O'Donnell. Ask there."

"Well, I suppose they would be familiar with MacGregor," I said.

She gave me a quizzical look.

"Not a maker of books. A betting shop. Ask to speak to O'Donnell's wife. But don't let on the reason why. Say that Dorothea sent you."

She gave me her business card and I scribbled O'Donnell and Salamander Street on the back of it.

"Salamander Street, in Leith. And hush-hush," I said. "There is another matter. I found this written on a document, a legal document. I recognise the Helm of Awe, but not this wording: can you tell me what it says?"

I showed her my copy.

"Is it from a graveyard?" she said.

"No. As far as I'm aware it has nothing to do with them. Why?"

"It says 'for the protection of the dead.' You'll find that on many a gravestone in the Highlands."

"How odd. Now you mention it, I have seen something similar."

I didn't add that such an admonition made no sense on the back of a title deed and instead reached for my wallet and attempted to pay her, but she refused to accept anything and wished me a safe journey.

Must break off as the train is arriving.

HOME FROM HOME

Late afternoon; Wild Hunt, Galashiels

The thing that struck me most at Arbinger was how at home I felt in MacGregor's study. The room had witnessed the creation of all his novels from *Wyvenhoe* in 1852 onwards and including the two versions of *Acts of the Servant* and its sequels, but following the recent restorations it was my first opportunity to see it as MacGregor saw it; or approximately so, at any rate.

It is, if you will forgive the sacrilege, my Holy Land, and standing at his writing desk it all felt curiously familiar.

Everything on the desk was placed just as I would have placed it—with the exception of a snuff box—and I saw that my own desk at Avebury was its pale imitation.

I suppose it should not surprise too much if, having spent so much time in MacGregor's company, albeit at one and a half century's remove, I should subliminally pick up some of his habits.

The writing desk and chair are the only items of furniture original to the room. Both were purchased from a chateau near Rheims and restored two years ago with a modest contribution from the society's funds and a generous donation from Blackwater Publications. For the moment, the rest of the furnishings are approximations of the originals, but one would need a good eye to notice anything out of place.

Diane had a photo album which she set down on MacGregor's desk.

"I thought you might like to see this," she said.

She opened the page to a photograph I had seen many times before but never in the room in which it was taken. It showed MacGregor seated in an imposing wingback chair with a terrier on his lap.

"The effect is extraordinary," I said. "I know that isn't the same chair but somehow it seems so right here. I wonder, may I sit?"

"Of course."

I took the chair and leant back into the smooth leather. The marble fire surround; the bronze grate; the painted wood panelling and architrave, were all original to the room and as MacGregor would have seen them.

"It's uncanny. I would not have thought one could be closer to him than studying his texts all day, but to see through his eyes..."

I could not find the words to finish and had to apologise as tears overcame me.

"I'm sorry; you must think I'm an old fool."

"Not at all. It is affecting."

"Thank you for understanding. Hello..." I had seen a painting beside the fire surround. "Is that who I think it is? I thought the chair and desk were the only original items."

"It is him. Lachlan MacGregor, his son. It was donated to us last month. I wanted to surprise you with it."

"Who was the donor?"

"They wished to stay anonymous. They claim it was inherited from a descendant of Lady Helena."

"Well, well. Who knows what else will appear. By chance I will be teaching at Belshade College from October. Lachlan was schooled there for a few years."

"Should I know it?" Diane asked.

"No, not at all; very minor Oxford College. It's only the coincidence makes it odd."

"We have two more rooms to show you: the drawing room and Lady Madeleine's bedchamber."

Diane led me on. The drawing room revealed Lady Helena's touch and we are fortunate that several of the items are original, having been donated by various museums and descendants. The Chinese wall paper is extraordinarily vibrant and full of character. Of course, Lady Helena outlived her husband by three decades and we do not know what changes she made after his death, so the room does not have as strong a connection to MacGregor as his study.

From the drawing room Diane led me up a stairway to the next floor. As yet the stairs have not been restored and the linoleum flooring was a stark contrast to the splendour of the two previous rooms. Diane halted at a door.

"And this was Lady Madeleine's bedchamber."

Again, there was that abrupt shift between shabby present and restored past, but this room had none of the warmth of the drawing room or the personality of MacGregor's study. Instead, everything seemed alien and unwelcoming even if I could fault none of the décor or furnishings.

"Such a tragedy," I said thoughtlessly. "Sorry. Only there are times I think of MacGregor not as someone who died almost a century before I was born, but as a friend. His grief after her death, and of course her own loss... it was appalling. I suppose none of the furnishings are original."

"The plaster on the external walls needed considerable repair," Diane said. "We believe damp came down the chimney while the room was closed up. However, the furniture and the bed frame are original, albeit a little fragile."

"You surprise me. The room was closed up with everything in it?"

"It was never used after Madeleine's death. And perhaps never entered. The room has an effect on some people. Two of the workmen were taken ill while plastering the walls and one of the women who made the bed coverings miscarried."

"How awful. It does feel cold. Have you read Madeleine's letters back to her father and mother?"

"I have not."

"She hated Arbinger. This room especially. Her letters are tragic, given what happened to her."

I was rather keen on leaving as soon as possible and suggested the Madeleine Shrine more as an excuse for fresh air than anything else.

"Are you married, Mr Warbrook?"

"Yes. I mean no. Divorced actually. Why?"

"It's said that MacGregor paid Madeleine more attention after her death than while she lived."

"MacGregor said as much in his own journal, but I do not think we can wholly condemn him. He was a man of his time. I confess I have never noticed if you are a Misses or a Miss."

"I am a widow."

"I am sorry to hear that. He must have been young."

"Young and foolish. He, too, was a man of his time."

I admit I did not understand her, though I sensed the bitterness. I followed Diane back to her office and waited while she telephoned for someone to escort me to the shrine.

"David will be here in a moment. You are happy with what you have seen?"

"Indeed. Of course, we are a long way from having

anything we can show to the public, but as a private museum it is exemplary. You may know it has long been my ambition that Arbinger should be open to the public, at least in part."

"I appreciate your ambition, but public admittance would conflict with creating a safe residence for our clients," Diane said. "However, legislation gets evermore restrictive and there will come a time when adapting an old house to modern retirement needs is no longer practical."

"You mean Dorothy Parkin would sell?"

"We may have no option. But it is some years off."

There was a knock at the door and a young man came in. His looks were striking with dark eyes and curly black hair.

"David. This is Nevil Warbrook, secretary of the MacGregor Society."

I had seen the young man's face somewhere but could not place it. It made Diane's next statement more astonishing than it might otherwise have been.

"Nevil, this is David Strange, our junior gardener. David, show Mr Warbrook the Madeleine Shrine. You can unlock it and take him up the tower."

Diane gave David a set of keys.

"After ye, Mr Warbrook."

David's voice was authentically Border Scots, unlike Diane's accent which was anglicised. It reinforced my suspicions that while I did not know David I might know one of his ancestors.

"Have you worked at Arbinger long?" I asked as he led me across the driveway toward an avenue of trees.

"Five years," he said. "But my family has worked for the estate a good while."

"Then one of your ancestors was Jock Strange, no?"

"Black Jock, aye. I forget how many generations back."

"Black? I haven't heard him called that before."

"Family secret, Mr Warbrook. It weren't for colour of his hair, or we'd all be so-named."

"I suppose not. A bad reputation then?"

"I don't know the whole of it. My grannie would tell ye. She reckons he failed Lady Helena, but this was long after MacGregor's death and Jock was an old man by then. I dinna ken the rest of it."

I was intrigued how Black Jock earned his sobriquet, but didn't have time to dwell on it as we were at the shrine. The starkness of the limewashed stone impressed.

"Have you seen it before?" David asked.

"A few years ago. It looks so different now. This will be my first time inside."

"Taken a fair few crowns to get it sae guid. Reckon the view is grand."

"You haven't been up?"

"Dinna have a head for heights. You're more'n welcome tae gae up."

David unlocked the door and showed me a semicircular room. A staircase spiralled upwards to the left while to my right was a second, much smaller door covered in iron strapping.

"Rather excessive for a cupboard under the stairs," I said. "Assuming it is a cupboard."

David was amused. "Nae cupboard. Didna hae much to do with the rebuilding work, but workman reckon there's a well 'neath the tower. Though the water table's that high, like as no' any good-sized hole becomes a well."

"Water below and sky above," I said. "A line from one of MacGregor's poems. As you say, perhaps no one intended it to be a well."

"I'll wait here for ye."

I climbed and after a few dozen steps I was glad of the stone handrail moulded into the wall. Without any intervening floors it was hard to gauge one's progress and the only light came from narrow embrasures.

"The door at the top is unlocked," David called.

I have a reasonable head for heights, but I had noticed the angling of the walls meant the stairway became ever-more constricted and I dislike confined spaces. However, it was my first time climbing the shrine and I told myself I would never need do it again, so persevered. Eventually the stairs turned one last time and I found a wooden door latched with bronze. It opened without difficulty, and I stepped onto a ledge surrounded by wrought iron railings.

"You made it."

I glanced down to see David on the grass far below.

"As you say. It is higher than I expected. I..."

I had swayed slightly and held to the railing, trusting the builders had made everything secure. The view was extraordinary. I could see down the Tweed to Melrose in one direction and Galashiels in the other, but marvellously there was no sign of the dreadful sprawl that now surrounds both towns. That was hidden by intervening folds of the land.

"Mr Warbrook?"

"Perfectly fine, thank you," I said, though I admit that I had felt a little peculiar. Probably just lightheaded after climbing all those steps. I let go the railing—it was damned cold against my hands—and circled the tower. A 'beacon' MacGregor called it in his journal, and it was clear now why he entrusted it to a contractor for the Scottish Maritime Board. It was indeed like standing atop a small lighthouse.

It was also exposed and after a few minutes I was feeling the cold. I had seen all I needed to and there is no doubt the renovation work has been excellently done. I descended, rather faster than I had gone up and was happy to meet David Strange again.

Must find out what his grandmother knows about 'Black' Jock.

My train should be due about now and there is nothing to detain me here. The pub is a drear as its name suggests and even the hounds of hell could not entice me to stay.

Evening; Dudley Hotel

I had hoped to finish describing last evening on the train back from Galashiels, but Border Trains have little regard for passenger comfort or convenience. The ride was awful—

the whole carriage (there was only one) shook at every rail joint—and all the seats were taken. I had to stand and had nowhere to rest my notebook.

Anyway, I left Dorothea's tent feeling rather pleased. She had translated the runic lettering on the title deeds—albeit without casting light on their purpose—and I had a possible contact in Leith. I dallied for ten minutes at the Night Fair and was even tempted to pet a bored tawny owl and tip an athletic young woman juggling flaming torches, before I made my way back to what I thought were the steps to Melville Street.

The next thing I knew I had tripped down some steps and landed on my head. At least that's what it felt like, though my hands are bruised so I must have broken my fall. It was all very dark, though I could see lights in the distance. Then someone was pulling me from the ground and of all people it was that chap I met on Arthur's Seat. Marroway or whatever his name is. He shook me by the shoulders and stuck his ugly face in mine. His breath stank of something unholy.

"Albert Rich?" he demanded. "You know him. Where is he?"

I hadn't and haven't a clue who Albert is, but old one-eye wasn't having it.

"My brother," he said, as though that was supposed to help. "My dumb idiot brother. Bronn. Bronn! Maybe you know him?"

His accent, brought forcibly on me by unpleasant proximity, was not Scots but something closer to Bavarian. Unfortunately, I didn't know any Bronns either, but this only seemed to perplex Marrowface further and his shaking left me quite giddy. Then I heard girls laughing in French at which point Marrowface cursed and disappeared into the shadows. By now I had the vague idea I was in a churchyard and next thing I was surrounded by cooing French ladies saying, "Iz zame wan? Oui! It iz ze comeecal leetle Inglishman!"

So I was, for they were the party of French students I met on Tip MacCannie's tour. The ladies helped me up and brushed down my trousers which had been mired by the gravel path. My hands were sore, but they were more concerned for my head, and one began dabbing it with her *mouchoir*. I protested but it was apparent I was bleeding a fair bit. They got me back to the Night Fair and one of them found an elasto in her bag and patched me up. I never did return the *mouchoir* but at least I was sufficiently compos to pay for a taxi back to The Dudley.

No more peculiar imaginings, I'm glad to say, though Marroway has a face to haunt one's dreams. But who is Bronn? Don't suppose he meant O'Brien? But how on earth would Marrowface know O'Brien?

No. No. No. You bumped your head and had a bit of a fright. Nothing more.

Considered getting a taxi to O'Donnell's this evening, but the weather is dreich. There'll be time in the morning before catching my train.

10 May; Dudley Hotel

This is my last Arbroath Smokie of the week. Porridge would have settled my tummy better, but I can make porridge at home. A decent smoked haddock is another matter.

The proprietor has kindly allowed me to leave my luggage at reception until I am ready to catch my train. Before then I have business in Salamander Street and must call at Beavers to collect my kilt.

Weather looks changeable but in a Scottish summer one should expect anything.

THE CANARY OF SALAMANDER STREET

Lunchtime; Greyfriars Tea Merchants, Old Town, Edenborough

Frustratingly, Beavers have closed for lunch. Quite certain they didn't warn me on Tuesday, and they jolly well should have done. Not open until one-thirty so I'll miss the two o'clock train.

If I hadn't been delayed at O'Donnell's I would have got there before they shut—who on earth shuts for lunch these days?—nor would that ugly child be staring at me. The best laid plans of mice and men go oft astray.

The taxi driver outside The Dudley this morning looked askance when I asked for O'Donnell's on Salamander Street.

"Need a wee bit more'n that. D'ye hae a number?"

"House number? Not the foggiest. It's a turf accountant, that's all I know."

"Och, why'd ye no say? Ye dinna look a bettin' man."

"I'm not," I said but remarked that I was short of time.

"Soonest in soonest awa', sir."

"What?"

"Salamander Street is nae place tae linger."

"Really? I nearly went there last evening."

The driver sucked his teeth, but we were now moving.

"Extra charge fer gaen thurr efter dark, sir. Ye can coont yersel lucky fer yer change o mind."

I was wishing Dorothea had mentioned Salamander Street's reputation, though it added authenticity to my journey; booth-scryers always kept bad company.

"That is, sir, unless ye were efter a woman," the driver hinted salaciously. "No' that ye'll find the nicer lassies on Salamander Street."

"Certainly not," I said and nearly added that I was happily married.

Perhaps I ought to drop this attempt to capture the Edenborough accent. I'm not at all sure I am succeeding, and I am not in the mood to struggle on.

I recalled Dorothea's instruction to be discreet and had the driver drop me short of my destination. This he did, on the corner of a grim row of shops with flats above. Ominously, the nearest shop was McGillivray's funeral directors.

I paid off the driver and glanced about. There was a telephone box at the end of the row where I could call for a cab and between lay a lady's hairdressers named Hydra, a baker, and then O'Donnell's. The last two premises were a branch of Samson's, the gent's barbers, and a pawn shop. McGillivray's window displayed a black coffin and a headstone.

The interior of O'Donnell's was grim. Television sets lined a shelf high on one wall above a chalkboard filled with tables and times and the names of racecourses and below it a row of cheap plastic chairs. Against the other wall were six slot-machines ablaze with flashing lights and whirling carousels. Two customers craned their necks at the television sets while a third pumped one of the carousel machines. The proprietor sat at the far end of the room behind a wired-glass screen. The last time I entered such an establishment was during my student days at Oxford and while the carousel machines and television sets were new to me, the smell of hope and despair was familiar.

No one paid me any attention until I was within a few feet of the counter when the attendant finally looked up.

"Good morning," I said. "I'm hoping to speak to Mr O'Donnell."

He stared at me, then withdrew a pencil from behind his ear.

"As you might guess," I continued, "I'm not from around here. I was instructed to speak to Mr O'Donnell, though it's Mrs O'Donnell who may be able to help me, by a woman at the Night Fair in Nor'loch Gardens."

I now had his attention and he glanced furtively behind me into the shop.

"A lady?" he said warily and by his accent I understood this probably was O'Donnell himself.

"She said I should be discreet. Her name is Dorothea. She..."

O'Donnell silenced me with a finger across his lips and picked up a telephone. He spoke softly in Eirish then ushered me through a lift-up section of the counter and thence to a backdoor.

"Go on up with you. She'll see to it."

I did not stop to ask what he supposed 'it' to be and

climbed a narrow stairway. Part way I was aware of a woman standing on the floor above.

"Hello? Mrs O'Donnell? I hope you don't mind. Rather a fish out of water. Dorothea..."

"Shush. We can speak in here."

Mrs O'Donnell let me into a room overlooking the street where I had just entered.

"And why would Dorothea send you here? How is she anyway?"

"She seemed well when I saw her," I said. "At the Night Fair on Tuesday night. I suppose she thought you might be able to help me. If I may, I'll get to the point; have you read anything by Tamburlaine MacGregor?"

"Well, that'd be the quarest question anyone asked. Sure, is it not fortune in love and money that brings you?"

"Quite sure. Not that I've much of either... but enough to pay for anything you might give me."

"Well then, sit down. Sit down."

The room was brightly lit, though that may only have been a response to the dismalness of the room below. The window was half open and traffic noise came through a lace curtain. More unusually, the window was occupied by an antique rune stand. Mrs O'Donnell noticed my gaze.

"My stones are warming," she said.

"Or they lose their power," I said. "May I have a look?"

"You can look but don't touch."

"Wouldn't dream of it," I said.

Her stones were not the usual runic design but appeared to be Ogham.

"I was born in Galway," she said by way of explanation.

Ogham is the ancient Irish writing system, so I suppose it is quite appropriate. Meanwhile a soft chirping drew my attention to a canary flitting in its cage.

"I'm not after any divining," I said. "I'm an editor restoring MacGregor's novel: *This Iron Race*. Dorothea thought you might have read it."

"Years ago," she said. "But I didn't think much of it."

"That may be because of the butchery done to it by his publishers," I said. "I'm hoping you recall a character named Eolhwynne? She was a spaewife and I need someone who actually practises magick to tell me how well MacGregor depicts her."

"Jaysus," she said. "It's not like we're all alike. One spaer is as different from another as any woman is."

"Sorry. Of course, that's not what I intended to imply. But did his depiction ring true to you?"

"I still have my copy from college," Mrs O'Donnell said and went to the window. In the corner, half in and half out of the sunlight was a bookshelf. I thought it a strange place to store books as surely they would fade in such bright light. The canary chirped loudly, and a motorbike roared by in the street below. I began to stand, though I'm not sure what I intended, but then Mrs O'Donnell shrieked and leapt back into the room.

"Oh Jaysus, would you see it."

Something large and black flapped between the window glass and the curtain. The lace billowed up like a shroud.

"Go'way. Go'way!!!"

I hesitated. For some reason, the canary objected to the intruder's presence and set up a terrific din of chirps and trills. The other bird called, and I realised it was a jackdaw. Then it found the gap between curtain and wall and flew into and around the room. Mrs O'Donnell backed into the corner. I, feeling a little braver now I could see the enemy, grabbed an umbrella and waved the pointed end at the bird. It seemed intent on Mrs O'Donnell herself but I somehow managed to get between it and her whereupon I was almost duelling with the blasted creature. A door slammed below, and feet pounded the stairs.

"Hit it, hit it!" Mrs O'Donnell yelled in my ear.

The bird had pinned us into the corner of the room, and I suppose the way Mrs O'Donnell was clinging to me could be misread and Mr O'Donnell sadly did exactly that and next moment I'm flat on my back and he's delivering a tirade of Eirish while his wife does her best to explain. None of us saw the jackdaw escape.

Then Mrs O'Donnell screamed and pointed at something on the carpet.

"O mo Dhia!" she wailed. "Fuair sé bás."

"Ar mhaith leat labhairt ciall, bean," O'Donnell replied.

"Fuair sé bás," she repeated.

A puffball of yellow feathers lay in the middle of the carpet and the door of the birdcage hung open.

"It was a big black bird," Mrs O'Donnell said in English, presumably for my benefit. "It flew in off the street and attacked us. This poor fecker was bayting it off, and you bate him, you big eejit."

O'Donnell glanced down. My head lay between his ankles. I did my best to smile at him.

"Ah, Jaysus, Bridie. Why'd you not say?"

I did not remind him he had given neither of us a chance to say anything but accepted his help and got to my feet.

"That eye looks awful," Mrs O'Donnell said.

"Oh, Christ. Well, get something for him. I've to get back to the shop."

Mr O'Donnell descended, and Mrs O'Donnell fetched a basin of water and dabbed at my face.

"Ye've been in the wars," she said.

"I don't suppose you have a mirror?"

"Not in the house; himself won't allow it."

"Ah well. I won't be suing your husband. Frightful misunderstanding. And I'm sorry about your canary."

"It was no fault of yours."

"Poor thing must have died of shock," I said.

Mrs O'Donnell paused. "They kept them in mines; they were to warn the miners."

"It didn't die of firedamp."

"They are sensitive to what we cannot see," she said. "Why did it attack?"

"I suppose it was afraid," I said without conviction. Truth to tell it had seemed possessed, but I had no other explanation. "I wonder... I can't stay long as I have a train to catch. But about Eolhwynne: Dorothea really did think you might help."

My eye was already starting to close up and the room was taking on an out-of-focus and lopsided appearance. Mrs O'Donnell continued ministering to me as she replied.

"I can't see why she'd think that. I read the book, but it was years ago. Yes, I thought I recognised myself in the girl, but that's all. There. It will bruise but I can do no more."

"But thank you for trying. Dorothea said I ought to be discreet, given your husband's business. I imagine it would be tricky explaining to his clients that you have the gift of clearsight."

"It would," she said with a half smile. "There's a back way out."

I have collected my bags from the hotel and half-one approaches. Better call on the gent's toilets before I leave and see how my eye is. Heaven knows what Beavers will think of me.

Afternoon; departing Caldtoun Station

"Forgive my appearance," I said on entering having decided to address matters from the start. "You should have a kilt for me to collect. I have the receipt."

"May I ask who dealt with you, sir?"

"You mean the eye? Oh, just a misunderstanding. Nothing to worry about."

"I mean, who took your order for the kilt?"

"Oh! Oh yes. Tall chap. Clan Fraser. Didn't catch his name."

"That would be Hugh. I'll just get this for you, sir."

"You mean it's all done?"

"Of course. Are you purchasing anything with it? A sporran perhaps? Or hose? We have a range of *sgian dubhs*."

I hadn't given much thought beyond the kilt and while I have some perfectly good woollen socks, a sporran and a black knife would look the part. They were also a good deal less expensive than I thought and while the chap was collecting my kilt I picked out a badger-hair sporran and a small dagger to wear inside my sock.

"Here you are sir. A MacStrangie? We don't get many of them."

"From what Hugh said, I may be the first. Certainly, this is the first MacStrangie tartan."

"Would sir like to try it on? It should only take twenty minutes."

I glanced at my watch. Twenty minutes would make catching even the three o'clock train uncertain. I decided against.

"Hugh measured me thoroughly," I said. "If there are any problems...?"

"Return it to us within the month, sir, and we will make any alterations free of charge. And these?"

He gathered up the sporran and the dagger.

"Yes, as you say. They will add to the effect. And that comes to?"

I wrote him a cheque which he filed in the till and then he produced a small pill pot and a leaflet.

"If you are curious about your Scottish heritage, sir, we are offering a free ancestry test. The company is Bloodline. They use the latest genetic modelling. All you have to do is provide a sample."

"Of what?" I said, thinking one could easily overfill such a small vessel. At hospital, the doctor always gives you something decent to piss into.

"Saliva, sir. If you rub the inside of your cheek first."

"Oh. Oh, yes. Why not? Always assumed my mother's family came from Morayshire but who knows what might be lurking in the background. Of course, my father rather spoils it: English as toast and marmalade. In here, you say."

I chewed the inside of my cheek to dislodge a decent lump of flesh for the boffins to work with, and then carefully expectorated into the pot.

"And if you would fill out your details on the form so

the company can send you the results. It should take a month or so."

I jotted down my name and address and telephone number, then, with a large bag proudly bearing Beavers' name, I walked down to Caldtoun Station to wait the three o'clock train.

WAGNER
Selected Correspondence

September – November 1862

Dearest friend,

It is most excellent to hear from you, as always, but it is especially so after this long period of silence. Be so kind as to give my regards and my thanks to Lady Helena, your dear wife, who has brought you back to life and to hope and activity!

As to my own condition I fear you are optimistic; though it is not unreasonable of you to be so as my treatment is unreasonable. For you will surely have noted from my address that my long exile is not yet over. Once I found it curious that France, that enemy of the Teutonic nation, should give me a comfortable existence, but while that villain Louis Bonaparte leaves alone my dear German Confederacy it has become a commonplace to find refuge in the enemy camp. The good Teutons should really do something to save the most Teutonic of all Teutonic opera-composers from this terrible trial, but my complaints fall on deaf ears and even my dearest friends in Germany are oftentimes inattentive. Moreover, in Paris I shall again be pretty well cut off from all my German resources, however scant, and so I cannot consider remaining long and intend migration once more to Venice, or perhaps Vienna, if I am allowed so close to native soil.

Be so good as to send your poem to me and I will see what can be fashioned, but do not be tempted to consider how it might yet be set to music. Rather, allow me to make those alterations as are fitting to render it whole, as though libretto and score came from one source.

Regarding the time allowed I assure you King Ludwig was ever as impatient with the great Mozart and for the patronage of your King Charles I shall make all attempt to be of service.

Happiness and joy to you both

R. W.

Paris, Grand Hotel du Louvre (No. 364) September 4th 1862

Dear great friend,

Your reply came with such speed I thought surely it must have passed mine to you as ships in the night.

My circumstance is not yet changed, and it is this very state of impermanence which allows me to accept your request as it will provide a pleasant interlude when all I have to sustain myself are performances of excerpts from Tristan and The Ring for audiences who care not at all that they are butchered from greater works provided it is I who conduct them. I claim an organ grinder's monkey has more dignity than I when standing on the conductor's platform, for it is ignorant of the circumstance of its performance when I am all too aware of mine.

I have not yet read in full your poem, though am inclined to believe we are of common mind in wishing to bestow upon our respective nations an original myth from which all else devolves and that your village of Brigadoon is akin to the great Teutonic forest where come all things pertaining to ancient Germania. But I must urge that you forego the desire to hold every word of your poem inviolate for in the marriage of libretto and music both must be prepared to bend if one is not to be subservient to the other and you would make poor use of my talents if I were to be a mere accompanist. Indeed, I fear I would chafe at such constraints.

Do consider this as the advice of a dear friend who means the best and is long practised at his art.

Yours

R. W.

Paris, Grand Hotel du Louvre (No. 364) September 14th 1862

Most excellent friend,

Do not burden your good kind self too much with worry that you overwork me and permit me to ask forgiveness for the delay in replying to your last letter. I understand your concern for the operetta and all will be well, yet I have been temporarily thrown into turmoil through my return to

Vienna. Allow me, in part to explain matters such that you do not feel I have ignored you and also to divest myself of an unpleasant experience by its retelling here. I had journeyed by railway to Lake Constance and thence by boat to Bregenz on the Austrian shore, yet my journey was far from over and the worst was to come. I may not travel via Munich, as you know, and the Austrians, no doubt out of fear of invasion and owing to their usual lassitude, are slow to build railways between their cities and those of any other nation. Further, the direct road beyond Innsbruck, via Saltsburg, to Vienna lies for a short distance within Bavaria and I dare not risk even so small an incursion while there is a price on my head! Therefore I must approach Vienna by circuitous route. Perforce, from Innsbruck I was obliged to take the post coach over the Brenner Pass, intending thence to continue to Trieste on the Adriatic from where I might take the railway to Vienna. I intend this only so you may understand my circumstance and not in any way to suggest such journeys are arduous beyond despair.

Of my fellow passengers over the Brenner, two were sisters from Vicenza who had taken the cure at Lake Constance and were now returning home. A third was a young woman of pretty demeanour but whose hand across her midriff and lack of wedding band betrayed her shame. Naturally, she travelled alone as one does not set a chaperone to guard that which was stolen in the night. A gentleman passenger was an official of some railway company whose name, both individual and employer escapes me. The last among us was a striking fellow with wild eyes whose name he gave as Blond, or something close to it, and who gave us to believe was of Dutch birth.

On a journey, in carriages, etc., my gaze always tries, or so it appears to me, to read in the eyes of my fellow-travellers whether they were capable of or destined for salvation. A closer acquaintance with them often deceived me as to this point; my involuntary wish frequently transferred my divine ideal to the soul of another person, and which, in the further course of our acquaintance, generally leads to an increase of disappointment, until, at last, I violently cut short their acquaintance.

Thus, some three hours from Innsbruck in that desolation of the mountain pass silence had fallen within the post coach when the Dutchman suddenly rose from his dream to note that our progress had briefly paused. This pause happened again and presently the Dutchman called up to the driver.

Reply came that the matter was nothing to concern ourselves with and we settled again. Presently, however, the pauses became prolonged and then forward movement ceased.

The trouble, the driver now revealed, was that he did not know the road we had entered upon. This was absurd for there was but one road of any quality through the pass. Nevertheless, the coachman informed us that there was a lake below us where no lake should be.

The lake, now drawn to our attention, had an uncommon aspect, much like that of an oystershell, which was curious enough for the wind ought to have shifted the water upon its surface. Then the elder sister observed mist forming on the lake and this quickly rose and soon reached us. Meantime the air had grown exceeding chill. The Dutchman had persuaded the driver to continue, arguing that as this was the only road it must be our road, but we had not gone any distance when a veritable swarm of birds engulfed us, and we could go no further.

Though he was not of our rank, with the exception of the young woman whose shame brought her station below his, it was felt to be an act of human charity to grant the driver refuge with us; but it proved most fortunate before he did so that he screwed down the brake for soon we were lurching and shuddering from the efforts of the horses to escape the avian assault. The Dutchman, having ascertained that only the brake held us, then tied a shawl borrowed from one of the sisters about his face and bravely leaping out secured the wheels on all four corners with scotch stones before returning.

We were agog and somewhat fearful at the noise, for the

birds hammered on the windows until we drew down the blinds to shield us from their wicked gaze and prayed the glass held against them.

Presently, having worn out their strength, the birds departed and soon after the mist lifted. We emerged to find ourselves in sorry state for one of the horses was blinded and must be despatched and the other, while its eyes were protected by blinkers, had been savaged on every quarter. For a brief time, it stood shivering before it collapsed and expired. At this the young woman wailed helplessly and said we were doomed, and that the lake was the door to hell.

This, naturally, returned our attention to the lake which we all agreed was now much smaller and no longer of shell-like appearance. The driver then affirmed it was a lake he always passed on this road.

But we were now without horse and the driver argued we should wait by as the road met with fair traffic and a carriage or post wagon was bound to pass and render assistance. An hour endured without disturbance and then the Dutchman suggested he return on foot with the driver to Innsbruck and procure whatever means of rescue they might obtain there.

This was agreed on and it was also agreed that rather than continue we would all return to Innsbruck.

This we did, after many hours, and the following day, despite some misgivings, I travelled over the Brenner in company with the two sisters and the railwayman. The Dutchman and the young woman had made other plans, but I do not know or consider it my duty to care what they were.

I cannot now think it was anything other than a freak disturbance of the air which occasioned the birds to attack. As for the lake, accidents of the ground are common in mountainous parts and no doubt the swollen waters were brought about by a partial damming of its course.

Nevertheless, my dreams are oft disturbed by the hideous cries of those birds, and I should be grateful you do not pass what I have disclosed to another.

Meanwhile, I shall give due attention to the score for Brigadoon in the next few days. You may write to me poste restante at Vienna as I am betwixt and between permanent address.

Your friend,

R. W.

Vienna, September 29th 1862

Oh, greatest of friends,

You must not chastise yourself. I wrote you very wildly last time. Perhaps it vexed you so I should like to fill up with all possible timeliness what it behoves you to know for you could in no way have known of my troubles. In any event I have made some amends for the delay ensuing that which I shall heretoafter refer to as the incident of the Brenner Pass and have sketched a leitmotiv phrase to accompany the Laird of Brigadoon, which I interpolate.

[Musical annotation]

Meanwhile, I have surmised some cause for the avian attack on my post carriage. For my birthday last May I was delighted to be invited to the von Bülow's. Hans has been my occasional patron and his delightful wife, Cosima, is the daughter of my great friend, Liszt, who you must recall meeting at the Paris Conservatoire—he certainly recalls you—when he performed Beethoven's Emperor Concerto (surely you do remember?). I was not the only guest of the von Bülow's and a pretty girl, albeit with a trace of the Jew in her appearance, thought it favourable to release five calling birds from their cage so they might fly about and regale me with their tones—she knew I was a lover of birdsong—but of the five only four flew as required while the fifth moped in a laburnum tree from whence it later fell and was devoured by Frau Cosima's dog.

It may seem unlikely to you but that is the only time I can recall when I have offended what Aristophanes called Νεφελοκοκκυγία.

I have still no permanent address in Vienna though have

settled on the vicinity of Penzing where I intend to rent a villa. I shall also return to an earlier scheme of having Tristan and Isolde produced at the Vienna Court. This I attempted some years ago without fruition yet may now enjoy greater fortune. If I fail once more some will declare my opera cannot be performed, but if I do not make attempt it shall not be performed anywhere for none will see favour in it.

For the rest, Vienna suits me; not the "artists," but the people, in whose good books I stand quite incredibly high. A new fancy-shop has just opened with the sign of Lohengrin, and every porter is delighted when he learns whose boots he is blacking. It is quite a remarkable populace and has given me a good few nice impressions already.

Otherwise, I have nothing rational to tell you today other than you will soon hear more of Brigadoon. A thousand cordial thanks for your letter.

In the time being please reply poste restante, Vienna.

Your friend,

R. W.

Vienna, October 12th 1862

I shall add that I remain troubled by strange dreams which affect my mood at all hours. Vienna long ago in a fit of progress banished that particular breed of person who may give respite from night terrors and other supranatural effects, and all a man might find for remedy are quack medicines and laudanum, of which I will not touch.

Therefore, and I must couch my words carefully as while I myself may avoid German lands I cannot very well direct the business of the post offices and so must suspect my letters read and therefore not give cause for any in Vienna or afar to think me engaged in practises that are frowned on and regarded with dismay, if you in less enlightened climes might know of a remedy for my complaint or know of one who might advise such, I should be eternally your grateful friend.

R.

Dearest great friend,

I bow to your power of words for though I understood not one whit of what you sent me it has been under my pillow since, and my nights are again filled with peaceful slumber and birdsong is once more harmonious to my ears.

Yet it is also with your words I struggle and must ask again that you permit some small change to your text to suit the needs of musical drama. You will recall that I long held the music as secondary to the drama, yet I have had cause to reflect on that regard through the example of the great Schopenhauer and now recognise that music is not secondary to the drama but coexists with the text in a harmonious whole much as the flower requires the bee and the bee requires the flower.

I fear you will again refuse me, though to what purpose you remain so stubborn I cannot tell. There is something in your words that escapes me yet also leaves me uneasy. I may not demand yet must remind you of your estimation of Das Rheingold which you called the work of genius. Genius indeed! For how else ought I describe myself but in the words of my dear friends who see magnified in me their own not inconsiderable talents; therefore, let me with good grace take their words and say that I am a genius, if one not yet recognised in his own land, and then let me take your words and pass upon them what I granted the libretto of Das Rheingold.

Music is the equal of the drama; that is my thoughts to you, and I should do you a disservice by not advising you.

Notwithstanding the above and my continued exertions in your favour, I must enquire to whom I should address claim for remittance at King Charles's court, unless this shall be a private arrangement between ourselves in which case I must urge you to consider an early settlement of part-payment to the sum of three-hundred thaler.

Your great friend

R. W.

Vienna, October 25th 1862

Most excellent dear friend,

I must beg of you, be patient. The score proceeds well and all will be in good time for Christmas, as promised. I have the first act scored and all of the major themes established. I believe you will particularly appreciate the theme for the village itself when it first emerges from the mist.

[Musical annotation]

Meanwhile those troublesome dreams of which I spoke have quite abated and once more my nights are peaceful, for which much thanks I give again to you. If I may say, I see a great deal of my old friend in the character of the Laird of Brigadoon: that puckish good humour and delight in mischief-making have, I trust, returned to you after your long unhappiness as they are so evident in the laird's toying with his human guests. Indeed, it is your own great happiness which I believe has allowed you to appreciate that my own happiness is marred, and I regret to say that you were quite right to observe that I have made no mention of my wife in these last letters.

The matter is that Minna and I have parted irreconcilably—no, do not trouble yourself to feel bad on my account for I have long resigned myself to this state of affairs. It is some years past since we had in any true sense been man and wife and while I would admit my long exile from Germany played its part in our estrangement—Minna was never happy without her borders—the blame does not lie wholly there. God, how many needless upsets in the house might I not have spared myself and wife had I, or rather we, set upon this course some years ago rather than continuing more in hope than sound judgement. Had we been blessed with children, or even one child, we would have taken our burden up gladly, but without there seemed little point perpetuating what had merely become a trouble to us both. Naturally, I shall maintain her until such time as she may remarry, though the burden of keeping two households is a great one. She has now returned to Germany where of course I may not join her even if there was hope of reconciliation. Meanwhile, I do not lack for company of any kind and after so long among the French the Viennese are proving a delight.

I cannot yet say that I am truly content, but a man has his work to detain and distract him whereas a woman only has her relatives and society to call upon.

I have sundry suggestions for changes to the libretto, which I understand you will be reluctant to accept but must beseech you to consider in the greater interest. These I will itemise separately.

Your devoted friend

R.W.

Vienna, November 4th 1862

My dearest friend,

You astonish and exasperate me in equal measure. How can we have arrived at such a pass whereby a misunderstanding of your purpose and, I must insist, a gross underestimation of the time necessary to accomplish such a feat should cause so much distress and ill-feeling between us. I must urge you to reflect that whatever you have promised your master was done without due reflection of that required on my part for its completion. In short, it is quite impossible to stage a production of Brigadoon for Christmas. Even were the score complete, there is simply not time for rehearsals and the learning of lines and so forth. You should consider that I, unlike your good self whose skills lie elsewhere, am all too aware of the frailties of performers and the difficulties of staging a production and when I say such a thing is not possible it is a statement of the fact.

What may be possible, and surely will suffice, is a dramatised reading whereby much of the stagecraft and the learning of the text may be dispensed with and a reduced company of musicians, of perhaps a dozen at most, will accompany the singers. As I am of the conviction this is the best that may be achieved by Christmas I shall complete the score accordingly, with allowance that a complete orchestration may be attempted at a later date. I urge you to accept that this is all I may achieve in the time allowed and that had I understood your intentions from the outset I would have urged caution and made clear that your expectations were too great. As matters now lie, my hope is that this news does not sit ill with you, and we may move on with greater understanding between us and without harm to that friendship which I know we hold most precious.

Winter has now set in and the mountains all about are lost beneath the snow, yet Vienna's gaiety continues. Paris may be where all serious art is done, but the Viennese have the best will towards me, albeit a total absence of the singers I require. Yet my only hope remains here, all the same.

You need not fear I shall lack for company at Christmas time and therefore shall refuse your kind offer and wish you and your wife all happiness at Arbinger once the matter of performing Brigadoon is complete. I must also extend an invitation for you both to come to Vienna where it seems your fame has preceded you for I was accosted at a gathering last week by a gentleman professing to know you but whose manner I found most strange.

This was at the house of Peter Cornelius, the nephew of the great painter, and though I do not know how this gentleman came to be there he was most insistent on making my acquaintance. He gave his name as Merovius but was vague as to his country—it was possibly Flanders or Brabant as his German was intelligible but not that of a native—and his most distinguishing feature was a monocle of smoked glass worn to disguise the loss of an eye, though there was no scar to suggest how the eye might have been lost. I wonder, does he sound familiar? A one-eyed gentleman, possibly from Flanders, answering to the name Merovius, or similar, ought to be distinctive enough to lodge in anyone's memory.

Once he had introduced himself—naturally, he already knew who I was—he proceeded to say that you and he were acquainted and that he had come to warn me not to continue with the operetta. I was, of course, astonished at this impertinence and also that he should know of the work, since I have done as you requested and told no one and it seems unlikely he should have heard it direct from you. Perhaps someone at King Charles' court has let word slip, but that is beside the point for here was Merovius saying I should have naught more to do with you or with Brigadoon.

Naturally, I was angered at his manner and cut short our meeting whereon he left in much indignation and muttered something under his breath which I could not hear.

Later I asked Cornelius of the ill-fellow, and he claimed not to know or have invited him. If you do not know of this gentleman be advised that he seeks to damage your reputation, though of course he had no effect upon my estimation of your good self.

It is all most mysterious, and perhaps unsettled by the meeting I slept ill that night and was visited by bad dreams. I still keep your note beneath my pillow but wonder if its efficacy is wearing off. If such a thing is possible, I would ask you for a fresh enchantment so I may sleep more easily.

Your good friend

R.W.

Vienna, November 16th 1862

My dearest unique friend,

I write in earnest as I have not yet had reply from you and am beset by a marish dream brought on by my encounter with the loathsome Merovius. In the hope that in your wisdom and knowledge of the workings of the mind and of unnatural things may I describe it herein so that by sharing with another I might lessen its hold upon me.

I beheld myself in some monstrous version of the opening scene in Das Rheingold in which I took the part of Alberich and climbed to a perilous summit where reposed three maidens who I recognised as my Minna, Cosima von Bülow, and Madame Mathilde Wesendonck of Zürich, whose husband, a wealthy silk merchant, has been my benefactor on numerous occasions—I mention this only so you may know of the connection—and as I neared them I saw they attended upon a child bathed in light and it seemed to me I was bound to waken this child and take him from these three women.

I cannot say how much this is a mystery to me, other than perhaps I grieve that I have not yet a child, but as I closed upon the three women I found them not as I had supposed, for Minna had much aged while Mathilde suckled the child at her breast and Cosima appeared scarce older than a child herself. Further, I now had a competitor for climbing with me and attempting to throw me back was Herr Merovius who had forsaken his monocle and whose absent eye was now only a void where the orb had been. He, so it seemed to me, took the part of Wotan, yet he is not in this scene in Das Rheingold! and so you see this dream is some curious amalgam of many parts and whose true purpose I cannot discern, except that I was to steal what belonged to the maidens even as they refused my advances. Yet I could not help myself and for all that Merovius held me back I climbed until I had attained the summit and had the golden child within my grasp, whereon the three women rose as one and threw me backwards into the abyss.

You will be relieved to hear that I then woke rather than being cast to my doom, but I lay in the darkness fearing for my life until the moment ceased, and my heart was at ease. It was then I recalled the music I have written for the Laird of Brigadoon, or Oberion as you call him, and the refrain then refused to leave me in peace until I had risen and with a candle begun to complete the score for the operetta with the music now pouring through my heart.

That was two nights ago, and I have not slept since, in part for fear the dream returns and in part because I am feverish with musical composition, despite which I am weary beyond belief in thought and bone. I beseech you; if you know of a remedy and may obtain it I should be eternally in your debt as I may not long endure this strain upon my nerves.

Despite my enervated condition, the work is good, or so I believe, though it seems improbable I have the reserves to complete it in the time allowed.

Your friend
R.W.
Vienna, November 22nd 1862

Most excellent friend,

Your reply received with much thanks and relief. I have slept blissfully for the first time in five days, and though weak I think myself much recovered. Is it too much to ask that you share the secret of their workings, or must these enchantments remain a mystery to be efficacious? No, you need not answer if you do not wish to.

It is snowing without, but I think I shall go to the café later as it will be good to clear my thoughts before contemplating with a clear head what these last maddening days have wrought upon the composition of Brigadoon.

Your eternally grateful friend
R.W.
Vienna, November 27th 1862

And one thing more!—

By chance I met with Cornelius at the Blue Parrot Café and learned he has enquired after the mysterious Merovius. It would appear the gentleman—I use the term advisedly—departed Vienna for Paris two days past. I am glad as the further he is from me the happier I shall sleep. I shall return to composition instantly.

R.

HOME

Bedtime; Avebury Trusloe

Cancellation of an earlier train led to overcrowding, and I was obliged to share a compartment with four business types who talked endlessly of finance and leverage all the way to Jutland Street. I tried reading but couldn't concentrate in an atmosphere of percentiles, margins, and aftershave. Then endured a miserable tram ride across Lunden to Hyde Station where I found the service delayed owing to signal failure at Reading. Found myself wishing I had taken the direct train via Oxford. Arrived Swindon shortly before ten and very jaded. Taxi home cost thirty crowns but cheaper than a week in the car park in Swindon and no risk of vandals. Driver wanted to know what I though of Swindon's chances against Doncaster this weekend. Said I hadn't the foggiest what he was talking about. Apparently there is an important football match tomorrow that will decide Swindon's entire season. I said I couldn't even tell him who their captain was. Started to rain as we climbed onto the Downs and on reaching home the driver claimed a health and safety issue on account of the wet and unlit road and I had to retrieve my bags from the boot by myself. Too tired to argue that part of his service included getting my luggage and assume this was revenge for my ignorance of football.

House is malodorous. Suspect one of the cats has left something somewhere but I'm not searching tonight. Also, reappearance of a black feather in Gerald's old room but am too exhausted to deal with it. Eye looks dreadful but I'm more bothered by my forehead. Must have bashed my head rather harder than I thought but a degree of addlement explains my peculiar impression of Merrowey at the Night Fair. Still no idea who or what Albert Rich might be. End of antibiotics on Tuesday. Finger fully mended and looking forward to a pint during Wednesday night's dominoes.

Bone-tired so off to bed.

GOOD NEWS!

11 May; Red Lion, Avebury

I have this morning received confirmation from Belshade College and am to start in October on a salary, pro-rata, of 28,000 Crowns. For the last five hours I have been walking on air and now write this in the snug of The Red Lion with a celebratory glass of Merit at my elbow.

There is one surprise. Vanity in refusing to wear my glasses during the interview and the gloominess of the principal's office misled me. On re-reading my acceptance letter it appears he is not Audley Stonebreaker, but an Audrey Stonebreaker. This does explain why she kissed me on the cheek as I was leaving—a startling gesture at the time—but, alas, has me perplexed at the hairiness of the upper lip. In my defence, Miss Stonebreaker is, I suspect, a heavy smoker for her voice was unusually gruff for one of the fair sex.

Perhaps I ought to be a little troubled by her sudden intimacy, though I laughed it off at the time. Miss Stonebreaker is a large woman, and I fear I did not check if the door to my attic room has a lock. Ah well. Let us hope she takes a gentleman at his word.

Aware that I shall need a new watering hole near Belshade College I asked Jonathan Grebe if he could recommend the Abandoned Arm in Beckley while he was pouring my pint.

"The what?" he asked.

"The Abandoned Arm? Pub a few miles north of Oxford. Just wondered if you'd heard of it."

"Can't say I have. Queer name for a pub. Where'd you say it was?"

"Beckley. Small village."

"Beckley? Beckley? Oh, I know the place. Ha. Who gave you that name?"

"Chap at Belshade College. I'll be working there this autumn. I'll need a local pub and he recommended the Abandoned Arm."

"Did he? You'll have a job finding it. Now, if you want the *Abingdon* Arms then it's a decent pub. Reckoned to be haunted, mind. Never heard it called the Abandoned Arm."

"Ah. Misunderstood him. Struck me as an odd name."

Jonathan passed my pint.

"Suppose it might have been called that one time. Pubs change their name from time to time. Unless it's a name like The Red Lion which never goes out of fashion."

"I suppose so. I shall ask for The Abingdon Arms. Thank you."

The Abandoned Arm did have a macabre ring to it. As custodian of The Red Lion Jonathan is an authority on haunted pubs. In fact, I intend enlisting his aid to write an article on my favourite hostelry: for the moment, let me just say that The Red Lion is the only public house I am aware of built around its very own well. Some say it is the fifth entrance into the great stone circle at Avebury, though not by tunnel or any physical means. A ghost path, some call it. A tall tale to alarm the tourists is my explanation!

But I digress. What I wanted to set down are my thoughts on the newly deposited material at King James's Library: the supplement, as Mrs Broody called it, having spent a few hours going through my notes. Alas, I don't have copies of the original material as KJU forbids photo-mechanical copying on the—spurious, I suspect—grounds it causes chemical damage to the original material.

Thoughts regarding the letters from Richard Wagner. Very little I can say. Jotted down a few words from them but I can make no sense of the translation. Something about blackbirds, mention of Cosima, though I think this was before his affair with her and eventual marriage, mention of a Peter Cornelius who I must look up in the Oxford Dictionary of Biography, and quite a lot about "Brigadoon," so presumably it all relates to Wagner's score and the unhappy results. Annoyingly, Van Zelden will have an advantage over me as I believe Dutch is very close to German and he can probably read them unaided. Of course, one hopes KJU might get around to translating them, but I doubt they are a priority.

I've had better luck with the lost acre on Hunter's Bog.

There's an obscure reference to the purchase of land in a letter from MacGregor to his land agent quoted in Evelyn Bishop's *A Writer's Life*. I don't believe anyone has tracked down where the property was, but it is possibly the acre on Hunter's Bog. It will require a visit to the Edenborough Land Registry to make certain but that will have to wait a few months. I have a canal trip to look forward to (if that's the right word) and then to Wales for another Creative Haven.

Must shop in Devizes on Monday. The cats are down to the last tin of Kitty Nibbles and my own stores are almost bare.

Postscriptum: as I suspected, a week of Scotch breakfasts and the human tendency to gain weight in cold weather has set progress back somewhat. Fifteen stone, ten.

Sunshine

12 May; Green Dragon, Marlborough

Had I waited a few days I could be enjoying a welcome glass of Thatcher's Weed in Marlborough, but I am still on Phloxymycin so stuck with a pint of Merit non-alcoholic beer. But the weather is warm and having walked over the Downs it cures the thirst.

My eye remains shocking and the graze on my forehead has yet to heal. Both drew comment at Holy Communion this morning. Molly was terribly worried when I said I was walking over the Downs and suggested I ought to be taking things easy. I reassured her I just needed a bit of sun after a week in Scotland. No buses on Sundays but I'll find a taxi later.

I have in mind writing this up for the parish magazine, so I'll make a few notes.

Long before it became the coach road between Marlborough and Bath, the track over the Downs had other uses and other names, two of which have come down to modern times. One of these is the Herepath, a Saxon word referring to the military roads or tracks used in the ninth century when Saxon fought with Dane, and serving much the same purpose as Napoleon's *Grand Routiers* in France. The meaning of the other name, Green Street, is now lost, however the track is far older than the Saxons, for the builders of Avebury brought the great sarsen stones down its western slope.

Wearing my tweed jacket against the expected breeze, and with camera, notebook, and thermos of tea in my rucksack, I left Avebury by the eastern gateway, or pythen, as it is called in the local dialect, and headed for the Downs. Beyond Manor Farm—where I saw Nancy Curlew in her Japanese Shogun arguing with Abel Samwise—the metalled road gave way to chalk and began to climb. In parts, the chalk is deeply rutted by countless generations of travellers over the Downs, and I nearly turned an ankle on a rough patch. Pausing while the pain subsided, I photographed Manor Farm and the ramparts of the henge at Avebury. I was already warm and suspected my tweed jacket may have been unnecessary, but there was no turning back.

With my ankle better, I continued toward a skyline of open fields and beech groves planted two centuries ago. Alas, we live in a land filled with delights left by our ancestors yet are rarely persuaded to leave anything of delight for our children's children. Instead, we are content to leave them our problems and our debts.

But I should not protest: Gerald is convinced I shall leave him nothing but poems and unfinished novels.

I digress. Impassable now to all but tractors and four-wheel drives, what tales this road must have of swearing, sweating coachmen, and sweating straining horses! In the wet, the chalk is greasy and in the dry hard as fired clay and bruising to the foot. For many horses this climb must have proved too much and perhaps their remains still lie under the roadside sod. With the horses and rattle of the coach now gone, the road is quiet. Only walkers disturb the peace and even they pass with no more than a nod in greeting. Ahead a keen barn owl perches on a fence post and rooks pursue a buzzard.

The top of the climb is marked by the crossing of the

Ridgeway, an even older path that has wound over England's southern uplands for five millennia. Beyond the crossing is a broad pasture filled with the brilliant song of the skylark. Here amidst the long grass one finds the first of the sarsen stones, before the path crosses a style and enters the head of a dry valley where ancient floods have deposited the sarsens, as though upon the tide's edge.

Seemingly many, the sarsens are much diminished from ancient times. Apart from those taken to Avebury they have been quarried for many centuries and extraction only ceased a few hundred years ago. Today, the valley is protected for its antiquity and flora and undisturbed save for the sheep who keep the invading gorse and hawthorn at bay.

Here, beside the valley, is a further clump of beech trees that provides welcome shade. Though only some two centuries old they seem older, ancient even. Perhaps their gnarled limbs remind us of ourselves in old age. Part hidden in their shade is an eighteenth-century lodge, now abandoned but once the meeting place for shooting parties, "with (according to a 1906 sale catalogue) a capital sitting room for luncheon parties." The lodge is the only obvious sign there was ever human occupancy on the Downs. A well gave water for the lodge but whether it did so for the coaching traffic is unknown as it may have post-dated the road's demise.

It is curious that even in this seemingly dry valley water lies only a few feet below the surface.

Refreshed with a cup of tea, I continued and recalled Samuel Pepys came this way on the 15th of June 1668 when he rode all day "with some trouble, for fear of being out of our way, over the Downes, where the life of the shepherds is, in fair weather only, pretty". The road has been quiet now some two-hundred and fifty years since the building of a turnpike a few miles south left it to the shepherds and the skylarks and even on a spring day the Downs has an otherworldly atmosphere.

Stepping off the path I found a vantage point to photograph the valley and its river of stones and as I framed the image I had a sense I was not alone. Sure enough, someone was sitting on a distant stone—the largest stone of them all—quite still and staring out at the horizon.

The path began climbing once more. There was not a breath of wind and the rasp of crickets vibrated from every clump of grass. It was now far too warm for my jacket, and I slung it over my shoulder. Then, as though to increase my discomfort, I passed a reservoir, wholly within a great bunker and protected by fence and security cameras. I had not thought water needed such guarding, but the powers that be think otherwise. Denied water, I sucked on a boiled sweet and looked forward to the inn at Marlborough.

Fortunately for me the track descended, and I found respite beneath a clump of beech trees where I sat for a second cup of tea.

I am not the first to break his thirst upon the Downs, as an old engraving places a roadside inn somewhere near this spot. The exact location is lost, but the name of the inn is plain from the proud swan upon the sign.

The clump of trees marked the end of the loneliest part of the old road. Now I was on the eastern slope and approaching civilisation. The path met with horse gallops, and I was surrounded by a broad swathe of grassland. Also gone was the chalk underfoot, replaced by loose stones which made for unpleasant walking, and I soon took to walking on the grass instead.

The last few miles are something of an anticlimax. The distant views remain, but the peace and isolation has gone. Soon the path meets the modern road between Swindon and Marlborough and then passes beside a golf club where I was tempted to steal a buggy and ride the rest of the way. The open view of the golf course changed to rows of fine and expensive houses, followed by a handful of shops before the road turned onto Marlborough's High Street where the sign of the Green Dragon beckoned.

My jacket had left a damp patch where it hung over my shoulder, and I was parched. As any traveller having arrived by the high road, I entered the tavern to break my thirst. Later I shall accomplish in fifteen minutes by taxi what has taken three hours on foot. Though I fear what we have gained in speed and convenience has cost us a great deal of romance and adventure my feet shall enjoy the rest.

Hmm. Not bad for a first draft.

Evening; Avebury Trusloe

Feet were tender after my walk but nothing that a good bathe in warm water and vinegar couldn't sort out. Spent most of the evening editing *This Iron Race, volume two*: progress is hardly spectacular, but I'm getting there. Boris is off his food. Hope it's nothing serious. Finished off the last couple of shots on the film after I got home so that can be dropped at the chemists in Devizes tomorrow.

Time for bed.

A WARNING

13 May; Caen Hill Café

Rather grim scene outside. Boat moored in one of the basins between the locks caught fire last night and there's police guarding it and lots of yellow tape everywhere. Horrible smell lingering and it had gathered a crowd of onlookers. Suppose there's a lesson for yours truly. Don't leave the gas on overnight and don't rock the boat while cooking. Reminded of that family I met here the other week, with the boy who threw himself in a puddle. Not that this was their boat. More like one of the itinerant boats—liveaboards, I think they're called—as it was scruffy and had half a garden on the roof. All burnt to a crisp now. There was a child staring at the boat with the saddest face.

I needed a decent canal guide as those from the library are years out of date and recalled the café had a few books on its magazine rack. There's also a small chandlers behind the café and I'm advised to get a spare lock key, whatever that is.

Boris didn't eat anything last night but dived out of the door this morning as though his life depended on it. Bought a few tins of Premium Purr. It's far more expensive than Kitty Nibbles but hopefully will get him eating again.

The sandwich went down very nicely, and I might order more tea after taking a look at their bookshelf.

Later; car park, Black Horse, Devizes

It's odd how dreadful stories affect one, even when one has no connection to the events.

I have a recent guide to the Kennet and Avon Canal, complete with maps of every blessed mile. Even has reviews of all the pubs en route. The chap I saw last time at the café was absent, but the owner was most helpful as I only had a vague idea what I needed. He was also in charge of the chandlery, so I asked about a lock key.

"Only, it seems I'm guaranteed to lose one," I said.

"We've got a few second-hand," he said and pointed under a shelf. I leant down and picked through a collection of shapeless metal.

"I don't suppose you could tell me what they do? Been commissioned to write pub reviews along the canal. Never been boating in my life."

"Not going it alone, are you?" he asked.

"No one wants to go with me, and I can hardly afford a skipper."

Each piece of metal had a handle at one end and a socket at the other, rather like a spanner except bent through several angles.

"Reckon you'll want two spare; accidents will happen."

"Yes, but what do they do?"

"Use them for raising the paddles on the lock to let water in or out. Lose your lock key and you're not going far. They don't float, see."

I found two less worn than the rest and laid them on the counter.

"Six crowns," he said without glancing at them.

I gave him ten crowns and asked about the stricken boat.

"Looks like a nasty accident."

"I wish it were. Arson, they reckon."

"Gosh, I hope whoever was on it got out."

"Bad job, the bloke who had it. Reckon it was him started it. Lived aboard because his wife had thrown him out. Tragedy is, they had a young daughter, and she was with him last night. No one's seen her. Or him. Police haven't been aboard yet. Doesn't look good."

"Gosh. How awful. You mean they might both be..."

"Could be. No one knows."

I left him with a guidebook and two lock keys under my arm. Only hope they've cleared the boat by the time I come through on my way to Reading. Really is too morbid. I shall pray for the girl tonight. And for her father.

There. Wanted to write that down before I drove home, rather than have it prey on my mind.

Boris

14 May; Avebury Trusloe

Opened the backdoor this morning in my dressing gown and pyjamas to let the cats in but only Tusker was waiting on the doorstep. No sign of Boris.

"And where's your brother? Or should that be partner in crime?"

Tusker gazed at me with inscrutable yellow eyes, then, as he sidled past me into the kitchen, he brushed against a bare ankle. Never does that usually and it seemed almost friendly.

I went outside and called for Boris. A handful of rooks and jackdaws took flight with a cawing and clucking of protest, but there was no sign of him. As I returned inside I saw Mr Pumphrey next door and waved a greeting.

"One of my cats is missing," I said.

"Is it now. Mebbe it's found a chair to scratch," he said and went inside.

I don't think he has to be quite so obvious in his dislike of my cats.

I returned inside to give Tusker his breakfast but left the door open, thinking Boris would turn up. That was an hour ago. Tusker has curled up having given no clue to his brother's whereabouts. I have eaten toast and scrambled eggs washed down with a pot of tea. Considering another slice with a dab of Scotch Bonnet marmalade I picked up last week. It has a hint of whisky about it and, joy of joys, I am finally off the antibiotics. Dominoes tomorrow evening at The Red Lion and I can enjoy a pint or three. We're playing the White Bear from Devizes, and they usually give us a good game. Sid and Bert will no doubt be keen to say my absence last week was no handicap, but I think they are just envious work takes me away so often.

Planning on a full day's editing. Time is passing and Hare & Drum want their pound of flesh. Must decide soon if I'll continue my editorship with *Works of the Master*. Would be handy to know how much work is involved but that means H&D releasing the first draft manuscripts and I doubt they'll do so just yet. More to the point, it would be useful to know how different the first drafts are from the published text. If I wanted to display MacGregor, the groundbreaking, taboo-breaking writer five decades ahead of his time, I'd continue as I am, but I'm not sure that *is* what I want to do.

Better check if Boris has returned, then I'll see to my ablutions.

Later; Avebury Trusloe

Tusker has not been himself all day. Normally he avoids physical contact with what I imagine he thinks is his human servant, but today he has gone out of his way, literally, to lie on my feet or rub his cheek against my leg. I can't think of anything I've done to be his new best friend and assume he is missing Boris.

Cats are cats, and it's not unheard of for cats to disappear for a few days and I believe there are cats that frequent several different families each quite certain he or she is their cat. That reminds me, I ought to ask Mrs Pumphrey. If any of my cats have gone anywhere it would be next door. She does spoil them dreadfully.

Though it wouldn't explain why Tusker hasn't joined his brother.

Bedtime; Avebury Trusloe

Still no sign of Boris. Had hoped Tusker would race out into the night anxious to find his brother, but instead he slunk out with a backward glance as if asking whether I really wanted him to go. Popped round after lunch to ask Mrs Pumphrey if she had seen Boris, but she denied it.

What do I mean by 'denied it'? Plainly she hadn't or she'd have said. Do I really suspect my neighbour of catnapping?

Managed to get a few thousand words edited this afternoon. Oddly comforting a cat dozing on one's feet. Though I never quite forget it's Tusker and liable to sink his claws in at any moment.

Had intended bringing a nightcap to bed to mark my first day off antibiotics but completely forgot. Not going down for it now.

Is it terribly wrong to trouble The Lord with a prayer for a cat? Surely there are more urgent matters in the world. Keep telling myself Boris is quite capable of looking after himself but I'm not quite convinced.

A HUNTING WE WILL GO

15 May; Avebury Trusloe

Opened the back door this morning to find one cat. Tusker meowed noisily, arched his back against my leg, and curled up in his favourite chair. I had anticipated, in fact rather expected such an eventuality, and overnight had concocted a plan. But first there was the matter of breakfast and my ablutions to complete. Then, fortified with scrambled eggs and toast, I approached the task. I approached warily, I might add, as it required considerable cooperation from Tusker and having just ended three weeks of antibiotics I did not want a second helping.

It seemed wise to complete the task in the back garden. If Tusker objected he had more room to escape and if I needed it I had more room to retreat. Fortunately, as I attempted to pass a length of cord around his flea collar he only put up a fearful wailing.

"Boris? Is that you, pussy?"

Mrs Pumphrey's voice came over the fence.

"Afraid this is Tusker," I said. "Boris is still missing."

"Whatever are you doing to him?"

Mrs Pumphrey's head appeared in view.

"Trying, with some success, to put him on a lead. I intend taking him for a walk."

"Oh no, no, no. Not like that. That little collar will never hold him. Wait a moment."

Mrs Pumphrey moved away.

"I rather suspect too much delay will result in serious injury," I called after her. "He isn't best pleased."

"So I hear!"

I gave up trying to leash Tusker and waited. Tusker stopped wailing and sat to wash his paws.

It was, to all intents and purposes, a lovely morning. Lots of birds about, including the usual crowd of jackdaws, but also swallows and house martins screeching and swooping overhead. The garden was getting to that point when one really ought to do something before it all gets out of hand.

Mrs Pumphrey returned.

"This was Charlie's," she said. "Don't know why we kept it. Bill's soft-hearted and Charlie was really his dog."

I had a dim recollection of a noisy Jack Russell terrier that had terrorised the neighbourhood for a year or two after Edith and I moved in. Fought everything until one day it took exception to council workers relaying the road and picked a fight with a road-roller. I suppose Mr Pumphrey probably did take it rather badly but, as Edith sweetly put it, it was very quick.

"Does it fit, Nevil?"

"I'm just doing the buckle, but I think it works a treat. Thank you. Of course, if he had a mind to I suspect he would be out of it in a jiffy."

"Take care he doesn't chew it. Don't think my Bill would approve of a cat wearing Charlie's collar and lead."

"I shall be ultra careful," I said. "Don't suppose you've seen his brother about this morning? I'm hoping Tusker can give me a clue where he is. A sniffer-cat, you see. That's the plan."

"I don't think cats really understand that sort of thing," she said. "But no, haven't seen Boris at all."

"They're usually inseparable. Whatever happened to Boris, I suspect Tusker wasn't far away at the time. Dominoes tonight so I'll ask around. Someone will have seen him."

"I'll mention it at my crochet class this afternoon."

"Would you? Thank you. How shall I return the lead? I imagine you don't want your husband knowing you lent it."

"I'll pop round later. Good luck." Mrs Pumphrey went indoors.

I was now ready. Tusker wriggled and danced round the lead, but the collar stayed firmly on his neck.

"Right," I said, with all the authority of a chap bidding a cat to do his will. "Lead on."

Tusker shook himself and sat down before sinking his teeth into Charlie's lead.

"Ah, no! Stop that."

Tusker relented.

"Find Boris," I said. "Where is your brother?"

It was much more successful than I expected, and Tusker made straight for a hole in the hedge at the bottom of the garden. Unfortunately, it was a cat-sized hole, and I halted my side of the hedge with him on the other. He mewled.

"That isn't going to work," I said and pulled gently. A ruff of hair rose from the back of Tusker's head and the lead slipped off him.

"Blast. Wait there."

Tusker did nothing of the sort but began walking towards the Longstones at the far end of the field. I retreated along the hedge until I could squeeze through and follow him.

Fortunately, he was not running. In fact, he seemed quite tentative. Pausing often and sometimes circling. I followed slowly, anxious if I got too close he might think I was about to leash him again. But he was perfectly cooperative off the lead until midway between home and the Longstones he sat down and howled.

"Find Boris," I said. "Go on. Where is your brother?"

Tusker rolled onto his back and stared at the sky. A jackdaw swung overhead, and he was instantly on his feet again.

I looked up and pondered whether there was any connection. Surely Boris couldn't have fallen prey to a jackdaw. Boris could eat a jackdaw. But several jackdaws? All at once? No, not even then. And surely Tusker would have defended him so there'd be evidence of injuries. Not to mention a lot of feathers.

No. The bird was coincidence. But Tusker wasn't happy and as soon as I'd checked for rabbit holes and anything else that might hide a cat, we were on our way home again.

Hope to get some editing done this afternoon but am aware my mind is not on the job.

GHOST?

Bedtime; Avebury Trusloe

Clouded over in the afternoon and by the evening a steady drizzle fell. I hoped Boris had found some shelter as he dislikes getting wet. Tusker spent the day curled up and snoring. I fretted and flicked through the canal books. Then remembered I had meant to check my correspondence with Hare & Drum to make certain I hadn't committed to *Works of the Master*. Essentially, I did everything to avoid getting down to actual work until it was five o'clock and nearly time to think about tea before dominoes this evening.

Decided it was okay to drive as I'd only have two at the most. After three weeks on Phloxymycin I'd been looking forward to a proper evening at the pub and now it's arrived I have almost no appetite for it. Sid and Bert and the team from The White Bear had already arrived. Sid gave me the eye as I came in and shook the rain off my coat.

"Thought you might not be coming," he said.

"Bit of trouble at home."

"Shouldn't worry," Bert said. "Reckon that cat of yours can look after itself."

I stopped attending to my coat and stared at him.

"How do you know about Boris?"

"Mrs told me."

The penny dropped. Bert's wife was the village's best crochetier, if that's the word. Mrs Pumphrey had been good on her promise.

"I dare say he can," I said. "But it's out of character. He might look like a bruiser, but he enjoys his comforts."

I went to the bar and ordered a pint of Cropwell's Bitter.

"You've given up on the Merit?" Jonathan asked.

"No longer required. Had a dose of antibiotics but all clear now."

"Ah, I thought you might have gone on the wagon."

"The wagon? Oh no, no, no. Why? Do you think I ought?"

"I didn't say that. Not for a publican to criticise his customers' habits. That's like a hangman complaining about criminals, isn't it."

"Bit of an extreme comparison," I said and gave Jonathan a two-crown coin.

I joined Sid and Bert in the window seat. The three from The White Bear were deep in conversation on the other side of the room. I knew them by sight and by name but outside of a dominoes evening I think I'd struggle to recognise any of them.

"So, yes," I said. "I have lost a cat and I'm a little worried. If both were missing I'd be somewhat easier—as you say they can care for themselves—but it's odd only one has gone. Usually they're inseparable."

"My Mrs reckons you should put posters in the village," Bert said. "Something like 'Lost cat. Answers to Tiddles. Last seen, etcetera, etcetera'."

"His name's Boris and he doesn't answer to it, though he will come to a tin of Kitty Nibbles."

"Good idea, though," Sid joined in. "I recall when that

posh cow at the Dower House lost her yorkie she put up posters all the way from 'Vizes to Broad Hinton."

"Did they work?"

"Sort of," Sid said.

"What does that mean?"

"Someone found it in the brew house field. What was left of it. Fox they reckon."

"Well thanks a bunch."

"At least she knows what happened to it," Sid protested. "Some folks are never grateful."

"I'll put up some posters," I said. "Thank you. It *is* a good idea."

"Photo helps," Bert said.

"But people know who I am," I protested.

"Of the cat you daft bugger!"

Sid chuckled into his beer. I think several others overheard as well and I felt a right chump.

"Just as well Tusker is the image of his brother," I said. "Not sure I have a photo of the cats."

"It's a hard-hearted man who hasn't a photo of his nearest and dearest," Sid said.

I think he was being sarcastic but couldn't tell. One of the team from The White Bear came over at that point and reminded us they were here for a dominoes match.

"Ah. My apologies," I said. "Life sometimes interferes in one's minor pastimes."

The chap, Nigel I think his name was, didn't take my remark well and thrashed me soundly in our head-to-head. I managed to win my second game but lost again in the third. I blame the final defeat on Bert. During the half-time interval he produced a copy of the Devizes Messenger.

"Thought you might be interested in this," he said. "Seeing as you're off gallivanting on the canal."

"I doubt you can gallivant at four miles an hour. What is it?"

"Caen Hill Locks," he said. "That boat fire. Police have found the kiddo."

For some reason I had the awful smell in my throat again.

"It was expected, though? I called at Caen Hill on Monday and saw the boat. Pretty awful. Police hadn't been able to go on board then. Wasn't there a chap as well. Her father."

"Missing," Bert said. "They reckon he killed the mite and set the fire to cover his tracks."

"How awful."

Bert pushed the 'paper across the table, and I glanced at it. I know it's a terrible cliché, but sometimes a shiver really does run up one's spine. There was a photo of the girl, and I recognised her as the child I had seen on the canal path.

I didn't know what to say. I certainly wasn't going to tell Bert I had seen a ghost. So, I said nothing but declined to take the paper home with me.

"Thought you'd want it, you being a writer. It's a good story."

"It's an appalling story. My week on the canal will be filled with restaurant and pub reviews, not ghastly murders. Especially not when it's a child."

"Suit yourself."

So, as I said, my mind wasn't on dominoes after that. Fortunately, Sid and Bert did rather better, and The Red Lion managed a 5-4 win.

It was still raining when we left the pub. Sid was getting a lift from Bert, so I drove home alone. Half of me wanted to race along and get out of the dark as soon as possible. The other half knew that Boris was somewhere out here, and I was terrified of running him over, so I barely got over thirty the whole way. Of course, the odds were, in the cold light of my bedside lamp, preposterous, but stranger things have happened lately.

Even so, I almost had an accident as I slowed for the turn into Avebury Trusloe. Motorbike was suddenly right behind me and just before I would have turned right he pulled out and roared past me. Had to brake smartly and shouted after the bloody idiot. Then I got into a bit of a funk and by the time I got home I was shaking like a leaf. Sat for a bit to calm down before going in. Made myself a cuppa and let Tusker out. He seemed slightly happier tonight and didn't hesitate when I told him to look for his brother.

I suppose it's possible that the girl on the boat had a sister. Or even a half-sister. And there's no telling if the photo in the paper was up to date so she could be older than the girl I saw. When I think about it, the idea that I'm seeing ghosts is far-fetched. Rational explanations must come first.

Postscriptum: three pints of Cropwell's Bitter.

16 May; Market Street Tearooms, Devizes

Need to while away an hour or two while the printers do their business. Obviously, I write this because there was still no Boris this morning. Tusker simply walked in, sniffed disinterestedly at the breakfast I had prepared him and curled up into a ball. I don't suppose he really is spending the night searching for Boris. It would explain why he is so tired during the day. Though it wouldn't explain why he isn't hungry when he gets home.

Bert is right of course, though he said it was his wife's idea, so Mrs Tanner is right: I need to put up some posters. Finding a photograph of Boris was tricky but I eventually found one taken in the back garden a few years ago. He was about two then, though full grown, and not much changed from now. The only difficulty is I had actually been taking a snap of Edith reclining on the lawn and Boris happened to be lying across her legs. Edith has always had rather fine legs and even into her fifties is still wearing skirts that many a woman in her thirties might look twice at. So, there's Boris sprawled across my ex-wife's shinbones looking utterly content and it's the only photograph I can find of him.

I was in a quandary but eventually I took a pair of scissors and cut off Edith's legs just above the knee. I don't have many photographs of Edith and hardly any showing her knees so it was a bit of a sacrifice, but once the printer has used it I can always tape it back together.

For the rest of it, I just gave him the wording and he promised to get it all done by three this afternoon.

The father of that poor girl is still on the run. It seems several people have reported seeing him and an arrest is imminent. Nobody has a good word for him, which I suppose is not surprising, while she was a perfect angel.

That's all gleaned from eavesdropping on conversations at the café.

Shouldn't have written 'angel.' Makes me think of ghosts again. Still another hour to wait. Might wander into the library as the only reading materials here are the newspapers and I've had enough news.

SPREADING THE WORD

Bedtime; Avebury Trusloe

Sid caught me pinning a poster to the village hall notice board.

"Nice pair of pins," he said. "Anyone we know?"

"They are my ex-wife's. And that is Boris."

"Reckoned it was. Most folks'll look at those legs though. What were you doing letting that woman go?"

"I hardly let her go. I think we all know who to blame for her leaving."

"Do we now," he said. "I suppose blaming Glendale and his stud farm makes it easier."

"It's a riding stable, not a *stud* farm."

"Depends on who you ask. See you inside."

I got quite annoyed at that point and pressed so hard the head of a drawing pin broke, and the shaft pricked my thumb. Luckily, it didn't go in deep, and I was sucking the wound when Prudence arrived.

"Oh dear, Nevil. Are we that unkind?"

"Whatever do you mean?"

"You remind me of my little boy, sucking your thumb like that."

"If you must know, I stabbed it on a drawing pin."

She was instantly paying attention to the poster.

"Is he yours?"

"That's why I'm saying he's missing."

"You're being catty," Prudence said with self-conscious wit. "He's adorable. I'll put word round for you. Someone must have seen him."

Boris always has that affect on women. I've no idea how he does it. Even his photograph charms them.

Prudence went inside, reminding me as she did so that the first aid kit was in the porch if I needed it. I decided it was wise and found an elasto before going into the meeting room.

Prudence and Sid had already set out the chairs for the evening and Prudence had the kettle on. The other members arrived over the next ten minutes, and we began with a pouring of tea and me reading the minutes from the last meeting.

Fred Thirsk was, as we all expected, missing. News is he is recuperating but we shan't be seeing him at any meetings for a while. Terry proposed a motion to thank him for his long service to the council, passed unanimously, and we set a budget of thirty crowns for a gift. Terry added that the bell ringing teams have yet to elect a new Captain of the Tower. Then he said he had received the first quote for the repairs to the bell frame but declined to share it with us as he was still awaiting other quotes, including one from the firm who repaired the frame at All Saints in Fyfield.

Paul stopped him at that point to ask for an approximate figure based on the quote received.

"It would at least give us some idea of the costs involved," he said.

"I don't think it will," Terry said. "I spoke to the chap who was head of Fabric and Works at All Saints at the time, and he reckoned some quoted twice what others offered. I suggest we hold back until we have more quotes in. No sense getting all worried or too hopeful just yet."

Molly agreed with him, and Prudence surprised me by also agreeing. Paul backed down.

Prudence had precious little to report from the Spiritual Outreach Committee and when we got to the ongoing matter of the church crèche she beamed at Molly and reminded us that Molly had offered to approach the New Barn School.

"I'm sure that's what you proposed," said Prudence.

"I've been busy at the guesthouse," Molly said, but just as Prudence was looking smug added she had spoken to them.

Prudence sniffed.

"Far from being antagonistic, Jenny Atkins said they would love church involvement. I also spoke to a couple of parents with children at the school and they said how much they enjoyed the Easter Sunday procession to West Kennet."

"I still have misgivings about The Henge Shop and their support for the school," Prudence said. "The church cannot support anything with pagan influences."

"We put up mistletoe at Christmas!" Terry said. "How *pagan* is that!"

"The Henge Shop also supports the post office," Molly said. "Are we to have nothing to do with them either?"

"You can say what you like," Prudence said. "I think it is inappropriate."

"Can I say something?" Lucy Chadwick asked.

Paul said he would value her opinion. Damned creep.

"It might be best if Peter approached the school as this is such a sensitive issue. I do know that the New Barn has better facilities than we can offer: an outdoor play area for example and economical heating."

"My objections are spiritual," Prudence said.

"I'm sure Peter is sympathetic to *spiritual* concerns," Lucy said.

Frankly, I could have cheered at that point as Prudence was suddenly deflated. I noted in the minutes that the matter had been passed 'upstairs' and then Prudence turned to me.

"The Outreach Committee have also discussed the coming solstice," she said. "We all know what that means for the village, and this is the last chance to discuss the church's involvement."

"Y'mean barricade the door to stop 'em getting in," Sid said.

"Not at all," Prudence continued. "We think it should be quite the opposite."

I couldn't follow Prue's reasoning. One moment she was forbidding any involvement with the New Barn School and next she's inviting solstice revellers into the church. Naturally, it wasn't quite that simple and there was a sting in the tail for yours truly.

"It is the function of the Spiritual Outreach Committee to connect with those who are without Christ, and we cannot do that behind closed doors—I speak metaphorically: I am not suggesting the church should be open."

"Didn't we try this on May Day?" Terry asked. "Paul got flattened for his troubles."

"I don't think my experience is a true judge," Paul said.

"The committee accepts that mistakes were made, but we must not be discouraged," Prudence said. "We need to understand what those coming for the solstice are seeking and then guide them towards God."

"Good luck with that," Terry said.

"I think we are being too harsh on Prudence," Paul said. "It is clear that there are many lost souls among those coming to Avebury and the church should reach out to them."

"Thank you Paul. I was reminded of the success of Nevil's Lenten talks and how he found so many echoes of Christian faith in the landscape around Avebury."

Sid raised an eyebrow. I think he saw what was coming.

"We thought Nevil could write an eyewitness account of the celebrations for the Parish Magazine. Talk to some of them. Find out what they believe and what they seek."

Sid rolled his eyes. I was torn between dismay and feeling rather surprised that after her opinion of my Lenten talks Prudence should be turning to me.

"I think that's an excellent idea," Paul said. "And I'm sure Peter would approve."

"I'm sure he would," I said. "But I'm not sure it's me. I even avoid the pub on that night."

"We don't want you to act like them," Prudence said.

"You would be more of a missionary."

"I don't think they take kindly to being converted. Look what happened to Paul."

"We're not asking you to convert anyone," Prudence said.

"It would be a fact-finding mission," Paul said.

"Like ethnological research," Molly said.

"Like what?" asked Sid.

"Ethnology," Molly repeated. "It's the study of people and the differences between groups of people."

"So I would be an observer."

"Just so," Molly said. "In a spirit of understanding and mutual exchange."

"While keeping in mind that Jesus advises he is the sole path to The Father," Prudence said.

"Actually," Lucy interjected, "Peter believes Jesus' words are taken out of context. He was not referring to all people everywhere for all time but only those in that time and place."

"I prefer the *orthodox* view," Prudence said.

"So: you want me to find out what they are worshipping, how they worship, and anything we can do to put them on the straight and narrow path?"

"That puts it rather well," Paul said.

"And I should approach them without disapproval or attempt to cast doubt on their beliefs."

I was slightly warming to the task.

"But take a Bible, just in case," Prudence said.

"I don't think Nevil will be preaching to them," Molly said.

"I mean for his protection."

"From what?" Terry said. "It's not like they'll sacrifice him to Beelzebub!"

"That choice is Nevil's," Paul said.

"You cannot reach out to people by fearing them, or their beliefs," Molly said.

"They bloody put the wind up me," Sid said.

Molly smiled at me.

"If anyone can do it, you can," she said.

17 May; Red Lion, Avebury

Bright start this morning. Warm and dry night as well so wherever Boris is at least he isn't suffering in the cold and damp. That is some comfort, I suppose.

After breakfast I went out armed with drawing pins, a sheaf of posters, each laminated in plastic to withstand the weather, and a hammer. My thumb is still painful after impaling it last night. I intended a few posters on the nearby lanes and then a wander into the village to ask the village shop and The Henge Shop if they would mind me pinning a notice up. No point asking the Antiquities Trust Museum as only tourists go there.

The first place for a poster was my own gatepost and I was tapping away when the postman arrived in his van.

"Missing dog?" he said.

"Cat, actually."

"That's all right then. Don't like dogs."

"Must be awkward for you," I said.

"Why?"

"You are a postman. Don't dogs bark at postmen?"

"They bark whether you like 'em or not," he said.

I couldn't follow his reasoning so asked if he had anything for me.

"Warbrook, is it?"

"It is. Foxglove Cottage."

"I have to put it through the door."

"Couldn't you give it to me? I'm standing outside my house which, as you see, is Foxglove Cottage."

"I am contracted to deliver post to each address, sir. You standing by a gatepost don't constitute an address. Besides, you might not be who you claim to be."

"Well, I think I can easily prove I am who I say I am, and I can prove this house is mine, but if you insist post it through my door. I am busy."

He walked up the drive and posted the letter.

"Nevil, isn't it?" he said on the way back.

"It is. As on the letter."

"Nice pair of legs. Best of luck finding the cat."

I finished hammering and wandered along the lane towards the meadow and the path to Avebury. I could hardly put posters willy-nilly on people's gates and fences, but I hammered one onto a telegraph pole and put another on the gate into the meadow. I was doing rather well.

The meadow is a joy this time of year. No trace of the winter damp that lingers here and the grass was jewelled with buttercups and orange butterflies. Damsel flies hovered, bright as sapphires over the Kennet which babbled brightly under the wooden bridge. Had I waited I might have seen a kingfisher or a trout, but I was on a mission.

I was busy putting a poster on the gatepost where the footpath joined the end of the High Street when a woman walking a terrier stopped as if to pass the time.

"Hello. Are you Nevil Warbrook?" she asked.

"I am. Sorry, I'm not sure I know you."

"Jenny Atkins," she said. "Molly is a mutual friend."

"Ah, yes. We were only talking about you last evening."

"I hope it was complimentary."

"What?"

"I'm teasing. I know Molly is on the PCC. You want the crèche out of the church."

"I wouldn't put it quite so bluntly. But yes. It isn't really right for such an historic building."

"Beautiful cat," she said. "I hope you get her back. Is she a Persian?"

"She is he. And no. More this and that rather than pedigree. He has a brother, Tusker. He's safe and sound at home. Probably sleeping. Not seen Boris in three days."

Jenny stepped closer and took a good look at the poster.

"It says Doris. Definitely Doris."

"No, no. Printer was most careful. And I checked them myself yesterday."

"It still says Doris," Jenny said. "Look."

I did and as though by magic the B of Boris softened and blurred in the D of Doris.

"Well blow me," I said.

"We always read what we expect to read," Jenny said. "Doesn't matter though. I mean. It's not as if Boris comes when you call him. No cat does that."

"I suppose not. But quite a few people know Boris and I suppose they'll think it great fun he's now Doris."

"But that's good," she said. "More memorable. They'll be more likely to look out for him."

"You think so?"

"Certain of it. If you see Molly, tell her we're waiting to hear from her at the school."

"Ah," I said. "Actually, Peter Chadwick is going to write to you. Or speak to you. Not sure which. There's a bit of resistance among some members of the PCC. They don't like that you're supported by The Henge Shop."

"Oh, that's so silly. We hardly do any necromancy with the children and the Tarot is just for fun."

"Now *you* are teasing," I said. "I also attend the New Barn School and I know you do nothing of the kind. I'm in Angela Spendlove's art class."

"Oh. They're meeting this evening, aren't they? I must get out my brushes."

"You're in ASP?"

"Founder member. So I'll see you later."

I'm tempted to say it's a small world, but it really is a small village. The Henge Shop is happy to have Boris's poster in the window and charged nothing. The village shop insisted on the same rate they charge for small ads: not much of a public service. Hoping to ask Jonathan if I can pin one to the pub's notice board. Work has yet to start on the refurbishment of the old antiques shop so my last port of call will be the Methodist Chapel on the Herepath. Still have a dozen posters spare so I'll ask a few friends in the village if they'd mind advertising for me.

Wonder if I can get a refund for the misprint. Damned certain it isn't my fault Boris has come out as Doris.

Later; Avebury Trusloe

Back home after an evening with the Avebury Society of Painters. Had to field several questions into my absence last week and said that work had taken me to Edenborough. I mentioned MacGregor but it didn't raise any great interest.

Apparently Angela brought her pet Afghan hound in with her, and it was the model for the evening. My clockwise neighbour in the circle of easels complained that the dog wouldn't sit still but my neighbour to the other side said that was rather the point as the class were to capture movement.

"Don't suppose you have any idea what tonight's task will be?" I asked of the widdershins neighbour.

"Don't recall," she said, "but Angela didn't ask us to bring anything so you should be all right."

I was relieved to know I would be no more handicapped than anyone else for missing a week.

This all happened while we waited for Angela. Apparently she was delayed by family issues but after ten minutes filled with chit-chat she arrived with a large bag.

"So sorry to keep you waiting," she said. "Grandmama was needed so of course I had to drop everything."

Actually, I'm rather surprised Angela is a grandmother, but I suppose I too am easily old enough to be one. A grandfather, I mean. Alas, Gerald seems to have no desire to settle down and even if he did it would probably be on the far side of the world. Gerald was eleven when my father died so three generations of Warbrooks at least managed a passing acquaintance with each other before the reaper called.

Angela's bag contained an assortment of scarves and head scarves which she handed round.

"Take one, take one," she called. "It must be big enough to tie around your head and heavy enough that you can't see through it. Tonight, we will be doing automatic drawing. Drawing from memory and using only your inner senses. No peeking at the work in progress."

I found a headscarf in the bag and tested it around my

head. It seemed up to the task and had a faint aroma of lavender. I've noticed that Angela rather likes lavender. She often wears a sprig in the buttonhole of a cardigan.

"At least if it's in my memory I can keep the blessed thing still tonight," my clockwise neighbour said.

"If it doesn't sit still you can always imagine shooting it," I said light-heartedly.

"Actually, I was thinking of drawing my husband."

"Ah. Perhaps better not."

"I don't know. It's an appealing thought. But it wouldn't be a memory, would it."

"Hopefully not."

"Now, everyone," Angela began. "Before you wear your blindfolds I want you to place your feet firmly on the floor and reach out to the corners of your drawing paper. You must remember how you are standing so you can proportion your drawing. I know it's difficult for some of you to stand for a long time, but it would be much easier if you could keep your feet in the same position throughout the exercise."

"Bet she hasn't got my feet," my clockwise neighbour said.

I was pondering this as Angela continued. She asked us to draw a relative, or friend, or acquaintance we hadn't seen for a while and for whom we had strong feelings.

Apple Tree put up a hand.

"You don't need to be formal, Apple dear. This isn't school. And if you call me *miss* I will positively scream."

"I was wondering, *Angela*," Apple said, "If I could draw my pet rabbit. Only he died last week, and I miss him."

"Of course, dear. Everyone, pets count as friends."

Having spent most of the morning putting up posters of Boris my mind immediately settled on him as my subject. Of course, I couldn't just paint the image from the photograph as he was lying across Edith's legs and much as I might miss Edith I wasn't about to make an exhibit of her shins. During the day he, like his brother, spent most of the time asleep and the image of him curled on a cushion fixed itself in my mind's eye.

"You can begin," Angela said. "This is a twenty-minute

exercise and then we will be painting with our blindfolds."

"How will we know what colour we're painting?" one of the chaps asked.

"You will have to wait to find out," Angela said. "Twenty minutes everyone, starting now."

I was already tying the scarf behind my head. The smell of lavender was really quite strong but not unappealing. I had already gauged where each corner of the paper was and plunged straight in with the curve of Boris's back but had to check when my attempt to include his tail took my pencil off the edge. I tried again, this time making Boris a little smaller and managed to include everything from nose to tail without plunging into mid-air. The cushion didn't quite fit as it seemed I'd drawn him rather too near the bottom edge of the board, so I imagined him sleeping on a rug instead. Of course, when it came to drawing the details, such as his ears and whiskers there was an element of guesswork involved, but the abstract artists never bothered about the exact placement of body parts.

"Don't be cautious," Angela called. "Exuberance is everything. Be brave."

As she spoke I heard her getting nearer and then she was at my shoulder.

"Very good, Nevil. Is that Doris?"

"Doris? Ah, no. That was a printer's error. His name is Boris. And yes it is. Been missing three days."

"This is like an incantation," she said.

"How so?"

"A summoning. When ancient man painted animals he hoped to kill in the hunt. You are calling Boris to you."

"Am I? It really hadn't occurred to me. I just hope he is all right. So, it does look like a cat?"

"Oh yes. Definitely cattish."

Angela continued round the group, talking to each person in turn. I tried to add more detail but had rather lost my sense of where Boris was on the paper. Then after another few minutes Angela called time.

My effort was certainly more cat than not, but it seemed to be several cats all at once and not all the same size. Boris's tail was enormously long while his ears were tiny.

"Now I want you to use paint to create mass and texture," Angela said. "Again, you will be blindfolded but as you only have black and white paint you shouldn't get confused."

For a moment I was rather pleased because Boris is entirely black, but then I began to worry about turning him into a black blob. Before I could worry too much we had to prepare our paint and then it was back to the blindfolds.

"If you can avoid getting paint on the scarves it would make things much easier for me," Angela said. "I had to raid my wardrobe for this exercise."

I dabbed the brush in the paint, hoping to apply it thinly. Instead, the brush slid easily telling me I had overloaded it. I tried working quickly so the paint didn't run but was certain I had failed. So, I took a second brush and wiped it quickly across hoping to mop up any drips. Then I tried again, this time barely wetting the brush and working with quick dabs. Meanwhile Angela was slowly circling.

"Very good, very good, I'm seeing some excellent attempts here. Remember, you are painting what you are seeing in your mind's eye, in your memory. And memory is often false so don't be surprised if it looks different from how you think it should. Ah. Nevil."

"Hmm? What am I doing wrong?"

"I think you'll have more success with paint rather than water. There. I've moved your pots around for you."

I paused and rested a finger on the paper. It was decidedly too damp. I knew the paint would blur as soon as I touched it to the paper but had to continue anyway. I resigned myself to it not looking much like Boris.

"Ten more minutes everyone. Then you can have tea, and think about what to do with your paintings for the last stage of the evening."

My neighbour muttered something about a bonfire, but it was muffled by the scarf around her head. I painted cautiously and slowly, thinking that during the tea break I might at least get a good look at the work. Though I had little hope I could salvage anything. Angela called for five minutes, and I slowed even more, barely dabbing the brush on the paper until at last Angela called time on the first part of the evening and I pulled the scarf from my head.

Individual parts of 'Boris' bore some relation to a cat. There was an ear. There a whisker. There a nose. But they bore only a slight relation to each other.

"Impressionist, you reckon?" my other neighbour showed me her work.

"Who is it meant to be?" was the only sensible question I could muster.

"My late husband. He'd be spinning in his grave if he weren't cremated."

"Is that your cat?" Apple asked me. She had come round the circle of easels clearly intent on seeing my work.

"It is. But I haven't really captured him," I said.

"I mean on the poster outside."

"Oh, yes. Hoping someone's seen him."

"I think I have. This morning in the field by the Longstones. He seemed to be dancing."

"Dancing? That's not like Boris. Are you sure?"

"It was a black cat and it's near your house, isn't it?"

"Yes. The field is at the end of my garden."

"It was leaping up and spinning round. I thought it was caught in something. But then it disappeared. It was warm so it could've been heat haze."

"Thank you. I mean good. I'll go up there tomorrow. What do you think of your evening's effort?"

"Not much," she said. "But I like yours. It's not a cat. It's where a cat used to be."

Angela called out that tea was ready, and Apple had gone before I could ask what she meant.

Tusker behaved very oddly near the Longstones the other day. Did he know Boris was close by?

Postscriptum: two fingers of Budgitts whisky nightcap.

18 May; Avebury Trusloe

Cool and blustery start to the day. After breakfast I put on my coat and walked to the Longstones. It was hard to imagine anything 'dancing' in the field, let alone Boris. The squally wind sent ripples through the green barley and the Longstones stood like islands in a sea. Apple said she had seen Boris, or a cat like him, from the road. I suppose it's possible; certainly close enough. Can't recall any other black cats round here so if she saw one it may well be Boris. But maybe it only seemed black. How much could she see from a distance?

And why would Boris be dancing?

Back home now. Tusker is sleeping and my writing desk is calling me.

A SIGHTING?

Later; Waggon and Horses, Beckhampton

Telephone rang just before lunchtime. Quite a task dragging my thoughts away from darkest Africa where MacGregor's text had taken me.

"Hello. Avebury 5792, Nevil speaking."

"Mr Warbrook?"

"Yes, that's me. To whom am I speaking?"

"Delia Michaelmas. I'm in West Kennet. You've lost a cat."

"Ah! Indeed. Have you seen him?"

"I saw a black cat I didn't recognise. Near the Long Barrow."

"West Kennet?"

"That's it. Where are you?"

"That's why I'm surprised. I'm Avebury Trusloe. Is the cat still there?"

"It was an hour ago. I was walking Fitch, my grey-hound. I saw the cat, but it disappeared before I could get close. Then I saw it again. I think it was chasing butterflies."

"Butter—?"

"I know it sounds odd. But the field was full of orange-tipped butterflies. I'm sure the cat was chasing them. It might still be there."

"Thank you, thank you so much. Delia…?

"Michaelmas. Delia Michaelmas."

Lunch would have to wait. I jumped into the Rover and drove the two miles to the lay-by near the long barrow. Delia Michaelmas said she had seen the cat in the field to the right of the path leading to the barrow. I began walking up the slope. The day had warmed, and the wind dropped. Grasshoppers and crickets chirruped in the lush verges and red admiral butterflies flapped onto the path and lay with wings akimbo. Smaller butterflies danced through the grass ripening in the field. Then I saw Boris. At least, I think it was Boris. Just a black cat leaping up, as though playing with an invisible ball of wool, and disappearing into the long grass. I did not see it again.

Of course, I tried wading into the field to where I had seen him, but the grass was too dense and caught around my legs. I called, but it had no effect.

Behind me the cone of Silbury Hill punctuated the valley and beyond that the distant pale brown stone and buff brick of Avebury Trusloe. It seemed a long way, in cat-terms, from home.

I called for Boris until I was hoarse. Then arrived here for a drink and bite to eat. I'll go and look again once I'm refreshed.

Bedtime; Avebury Trusloe

Did not see Boris again. Perhaps I did not see him at all. Hard to tell. Returned home despondent and managed a few more pages on MacGregor. Tusker slunk out into the night with the look of a man about to face his executioners. Asked him to look for Boris. I hope he has better luck than me.

Postscriptum: pint of Thruxton's at lunchtime. Usual nightcap.

BELONGING

19 May; Red Lion, Avebury

Sermon on the nature of belonging this morning. Peter ought to take a look at his congregation and ask if he belongs here. All those blue rinses, tweed jackets, and walking sticks, not to mention the walking frames corralled beside the door must hamper his style, which is more interpretative dance than traditional Holy Communion.

Fortunately, it looks like the bell-ringers are going to elect Ruby Miller whose family has been in Avebury for three hundred years so I fancy the traditionalists on the PCC will still hold the balance of power.

Of course, I was mostly thinking about Boris who is not where he belongs. And Edith who is not where I think she belongs, though she wouldn't agree. And I thought of Gerald who has yet to decide where he belongs and perhaps never will. I also thought of myself and my tenure as editor of *This Iron Race*. Am I where I belong or should I admit the undertaking is more fraught than I supposed; or rather, as I admit to myself, not bearing the results I hoped?

It is not that I believe I have failed MacGregor, though I sense I am inadequate to the task except where MacGregor's intentions are clear and easily stated. Nor is there any great flaw in the work itself: it is among his greatest works if one judges it by imagination and literary skill alone. No, the problem is simpler than that but quite intractable: *This Iron Race*, as originally written by MacGregor, is proving to be unlike the work I, or anyone else, expected. It is too frank for its time. It is too 'knowing' of things that should not be admitted. Unlike anything by Valentine Stallworthy or Emilé Breton it is too bold in its condemnation of the rich and powerful and yet too subtle also, for it portrays the reasons for their faults.

What was it he wrote in *volume one*? Writing without heroes or villains, but only of ordinary men and women; 'players' he called them. Perhaps that's the real issue: he does not let us take sides.

I fancy I will make a decent fist of restoring a novel that few will read.

After the sermon I asked Lucy if she would mind me putting up a poster for Boris on the church notice board.

"Still no sign of him?" she said in that pitying voice people use when they think you should prepare for the worst.

"I wouldn't say that," I said. "Apple Tree thinks she saw him. And a dog walker at West Kennet claims she saw him near the long barrow. Of course, they cannot be certain it was him, but one is hopeful."

"Well, that's *something*," she said. "Of course, you can use the noticeboard. I hope you hear something soon."

She had more or less implied Apple and the dogwalker had borne false-witness, but never mind. Curious how so many clergy and clergymen's wives are sceptics at heart.

I ought to be drinking up and getting home. Intend an afternoon of editing. What with my week on the canal looming work must continue even on the Sabbath.

Postscriptum: two pints of Craftsman Bitter.

Post-Postscriptum: fifteen stone, eight.

Later; Avebury Trusloe

Tremendous noise at dusk. Turned out to be jackdaws seeing off a pair of jays. There is no fraternity among thieves. I think my general glumness at lunchtime came partly from missing Boris, and therefore being reminded I miss so many of my family from my late father to my absent son and ex-wife, or wife, rather, and partly from the scenes I'm currently reading in *This Iron Race*. MacGregor's depiction of slavery in Africa is unsettling. The character is a good man, for his times, and I believe MacGregor, by the standards of his times, had no time for racialism of any kind, yet something about the work sticks in my throat. Perhaps it is too true to his gaze and my gaze is not his.

I doubt Valentine Stallworthy ever described a single black character, unless it was a servant in the background. But still, for not portraying people as we think they should be portrayed, or simply for not being their colour, some will condemn MacGregor and condemn me as messenger.

Owls are noisy tonight.

Postscriptum: whisky nightcap.

20 May; Market Street Tearooms, Devizes

Letter from Devizes Surgery this morning. I am due for a review and my appointment is two weeks on Thursday. Fortunately, or not depending how you look at it, it falls neatly between my canal week and Pembrokeshire with Creative Havens.

Thumbing through the last week of my journal I fear I have been making up for Lent and abstinence while on Phloxy whatever it was. I suppose a certain relaxation was inevitable but better to be on best behaviour for the next... Blast. That won't work at all. I can hardly be temperant while reviewing pubs. CARP expects me to dine out at lunchtime and in the evenings. Somewhere I have a list of the establishments they want me to review. Oh well, Dr Saunders will be disappointed, but I can bear it. I wonder how much exercise one gets while boating. It can't be much effort waggling a tiller.

Couldn't bear the thought of the canal café today. Saw something on the local television news. Mother crying. Photos of the girl. Piece in today's Devizes Messenger reported they are still looking for the father and presumed murderer. For some reason it's all made me think of Gerald. Not heard from him since the begging letter. What with the coup in Borneo you really think he would telephone and let us know he's well, or at least still alive. It's selfish. That's what it is. Sheer selfishness. Even if he doesn't telephone me he could at least tell his mother.

Manageress is giving me the eye. I think she would like my table more profitably employed.

Later; Avebury Trusloe

As I sat scribbling away earlier the waitress was dispatched to usher me out the building. They do it discreetly of course.

"Another pot of tea, sir?"

"Ah. No. Best not. Long drive home you know."

I doubt she did know. The young have bladders like municipal swimming pools.

"I'll clear these away for you."

I could hardly object to her housekeeping, even if the teapot and cup and plate for my scone earlier legitimised my presence.

"Yes of course. Thank you."

"They haven't found him," the girl said.

"Who?"

"Him." She indicated the newspaper. "On that boat."

"No, but I'm sure they will."

"Hope so. What a horrible thing to do. No wonder his wife gave him the push. Not that she's an angel."

"You know her?"

"Live on same road. Everyone knows each other here. Girl was a sweet thing. If you want to stay you will need to buy something. Needn't be much but we are busy. Telling you polite because madam over there wouldn't."

"Thank you. And thank you for the warning. No. I think I shall head off. Things to do."

"See you soon."

"You probably shall."

I'll need to shop again at the weekend as it will be my last opportunity before picking up the boat. Even if I am eating out each day I shall want breakfast. Hope they've towed the burnt-out boat away by next week. Too awful having to sail past it.

Wonder what the girl meant saying the mother was no angel? Surely there can never be justification for what the father did. I mean his own daughter. No. I'm sure she didn't mean that. Why can't life be black and white? It would be so much more reassuring.

Postscriptum: a small nightcap.

Boris!

21 May; Avebury Trusloe

Boris is back. Sitting here with my toast and scrambled eggs half-eaten but felt the need to write it down to make it seem real, even though I can see him fast asleep on his familiar cushion.

No indication where he might have been this last week, though how I might possibly know such a thing I cannot imagine: he was not about to return with a holiday gift. He wolfed down his breakfast though does not appear to have been starving and apart from being a little stiff-legged he seems healthy. I do think his adventures have added a few grey hairs to his chin as he and his brother are no longer quite as identical as they once were.

Tusker is also fast asleep but in the opposite corner of the room. I wonder if he had become used to being a solitary cat and rather liked it. Hopefully, they will soon be best friends again.

I should mention how he returned. It was quite simple really. I opened the door as I always do, and Tusker leapt inside and went straight to his bowl. I was just going to close the door again when I saw a flicker of movement and there was Boris emerging from the hedge at the bottom of the garden. I stopped in surprise and then the moment rather overcame me, as I rushed into the garden in my pyjamas. Poor Boris. I rather think he had hoped for a quiet reappearance for he froze and seemed almost on the point of flight again. I steadied myself and kneeling down extended a hand and coaxed him. He kissed my fingers with his nose as though to reassure himself all was normal and rolled on his back and let me tickle his tummy. I suppose if my behaviour were unlike me—I am not in the habit of rushing into the garden before properly dressed—then his was unlike him as normally one would need gauntlets before attempting such indignities with him, but he was purring and mewling contentedly.

"Where have you been?" I asked. "Where on earth have you been?"

I glanced over the hedge but apart from the distant Longstones and the green barley the field was empty.

I had intended to drive to Pewsey today and investigate the canal prior to my boat trip next week but have changed my mind. I would far rather stay in and reassure myself Boris is perfectly well after his misadventure.

Bedtime; Avebury Trusloe

A fine day which, apart from my excursion before breakfast, I have spent wholly indoors. Editing continues and today has been quietly productive. Deadline with H&D is looking achievable even if I manage no work at all next week.

Tusker was only too happy to go out tonight, but Boris looked at me as though I were mad. I suppose I cannot blame him, but made sure the litter tray was topped-up. Whatever he has been up to this last week he seems to have mellowed as he let me scratch under his chin this evening. Try that with Tusker and it would be three weeks of Phloxymycin. Quite certain he has more grey hairs than a week ago.

Postscriptum: two fingers of Owl Service as a nightcap.

22 May; Avebury Trusloe

An unsettling start to the day, though Edith always had the ability to make me feel uneasy or downright guilty regardless of the o'clock. She telephoned just as I sat down for a morning's labour on the restoration of *This Iron Race, volume two.*

I walked into the hallway with several half-formed replies in my head as I assumed it was either a salesman, or perhaps Dessie or Pea unnecessarily reminding me of next week's boating assignment. Thus, I was ill-prepared when, instead of having someone to hurl abuse or irritation at, it was my ex-wife enquiring of her knees.

"Those *are* my knees?" she said again after my initial hesitation. "On the poster outside the village hall."

"Ah. I mean, yes. Though it was unintentional."

"You unintentionally pinned my knees on the notice board?"

"No. I mean. Yes, but it was Boris. I had lost Boris."

"Nevil?"

"Yes dear? I mean. Oh God. Sorry. Yes, Edith?"

"I am teasing. How long has he been missing? Are you worried?"

"Oh. Yes. I mean no. That is, I didn't realise you were teasing. I thought. Well. You can probably tell. But no, I was very worried as it's most unlike him and I was getting odd reports of him. I mean, people had seen him behaving oddly. But I'm delighted to say he returned home yesterday morning. Not yet had a chance to take down all the posters."

"All of them?"

"Yes. There's quite a few. About your knees. Dreadfully sorry but it was the only photograph I had of Boris. It must be four years old I suppose."

"At least, I'd have thought," she said. "We had only just moved into the cottage."

"Yes," I said hesitantly. "Happy days, eh?"

"They were. For a while. How is he?"

"Boris?"

"Who else?"

"He seems quieter. Bit greyer under the chin. Especially when he's next to Tusker. Don't look quite like brothers any more. He's eating though, so all seems well."

"You should take him to the vets. You never know what dreadful things farmers are putting down these days."

It was all very well for her to suggest I take Boris to the vets as she wouldn't be paying, but I suppose she has a point.

"I'll see how he is in a few days," I said, though now I think of it, it will have to be after I return from boating on the canal. "If he's not his old self I'll take him to the surgery in Devizes."

"It's not money you're worried about, is it?"

"No, no. Not at all. He is my cat after all."

"I do still think of him as a tiny bit mine. If it's expensive, let me know. Promise Nevil. I know you can be stiff-necked sometimes."

"I promise," I said, somewhat to my surprise. "If the surgery finds anything amiss may I call you?"

"Of course! Why ever would you not call me? Rupert is always out with the horses, so you needn't worry about him answering."

"Then I will," I said. "That is, if there's anything to report. Speaking of which, have you heard anything from Gerald lately?"

"Not for a few weeks, why?"

"I was a bit worried by this coup thing on the news."

"Coo who?"

"Not coo, coup, with a 'p'. Tanks and petrol bombs. You must have seen it."

"In Brunei?"

"Is it?"

"That's what they're saying."

"So not Borneo."

"Brunei is in Borneo. It's an island."

I was now deeply confused.

"All I really want to know is if our boy is all right. I've not heard anything. Have you? It would have been nice of him to let us know."

"But he's nowhere near Brunei. He's in Indonesia."

"So why do I think he's in Borneo?"

"Because that's the island."

I hesitated, aware that my knowledge was, to say the least, sketchy, but determined to be certain Gerald was all right.

"And the island is in Indonesia?"

Edith laughed.

"No, Nevil. Indonesia is in Borneo, I think. It's a huge island. Brunei is in Borneo as well, as is..., oh I can't remember. But no, Gerald is fine in Sumatra."

"Sumatra?"

"Yes."

"Excellent. So, I've been worrying for no reason. Still think it would be nice of him to let us know."

"But it's hundreds of miles away. I don't suppose it even occurred to him."

"It probably didn't. So, Gerald is perfectly happy in... Sumatra, and Tusker seems happy. Good. Good. Everybody's happy."

"I've got to go. Speak soon about Boris. Don't be unhappy."

Easier said than done. Naturally, I couldn't settle to work after that and ended up going for a walk towards Windmill Hill. Lovely day for those without a care in the world. Of course, that does not include me, so nature's glory was a bit of a waste.

Better get something for lunch and try and work this afternoon. Busy this evening at dominoes.

Bedtime; Avebury Trusloe

Horrible experience on way home tonight. Can't even begin to write about it now but I don't think Sid or Bert will be accepting lifts off me any time soon. I shall find time after breakfast tomorrow but for the moment I think I will pray for a good night's sleep.

Postscriptum: two pints of Slater's Ale in Wilcot and a stiff nightcap.

AN ENCOUNTER

23 May; Avebury Trusloe

The Blind Phoenician Sailor isn't quite the farthest flung of the several public houses in the Kennet Valley League but from Avebury it is easily the most awkward to get to. There is no direct route as the main road via Marlborough takes one miles out of the way, so one is forced to take a single-track road across the Downs via the villages of East Kennet and Alton Priors. It's a nightmare to drive, especially after dark. But I digress since that section of road did not bring any trouble last night. Though that may have been only by good fortune as, according to Bert when I dropped him by St James's in Avebury, I had driven it like a madman.

If I did, and I admit to no recollection of the journey from the canal bridge at Wilcot to Beckhampton where I dropped Sid, I would claim extenuating circumstances having been shaken out of my wits.

The evening had gone rather well. The Phoenicians, as they call themselves, are a solid team and after our last few away matches I was expecting something between a loss and a humiliation, but on the night the bones did well for me and I managed two wins and scraped a draw, narrowly besting the efforts of Sid and Bert who each won two games and lost one.

Despite the margin of victory, it was a hard evening as all the games were tactical with hardly anyone scoring high, and we did not get away from Wilcot until nearly eleven.

"What happened to you tonight?" Bert asked me on our way to the car.

"What do you mean? I did rather well: better than either of you."

"That's what I mean, you fool. Where'd this form come from? We could do with that against The Crown next week."

"Ah, if I only knew," I said. "Afraid this time next week I'll be moored somewhere along the canal."

"Or sunk," Sid said darkly.

"One could practically walk across the canal bed and still keep one's hair dry," I said, repeating something I'd heard at the Caen Hill Café.

"Damp though, should expect," Bert said. "Y'can feel the damp, even here."

That was true. The day had been warm but clear skies had sent the temperature plummeting and mist was gathering.

"Soon be out of it once we're on the Downs," I said cheerfully.

Sid had a torch which was handy, for the car park at the Blind Phoenician Sailor is completely unlit, but once we had the car door open the interior light allowed everyone to get comfortable and belted-up.

"Put the heater on will ye," Sid said.

"I'll try," I said. "Can be a bit temperamental."

"Eee, bugger that's cold," Sid protested as a blast of air hit him in the knees.

"Warm up once we get going," I said.

We had barely got going, with the village green on our left and a row of houses on the right, when the road pitched up and narrowed for the canal bridge. I had sat forward to see better as the headlights were reflecting back off the mist but at the last moment as I was about to commit to the bridge there was someone standing in the middle of the road. I braked and in desperation swung the car onto a gravel lane just before the bridge and we scrabbled to a halt. Don't know how I didn't hit anything as my door ended up hard against a wall.

"Ruddy hell! What was that for?" Sid bellowed.

"Chap could lose all pleasure in life," Bert said cryptically.

"Didn't you see?" I protested.

"See what?"

"The girl on the bridge."

It was only when I said the words I realised it was a girl. I suppose I must have realised the figure wasn't tall enough for an adult, but I had barely glimpsed a face as I braked and turned aside. Nevertheless, it must have registered as a young girl for me to say it.

What she might be doing at this hour did not occur to me.

"I saw no one," Sid said.

"I was rolling a ciggie," Bert said. "Gone to buggery now. Somewhere on the floor I expect."

"I was driving and paying attention and I tell you she was in the middle of the blasted road. What was I supposed to do?"

"Best see if she's okay then," Bert said.

"Thank you. A sensible idea. Bear with me. Bert, can you see out the back?"

With Bert's directions I managed to reverse to the road and as I did so the headlights swept across the tarmac over the canal bridge.

"Bloody hell. There is something," Sid said.

There was. But it wasn't the girl. It wasn't even human.

"What on earth is it?" Bert said.

"Bugger this," Sid said. "Who'd leave a traffic cone there?"

I had been looking for a child, but Sid had seen it right. Walking a few yards to the crown of the bridge he picked it up and after a moments' study tossed it over the parapet.

"Done," he said on returning.

"Not exactly a good citizen thing to do," I said. "Someone will run over that with their boat."

"With any luck it will be yours," Bert said.

"They'll fish it out soon enough," Sid said. "Leastways it's not on the road."

I drove on. The whole thing must have shaken me because I don't recall much after that. At one moment on a bend up on the Downs I heard Sid protesting and Bert falling sideways on the back seat but other than that my mind is a blank. The only thing I was certain of is that the girl on the bridge was the girl I saw by the burnt-out boat at Caen Hill. Except, it was more a feeling she was the same as I could hardly have recognised her in the dark and all we had found was a traffic cone. But of course, the girl couldn't be the same one, could she.

Anyway, after dropping Bert by St James's I drove home quietly and let myself in to the silent house. Tusker was happy to run into the dark but as last night Boris preferred his cushion. I still had the washing up to do but couldn't face it and instead poured a stiff whisky and made for bed before jotting a few lines in my journal and offering a prayer.

Dreamt I was motoring on a canal boat with six inches of water sloshing round my ankles and woke up feeling crapulous. Hoped my mood would improve for having written up my journal but it hasn't worked.

Must finish breakfast and then get ready for driving to Amesbury. Six weeks since I last visited Mummy and if I leave it any longer the guilt will start to eat away at me.

Lunchtime; Gingerbread House, Manningford Bohune

Judith Malmsey was quite correct; Mummy was indeed back to something like her usual self: which is to say she was gay and talkative and making not the slightest sense. There was something about motorcycle rides at night, which I assume was with her gentleman caller, and how thrilling it all was except when his friends turned up and chased him. She didn't like that bit at all.

Unable to contribute much to her fantasy; I said that I would soon be working at Oxford.

"Oh, darling," she said, rather too loudly for my comfort, "Your father will be so pleased for you."

I bit my tongue and did not correct her tense.

"Will you be at Israel College?" she asked with surprising lucidity.

"Ah, no. I will be tutoring at Belshade. But still, it's Oxford all the same."

Her face rather fell when I said I wouldn't be at Israel.

"Belshade is a perfectly good college," I said with all the plausibility I could muster. "I'll be teaching poetry."

"But you can visit your father, can't you," she said brightening again. "He will be so proud of you. Do you want to tell him or shall I?"

I hesitated. It seemed odd not wanting to tell Daddy about Oxford, but of course it was impossible to tell him anything.

"Perhaps you could tell him," I said. "When you see him next."

"Of course. He calls for me at night, you know."

"Does he? Forgive me Mummy, you lead such a busy life," I humoured. "Who calls for you?"

"Your father, of course."

I realised I had no idea who Mummy was talking about.

I doubt Daddy ever rode a motorbike in his life and even in the Aller we rarely got above a dizzying fifty miles an hour. Still, if Daddy really would be pleased about my appointment at Belshade I can pray tonight and ask God to inform him. I stand at least as much chance of letting him know as poor Mummy.

I kept an eye open for that pretty Spanish girl but saw no sign of her. Then I recalled Judith saying she had returned to Spain for some reason. If they were still finding black feathers in Mummy's room, and somehow I thought it more probable than not regardless of how oddly they might be arriving, no one mentioned it to me and after an hour of Mummy happily chatting her conversation got steadily more sporadic and I sensed her attention straying to the television where two middle-aged men were playing snooker.

"I had better be going," I said.

"To Oxford, dear?"

"Not just yet. Term doesn't start 'til October. Home to Avebury."

"Why ever do you want to go there?"

"It's where I live. You remember. With Edith."

"Oh yes. And there's someone else. Someone else."

"Gerald, I think you mean. Gerald, your grandson."

"No," she said firmly. "Not him. You're a very lucky boy, you know."

"Am I, Mummy?"

She didn't answer. The crowd watching the snooker on the television were applauding and after a pause everyone in the room joined in.

I am not, if I am honest, looking forward to next week. Can't imagine canal boating being anything more than tedium mingled with discomfort, no matter how well appointed the boat is, and a whole week of pub dining is too much. That being so, I knew I could get something amusingly exotic at The Gingerbread House, so I stopped here on the way home. Ordered buffalo soup with Peau Rouge flatbread. Hopefully, it won't be long as I am peckish.

The Perils of Soup

Later; Avebury Trusloe

Home again and feeling decidedly wounded in body and pride, not to mention my trousers are ruined.

Both cats are sound asleep, but I can't help feeling Boris is not at all his normal self since his return. Tusker must feel the same way as he has been quite stand-offish with his brother. Perhaps I ought to take Boris to the vet' but it must wait until my return from the canal. Meantime I'll ask Mrs Pumphrey to keep an eye on him.

Still only three in the afternoon and I hope for a few hours editing on *This Iron Race* before tea. Meanwhile I thought I'd return to my journal while the memory is fresh.

I did not wait long before a waiter arrived with a plate and a shallow bowl and, somewhat mystifyingly, a small metal tealight holder. These were placed before me.

"Shall I light the candle, sir?" he asked.

"Why not," I said, still not understanding its purpose. I was next to a window so hardly lacking light.

He produced a small blowtorch from his jacket and lit the candle with a tongue of hissing blue flame.

Some half a minute passed before a second waiter arrived with a trolley holding a tureen of soup and a platter of Peau Rouge flatbread.

"The soup?" he asked. I beckoned him to proceed, and he ladled a generous portion of thick brown liquid into my bowl and spread several sheets of Peau Rouge on my plate.

I had just realised there was no spoon when he produced two pieces of silverware from the trolley. One was a pair of tongs and the other was a spoon with a curious clasp mechanism where the stem met the bowl.

"An aroma spoon, sir," he said. "Herbs from the prairie complement the soup. Allow me."

The purpose of the tea light and tongs was now apparent as he held a pellet of dried material in the flame before securing it in the clasp on the spoon.

"Enjoy, sir," he said, and returned to the kitchen.

I hesitated a moment. The bulk of the spoon was awkward in my hand, and it took a few attempts to get my grip sorted. Then I dipped it into the soup and raised it to my lips. What can I say? The soup was extraordinary and aroma spoon or no, I was transported to the vast open plain where hordes of buffalo roamed, even though I have only ever seen them from an aeroplane or in American *bouvier* films. I savoured the taste and then dipped my spoon for more.

Whether the pellet of herbs was a little more aflame than it ought to be or if I weren't paying attention, I couldn't say, but the effect was searing pain in my eye, as when one is too close to the smoke of a bonfire. Of course, I dropped the spoon with a clatter and dabbed a napkin furiously at my tears. My cry of pain having alerted him, the French maître d' rushed to my table with the gestures of a swan attempting lift-off.

"Zer, may I 'elp you? Eez everything all right?"

"It is not," I said clasping the napkin to my face. "Bally smoke in my eye. Infernal contraption. Can't I have a spoon? A proper spoon?"

"Ze chef does not think the zoop does ze buffalo justeece wizout ze aroma, zir."

"Does he? Well, I'm afraid I must disagree."

I blinked rapidly and risked taking the napkin from my face.

"If zer will wait."

"Sir will wait," I said.

The maître d' retreated with the offending aroma spoon and returned with one of normal appearance.

"Thank you. Thank you indeed."

My eye no longer weeping, I returned to the soup. It was certainly no less excellent for lack of a smoking ember in my face and if I could no longer conjure up the prairie it certainly surpassed even the richest oxtail I had ever eaten.

However, disaster lingered for neither the maître d' or I had noticed that in dropping the aroma spoon I had dislodged the pellet of dried herbs, and this had continued to burn in secret. Its whereabouts became clear with a searing pain in my nether parts followed by the stink of burnt cotton.

I scrambled to my feet, knocking the bowl sideways with a brown tide over the linen tablecloth and dabbed water frantically at the affected area while emitting faint squawks of pain. The maître d' flew in again and this time I admitted assistance was required.

It took some explaining and even the chef emerged from his cavern with a scowl and a thick Flemish accent. I could not tell if he were more annoyed by my ineptitude—I would say inexperience—with the aroma spoon, or with the maître d' for allowing me to eat his precious soup without it.

The result of a three-way conversation in English, Franglaise and Flemish was a new table and a fresh bowl of buffalo soup and careful instruction in the correct way to hold an aroma spoon. Once the chef, who was clearly the villain of the piece with his claptrap ideas about cuisine, departed the maître d' offered to compensate for repairs to my trouser and I graciously accepted his offer. I did not enquire what I might be due for repairs to my person. There are some matters too delicate to discuss at table.

Bedtime; Avebury Trusloe

Some three hours of editing this afternoon. Believe I might spend next week on the canal with a clear conscience, so far as *This Iron Race* is concerned. After lunch I took to my kilt as the burn on my inner thigh was chafing against my trouser leg. It improved matters and I have now dabbed the affected area with cold cream.

Not much of an appetite this evening so had scrambled eggs on toast. Bit of a comedown after lunch but at least nothing is burnt.

Tusker is out but Boris is happy snoozing. As, I think, am I.

Postscriptum: glass of Navajo Whisky at lunchtime and my usual nightcap.

24 May; Avebury Trusloe

Telephoned Clutterbuck Surgery in Devizes immediately after breakfast and made an appointment for Boris. Reproaching myself for not doing so earlier in the week as I knew he wasn't quite his old self when he returned on Tuesday and only waited in the expectation, or should that be hope, he was recovering from the arduousness of a week away from home and would soon be back to normal.

Not that Boris and his brother are what anyone might call normal cats.

Made the decision when Tusker sauntered in after his night out doing whatever cats do and tucked straight into his breakfast while Boris continued snoozing on his cushion. Never known a cat do so much sleeping and while there was an argument he was merely tired after his week away that can no longer be true.

Beginning to wonder if he's eaten something poisonous. One hears of farmers using poisoned carcasses to kill foxes, crows, and buzzards, but it's frightfully hard to prove these things.

There was an odd moment as I gave them my address.

"Foxglove Cottage, Longstones Lane, Avebury," I said. "Avebury Trusloe, actually, but everyone knows it."

There was a pause at the other end.

"Avebury?" she said.

"That's right. Just off the Beckhampton Road."

"Are you sure it's your cat?" she asked.

I was perplexed and a little offended at the idea I might have unwittingly taken in a stray.

"Of course, he's my cat. Inasmuch as a cat belongs to anyone. He's just a bit off-colour. Assume he had a bad time of it living off the land."

The receptionist pointed out that it was late May and hardly inclement.

"I do think it's the vet's opinion that matters," I said.

"Of course. But we see a lot of patients from Avebury. Things happen there," she said.

"Well, it's the first I've heard of it."

"I've booked you for ten o'clock on Wednesday," she said.

I apologised and said that next week was impossible. She was put-out at offering a fresh appointment.

"I suppose tomorrow is impossible," I said. "Only I'm away next week."

"Fully booked," she said. "If you like I can put you on standby in case there's a cancellation."

"Thank you, yes. But if you would also give me an appointment for the week starting third June, I'd be grateful."

This was arranged. The only annoying thing is I had anticipated going shopping tomorrow morning and will have to stay in until at least two in case they call. I suppose I only have myself to blame for not acting sooner.

Tusker is scratching the door wanting to go out. Boris hasn't moved.

Victualling

Later; Market Street Tearooms, Devizes

There has been a change of plan. If I must stay in tomorrow in case the vet' calls I had better shop today. The town is less crowded in the week anyway, so long as one avoids the dreaded 'school run,' and Budgitts is a lot more pleasant without hordes of screaming children.

I had a glance at the catalogue from Waterfowl Cruisers earlier as there's no point buying something beyond the capacity of the galley, but I really needn't have worried. It is as well-appointed as my kitchen and the only question was what I needed that wouldn't be provided by my pub tour. That, so far as I could tell, came down to a decent breakfast to set me up each day. Therefore, I have loaded up with tinned beans, bacon, eggs, tomatoes, and blood pudding. Also have a half-dozen lamb's kidneys as a treat and a loaf of that sliced white bread that lasts forever. Considered getting a few pints of long-life milk, but it's vile stuff and I can probably pick up a pint or two while boating. I'm hardly venturing into the back of beyond.

Saw a copy of the Devizes Messenger in Budgitts. Still not found the girl's father. Speculation he fled abroad. Better stop as the waitress has my tea and toasted sandwich.

Postscriptum: arrived home to the ringing of the telephone. I hoped it was Clutterbucks offering an appointment for Boris, but it was Angela Spendlove.

"Oh, hello Angela, what can I do for you?"

"I'm telephoning everyone to say there's a change of plan this evening."

"Oh. Is the meeting off?"

"Not at all. It's a lovely afternoon so I thought we could do landscape painting. We haven't tried the outdoors yet."

"Ah. Of course. Al fresco."

"I've arranged with Nancy Curlew for us all to park at Manor Farm. She says Able won't mind. Then it's a hike up the hill I'm afraid, but the view will be worthwhile."

"Of course. Usual time?"

"I thought six-thirty, if everyone can manage it. So far no one's backed out. I've picked up the easels from the school so all you need is your usual kit."

"Six-thirty then. Manor Farm. Right ho."

Weather is nice enough. Only hope it holds for the next few hours. Carrying everything up the hill won't be fun.

SUNSET PAINTING

Evening; Avebury Trusloe

At just after the appointed time, I parked in the yard at Manor Farm, joining several other members who had already arrived. As soon as I got out Jenny Atkins and Apple Tree approached me.

"We were just talking about your cat," Jenny said. "We think we've seen him in the meadow between Trusloe and the village."

"Oh, well thank you. Actually, he's back."

"Oh good. But he must have only just got home."

"Tuesday morning actually. Exhausted mind you. He's spent the last three days sleeping."

"Oh, well it can't have been," Apple said. "I saw him this morning."

"I thought he was chasing mice," Jenny added. "He was leaping in the air and pouncing."

"Can't have been Boris," I said. "I assure you he's scarcely moved from his cushion. I don't think it can have been Tusker either as he tends to stay in during the day. But I'm sure it's someone's cat."

Their puzzlement was broken by Angela calling everyone.

"If you would like to collect your easels from my car. The sun will not wait for us."

Fortunately, Angela did not have us walking onto the Downs themselves, but only about halfway where the path briefly levels off and we set up our easels on the verge. The air was still, and we all had the pleasure of watching a barn owl silently swooping across the slope.

Of course, no one dared try to capture something as elusive as an owl and instead everyone settled to painting the landscape as the day sunk into shades of pink and amber.

"The light is changing all the time," Angela trilled. "You must paint what you see then remember you have seen it. If you try to chase the light you will still be working when the stars come out."

"The pillars of the sun," someone said as several shafts of sunlight fanned from beneath a cloud.

The owl drifted over the path, saw us, and turned about. Cows lazily shifted in their pasture and Avebury within its massive earthwork bathed in a cloud of gold.

"Broad colours," Angela said. "If you cannot see the details don't try to paint them. Think of the impressionists: Monet, Cézanne, Renoir."

I had a generous squeeze of green on my palette but there was no green in sight. Instead, it was as though the world had been reduced to every shade of yellow from crocus to umber with the sky streaked with rose red and pale blue. Only the foreground, where a fence paralleled the path, was defined with every distant thing half-formed, as though the land was dissolving in the gathering dusk. The only distinct point of colour was the sun itself.

It was, when I stopped painting to watch it, quite wonderful.

"I do believe you're inspired," Jenny Atkins said as I was putting what I hoped were the finishing touches to my work.

"Really? One just tries to do one's best," I said.

"No. I think it's really good."

Angela overheard and came over.

"It is a great improvement. Working outside helps you."

"It's no hardship on an evening like this," I said.

Indeed, it was not. For the first time with ASP I felt at ease and hope some of the joy I took in art back in my student days has revived. On returning home I placed my 'sunset over the village' on top of the fridge to dry and tore up my dreadful attempt to paint Boris and put it in the bin.

25 May; Avebury Trusloe

I have dipped into my boating supplies early and enjoyed buttered crumpets with Scotch Bonnet marmalade and French coffee for breakfast. There was a drop left in the pot and while finishing it off I thought I'd write concerning Boris.

I say Boris but ought I to write 'Boris' as I am wondering if the cat on the cushion by the kitchen boiler is an impostor?

Tusker is sound asleep in the opposite corner of the kitchen, but sleeping is the only obvious similarity as Boris is noticeably thinner and more, for want of a better word, careworn. I might even say older but if I admit that 'Boris' is older than Tusker then I am accepting this cat is not Boris and Boris is still lost somewhere. Jenny and Apple's testimony last evening also suggests that Boris, or at least a cat very like Boris, is still wandering about the village and behaving strangely: 'dancing' they said, and the lady from West Kennet—Delia, I think—said the same.

But then again, I can't imagine Boris dancing and I'm

not at all sure it was he I saw chasing butterflies near the long barrow.

Boris, whether he is asleep by the boiler or still out and about, is not behaving like Boris. Who was the wit who said that if cats could talk they wouldn't bother speaking to us?

My painting of the sunset has held up rather well. Often when one views in the morning what one achieved the evening before it can seem tarnished, as though the glamour of achievement has worn away; but no, I am still rather delighted by it. ASP have a yearly competition, and I should consider entering.

Last sip of coffee and I'll settle down to editing *This Iron Race*. Of course, won't be easy to concentrate as I am hoping for a telephone call and an appointment for Boris, or his impostor, but one shall do one's best.

Evening; Red Lion, Avebury

A delight of late spring and early summer is one can walk to the pub in the evening and, provided one does not get distracted by company, be home before it's truly dark.

I came down as I am tired of the typewriter and tired of waiting for the telephone. Even though I rather gave up on them around midday—I have a sneaking suspicion they close early on Saturdays—I was still hoping right up until five this afternoon and it is enervating waiting for a call and especially so when it doesn't come. Poor 'Boris'—and even if it is not Boris it is someone's cat—will have to wait until my return from boating.

I'm considering whether to take *This Iron Race* with me next week. On the one hand, I imagine there will be hours to fill; but on the other I shall be dining out most evenings, perhaps all evenings, and will have to write up my notes on each establishment. Of course, I will resent the time away from work, but it might be for the best. At least there is twelve-hundred to consider and the expense account.

There are worse ways to make a living.

Postscriptum: two pints Cropwell's Bitter.

26 May; Avebury Trusloe

I have stopped for a bite to eat and a sit down. Chadwick was in his element this morning, which is to say he was torturing the congregation even more than usual. The homily was on some unfortunate Chinese chap persecuted for being a Christian. Anyway, he had us all on our feet facing the wall while he prowled behind our backs urging us to pray for Chan, or whatever his name was. Only one who was let off was Fred Thirsk, who is still recuperating from his stroke. Feet were bloody killing me after only ten minutes, and he must have kept us there for all of twenty-five before we sat down. Whatever one was supposed to feel for the unfortunate Chan rather got lost in the discomfort.

During the social afterwards Sid approached me about next week's match with The Crown at Broad Hinton.

"Only I thought you're on the canal so it's not far."

"It may not be far, but I won't have the motorcar."

"Then give me a call and Bert can pick you up. Only be a few miles, won't it. We crossed it on way to Wilcot."

"Ah. Thank you for reminding me of that. Thing is, I won't have a telephone either and I'll probably be busy reviewing pubs and restaurants, so out most evenings."

"I'm just saying if you're only down the road a whiles and should you have nothing on, find a telephone and give me a call."

"Sorry Sid, but it's hardly like I'm a great asset to the team, as you are always so keen to point out."

"Well, if that's how you feel. I was thinking of Bert. It's too much for him playing four or five games when you're away. And if it comes to it, you're often aways."

Blighter was trying to make me feel guilty.

"I'm sorry but I have a living to make. If, and I mean if, I am free on Tuesday evening I will give you a call. But expect me to be absent. That's all I can say."

Sid's got a bloody nerve. If Bert can't manage five games why doesn't he take the extra?

Chadwick caught me just as I was leaving and asked if I spoke any foreign languages.

"Smattering of Italian," I said. "Schoolboy French. And I suppose I could brush up my Ancient Greek. Why, do you need something translated?"

"Possibly," he said. "Just planning ahead."

I've no idea what he's up to.

Arrived home eager for lunch but saw Mrs Pumphrey weeding her front garden so thought it a good idea to remind her of the cats and mention Boris was poorly.

"I thought I hadn't seen him out. Has he not got better?"

"No. Not at all. He sleeps most of the day and doesn't want to go out at night. I telephoned Clutterbuck's in Devizes; had hoped they would see him before I go but they haven't called back. Anyway, he's booked in Wednesday week."

"And Tusker?"

"Oh, he's perfectly fine."

"That's all right then. You remember Bill and I are on holiday next month."

"I hope you have a good time. Anywhere nice?"

"Ramsgate."

"Ah, well. Next month. Oh?"

I had remembered the Stackpole Creative Haven.

"We're going down on the ninth for six days," she said.

It coincided exactly with my week in Pembrokeshire.

"Thank you for reminding me. No trouble at all."

"Are you away then as well?"

"As a matter of fact, yes. But I can always put them in a cattery for a week."

"They won't like that," she said.

Admittedly that is true and the last cattery I tried refused to ever have them back, but I can deal with that next month. Might even persuade Edith to look after them.

Anyway, time for some lunch and then I must pack.

Postscriptum: Everything ready for tomorrow. Set the alarm for eight and need to be at Waterfowl Cruisers for eleven.

Post-Postscriptum: weight, fifteen stone, six. Finger of Owl Service for my nightcap.

AFLOAT!

27 May; Avoncliff

It is now five in the afternoon, and I am delighted to say the day has gone swimmingly. Snipe is moored securely to the canalside a hundred yards beyond The Aqueduct at Avoncliff, which is both an imposing stone bridge carrying the canal across the River Avon and the name of the first hostelry CARP wish me to review.

I am writing this sitting on the fore deck with a cup of tea—my first attempt at using the boat's galley—and a slice of buttered bread. The sun is shining; the reflections off the water dazzling; and the scenery picturesque in the extreme. I can't imagine what I had been so worried about.

Charlie, the boatman at Waterfowl Cruisers, could not have been more helpful. After taking my details and confirming CARP had paid in full, he helped carry my bags to the boat which was moored to a pontoon on the river. I was slightly disappointed that Snipe was one of their smaller boats, but I dare say I shall be grateful at some point as it must be more manoeuvrable. First he showed me the controls for the amenities, which, apart from a whirring pump whenever one wanted water from the tap and a chemical toilet, were quite normal. Then it was the electrical panel for the engine before we dealt with the controls themselves. These could hardly be simpler. A key for ignition and start button. The throttle to control the engine doubles as the reverse lever, and the tiller is only tricky if one forgets to point it in the opposite direction to that in which one wishes to go.

Of course, my main concern was the locks as I would be doing everything on my own and all the guidebooks recommend at least two people for efficiency and safety, but Charlie put me at ease by saying he would accompany me on the first few miles of the canal.

"Just need my bike aboard so I can get back," he said.

This was done and he showed me through the starting procedure. I was surprised how loud the engine was but of course it was only just below me on the aft deck.

"You'll soon get used to it," he said above the noise. "Keep an eye on the outflow for the coolant water."

He showed me a hole in the hull from which a plume of water bubbled.

"If it gets blocked, moor up and switch off. Shouldn't happen, but you never know."

Of course, I have had my eye fixed on the outflow for most of the last two hours, but I hope it will soon become a sixth sense. Otherwise boating will be very tedious.

"If you go forward," said Charlie.

"Forward?"

"The pointy end. I want you to cast off. Take the rope from the ring and throw it into the bows. Then push the boat off the pontoon. Don't push too hard, or you'll fall in."

I managed this without mishap, but my push was feeble, and after I rejoined Charlie in the stern it was an age before the boat swung far enough to allow Charlie to cast off astern. Then we were away with the engine throbbing beneath us and the propeller churning.

It felt suddenly, brilliantly alive. We were free of the land: independent. Charlie took us out into the river and gave me the tiller.

"Don't grip it hard. Just keep your hand on it. Try moving it to your left a bit."

I did and after a pause the bow moved slowly to the right.

"That's starboard, isn't it?" I asked hopefully.

"Only at sea," he said. "We stick to right and left."

That was slightly disappointing, but it saved me having to remember which was which.

"And back again," he said. "Straighten up. You see that wooden gate?"

I did. It was the first lock and the start of the canal.

"Slow down as you approach, and I'll talk you through the gates and paddles."

I had some idea of the procedure having paid close attention at Caen Hill. Nevertheless, I was surprised at just how laborious it was. The lower gate was closed against us because the lock was almost full from the last boat to ascend, so we opened the lower paddles to let it drain. This took several minutes but then we could open the lower gates and enter the lock basin. This was now a sheer-sided pit twice the width of the boat and some four yards deep. Water oozed from the algae covered brickwork and from the perspective of Snipe's stern I was reminded of Homer's *Odyssey* when the Argo passes between the Clashing Rocks.

It then got rather complicated with ropes. I recall at one point grimly climbing a slippery iron ladder with a rope around my shoulders. The ropes, Charlie assured me, would stop the boat moving with the current while the lock filled. But first we had to close the lower gate and paddles, run the ropes through iron rings set into the concrete sides of the lock, and then open the paddles at the upper end of the lock to admit water through the sluices. I'm writing this all down as I may well have to refer to it tomorrow.

The paddles open, water surged into the basin and at once Snipe began to drift backwards towards the lower gate. This, Charlie declared, was a bad thing.

"Your stern can get caught on the frame of the gate, see. Ends up under water and puts a damper on your holiday."

I viewed the lower gate with horror and found myself running towards the iron ring holding the stern rope.

"Walk!" Charlie yelled. "Don't want to trip and fall in." I did as instructed, collected the rope and hauled frantically to take in the slack.

"That's the idea. Hold it steady."

The force exerted on the rope was surprising and it took a deal of effort to bring the boat under control.

"Keep taking in the slack as she rises," he said.

The flow of water into the basin gradually eased as the

water inside drew level with that outside. I pushed against the upper lock gate, but it did not budge.

"No point being impatient," Charlie said. "It might look ready but there's still a quarter of a ton pressing again it."

Only when the water had completely stopped flowing into the lock could I lean back against the arm of the lock gate and ease it open. I was slightly faint with exhaustion, and it was only the first of eighty locks between here and Reading. Any thoughts I might enjoy a week of bucolic ease had gone.

Charlie kept me company for the next few miles and several locks through the pretty environs of Bath. Motoring between the gardens of plush stone villas and under quaint little bridges it was a world away from the hubbub of the streets and one could almost imagine this was a backwater of Venice. The Venetian aspect, along with memory of holidaying there with Edith, disappeared on the outskirts where unkempt allotments, scrubby grassland and dismal cottages replaced the gardens. Then, after a pronounced turn to the south, came a fifth lock. This time Charlie took a supervisory role and, while progress was much slower, everything proceeded smoothly.

"Well done," Charlie said. "Five down: fair few to go. You've got our number for emergencies. Engine, propeller, anything vital and mechanical, give us a call and I'll come out. Sooner you didn't attempt anything on your own. That includes the weed hatch."

He lifted a panel in the wooden deck to reveal a metal plate secured with wing nuts.

"Some hire companies are happy for you to check the propeller and clear any debris. We'd sooner you didn't. Can be a nasty accident."

"Wouldn't dream of it," I said. "Don't want to risk sinking the boat."

"I was thinking more of losing a hand," he said. "Seen it happen. Plus, there's vile disease."

"Ah. Then I shall leave well alone."

I hadn't a clue what the vile disease was but intended steering clear of it.

"I'll be off then," he said. "I recommend The Aqueduct at Avoncliff if you want a decent meal tonight. Should take you a couple of hours."

I was surprised to see it was already two o'clock and we had only done five miles.

Charlie took his bicycle off the boat's roof and cycled off on the towpath. I walked solemnly to the bows, pushed off rather more forcefully than before and stepped smartly aboard before returning to the stern. Once free from the surly constraint of the land, I engaged the throttle and motored into the warm and sunny afternoon.

MY FIRST REVIEW

Later; The Aqueduct, Avoncliff

I'm making notes on this evening's repast. Don't think they will suspect I am masquerading as a restaurant critic, but I have a handy cover story should they ask what I'm writing. I am researching a crime novel set on a canal. My protagonist is a restaurateur living aboard a boat after his divorce and he stumbles on a wicked crime. Unable to persuade the police to arrest the suspect, he is forced to pursue the villain along the canal until he catches him in the act.

I doubt it would impress Elfa Jonsdottír (not enough gore), but it will do for my needs.

Anyway, The Aqueduct can have no complaints at my review. The roast plover stuffed with forcemeat and figs was excellent and the cranberry sauce had just the right tartness—sometimes it can be too sweet—and the roasted green (I think) peppers stuffed with rice were a perfect accompaniment. Any wine would have a hard job competing with the richness of the plover, so I chose a bottle of Haus Hoffnungslos Beer which was excellent and pleasantly cool without being chilled into tastelessness.

Pudding was a little too rich after the excellence of the main, but tiramisu parfait with Belgian white chocolate had everything one could ask, and any overindulgence was my fault. I shall make a note that boaters should temper their enthusiasm for good food and drink with awareness that home and bed is a dark walk and a narrow gangplank away.

Food, five out of five; service, four out of five as there was a delay finding a table for one—not perhaps something many boaters will face—but once seated I was attended to promptly; facilities, two out of five as the lavatories left much to be desired; setting, five out of five as it really couldn't be better; value-for-money, can only give a three as it was a little pricey. Tomorrow I must find something more suited to the average pocket as not everyone has an expense account. Catering for disabled people—I'm working off CARP's checklist—not known, but I can't imagine there are many disabled boaters; it's exhausting even with four limbs: chef, the wonderfully named Paul Schimmelpenninck of Antwerp.

I think that will do for now. Have purloined a copy of the menu as an aide memoir when I write up these notes.

Postscriptum: one litre of German beer.

Small hours; Avoncliff

Just been on deck in my pyjamas to check the ropes. Woken by something knocking against the side and as soon as I was awake I knew the wind had picked up as the boat was rocking slightly. Not enough to be unpleasant but enough to be disconcerting when one is used to proper foundations. Lay awake for a moment hoping I might reassure myself all was well but visions of Snipe drifting downstream were too persuasive.

Happily, the ropes fore and aft were secure and I could check both without negotiating the gangplank in the dark. Tried to see what was knocking against the boat but my torch wasn't powerful enough. Suppose it's a lump of wood or something. Wind very loud in the trees. No stars out.

Considered getting the 'gaff,' which is a long pole with a hook on the end useful for snagging ropes from the water, and using it to clear away whatever is bumping against the boat, but that would have meant going below to put my shoes on—there's a narrow ledge between the boat's hull and cabin and one wouldn't want to negotiate it in slippers—but a gust of rain forced me below and my enthusiasm has waned.

Tucked up again now and my feet are warming. If I have to do another nocturnal check—and I think it likely during the week—I shall put my socks on.

Long day tomorrow: breakfast in Bradford-on-Avon and dinner in Devizes after ascending Caen Hill Locks.

Whatever is hitting the hull is still at it: Knock-knock; knock-knock; knock-knock. Half a mind to shout 'who's there' but it will do no good. Hopefully, whatever it is will drift away.

28 May; Boatyard Café, Bradford-on-Avon

Woke shortly after seven this morning; surprising given my interrupted sleep. Mindful of a long day ahead—it is imperative I reach the locks at Devizes before five as no boat is allowed through after that—I was quickly into the bathroom—bijou but perfectly functional—and underway with a mug of tea in one hand and the tiller in the other by eight.

I am fairly certain I can manage breakfast in the boat's galley, but my guidebook recommends The Boatyard Café in Bradford-on-Avon and as it was only a few miles away and would provide material for the CARP magazine article it was the simplest of decisions.

Annoyingly, I had misread the guidebook and was surprised to find the café guarded by a lock, the first I've encountered since Bath. Fortunately, another boat was waiting to lock-up and I recalled the advice at the Caen Hill Café that it was always quicker with two boats than one. A young couple were embracing in the stern, and I hailed them as I drew near.

"Good morning. Mind if I slip mine in alongside yours?"

The young lady had her back to me, but her chap looked up across her shoulder. He seemed bemused to see me.

"Hi. Yeah. I mean sure."

I wasn't certain but the young lady appeared to be having some sort of fit and I wondered if I had mistaken their amorousness for something else. Eventually she broke from her chap and dashed inside their boat emitting shrieks of laughter. Some people are most peculiar.

We waited five minutes for a descending boat to emerge from the lock and then motored inside. Their boat almost fitted the full length of the lock. I went forward and flung Snipe's bow rope onto the lock side, a yard above my head, then came back to the stern to do the same with the aft rope. Finally, I clambered up the ladder bolted into the wall.

The young woman had emerged from their boat and was now at the tiller while her chap organised mooring ropes. I had the impression she was ignoring me as the one time our eyes met she burst into giggles.

The young chap had already dropped the paddles at the bottom end of the lock and was now at the upper end.

"You ready?" he called.

"Oh, indeed, thank you."

I had hold of the ropes securing my boat, but the young man stared pointedly at the paddle operated from my side of the lock.

"Ah. Sorry. Yes of course."

I had to go back onto Snipe to get my lock key but soon emerged with it propped in my jacket pocket and climbed the ladder again. The key fitted and I wound manfully. It was stiffer than the paddles I had managed last evening and left me breathing heavily. I was also irritated by the noise of the pawl as it rode over the teeth of the winding mechanism. It stops the paddles from crashing down should one let go of the lock key but makes an unpleasant clanking noise.

Water began to rush into the lock from the sluice under my feet and the lock was filling. I took my ease just for a moment before the young woman called and pointed at Snipe. My boat was sliding backwards on the surge of incoming water and heading for the bottom gates.

"Oh, Lord."

I ran, forgetting Charlie's instruction, and tripped on a flagstone. The lock key flew from my pocket and skittered across the paving, fortunately without falling in the lock. Snipe was still moving toward the lower gate.

The young woman tried to grab Snipe by the stern rail as it slipped past her, but her chap warned her, probably wisely, to leave it alone. I had picked myself up and grabbed the stern rope. My feet slid under me, but after a tense moment Snipe stopped her charge on the bottom gate and as she rose in the lock I was able to take more of the rope in.

"Rather new at this," I said as cheerfully as I could.

"Are you boating alone?" the woman asked.

"Afraid so. 'Learning curve' and all that."

"How far are you going?" her chap asked.

"Reading."

There was an exchange of glances between them.

"I'm stopping here for breakfast, if you care to join me?"

"Ah, no. We've got to get on," he said. "But I'll help you tie up."

"Thank you. That would be most kind."

He took the bow rope, and we soon had Snipe secure.

"Good luck getting to Reading," he said, without a great deal of confidence.

"And take care," the young woman said as her chap rejoined her and they motored off.

That was half an hour ago and since then I have enjoyed a breakfast of eggs, bacon, blood pudding, sausage, and chipped potato, together with a pot of strong black coffee to shake off the charms of Morpheus.

Alas, I have barely sat here forty minutes and already I must be on my way.

Postscriptum: food, three stars as the eggs were a little overdone and the sausage bland; price, excellent value so five for that; service, five again; amenities three stars as they could have been cleaner. While a customer distracted the owner I discreetly took a photo of breakfast and surroundings for reference. Apparently photographing one's food is a 'thing' these days so I should get away with it.

Lunchtime; The Bridge, Seend Wharf

Motored eight miles since Bradford-on-Avon and managed four locks. Three of them alone. There are three more soon after the bridge from which this pub takes its name. Dr Saunders would surely be impressed by all my exercise, if not by my diet.

Dessie sent me a list of the establishments CARP want me to review—as I mentioned there is a strong link to CARP's advertising—and The Bridge is one of them. Unfortunately, I am still replete with breakfast—the Boatyard Café did not make their shortlist—and can't do The Bridge justice. But I suppose not every boater wants a three-course meal twice a day and a lunch review is perfectly acceptable.

Have ordered the spinach and nutmeg soup with toasted pancetta; wheaten bread drizzled with almond oil; and a generous glass of Pinot Blanc.

Pleasant view along the canal, though the nearby road is busy.

Earlier I tried propping my radio in the stern to ease the tedium but couldn't hear it over the engine. Alas, I suspect boating is not for me. May have seen a kingfisher but the deuced thing flew off before I could be sure.

Ah, lunch is served.

Postscriptum: food five stars, service three—I was waiting a long time—wine excellent, ambience three. Facilities not checked.

ALONE

Evening; Black Horse, Devizes

The afternoon has been disastrous in every possible respect. I am wounded; a lock key is at the bottom of the canal; my boat is hors de combat; and I have seen... no, perhaps I don't want to write about that just yet.

As I wrote, there were three locks almost immediately

after The Bridge and on the second one I discovered that one can lift the pawl to disengage it from the ratchet. This stops the awful noise. All went well until I was winding up the paddles on the third lock when the mechanism stiffened, and I gave the lock key an extra shove. My hand slipped and suddenly the lock key was a blur of steel as the paddle dropped to the floor of the lock. Then the damn thing flew off the shaft and with a glancing blow to my forehead rose high in the air and into the water.

Luckily, there was a boat waiting for me to exit the lock and they saw what happened.

"Are you okay?" someone leaning over me asked. I say 'leaning over' as I seemed to be flat on my back.

"Err. Umm. I..."

My incoherence said more than words and I was helped to sit up, though still on the damp paving beside the lock.

"The umm, boat... thing," I mumbled.

"Richard is looking after it."

I did not know who Richard was. The person besides me was a woman. A small boy stood next to her.

"Dickie, go and fetch the first aid box; you know where it is."

"Am I, umm? Oh."

I was indeed bleeding as my hand came away bloodied from my forehead.

"It's only a graze," she said. "You were lucky. Is there anyone with you?"

"No there isn't," I said more forcefully than I intended.

"It's okay. These things happen."

She meant the accident but in my addled state I took her to refer to my divorce, the death of my father, my mother's incapacity, my son swanning about in Borneo, and even my ineptitude regarding Madeleine: everything, in fact, which led to me being alone.

"Tied up your boat," someone I assumed to be Richard said. "Nasty cut."

"I said it was a graze," the woman said.

Dickie returned with that smug expression all children have when they adequately perform a menial task. The woman, who I had learned was Louise, cut off a piece of elasto and stuck it above my left eyebrow.

"I don't think you'll need stitches," she said. "But you might want to get it looked at."

Richard and the boy kindly took Snipe out of the lock and moored her for me. Louise suggested I rested for a while before motoring on. Then they left towards Seend.

My head still throbs but it's the least of my troubles.

I motored on as soon as I felt able, being anxious to make the foot of the locks at Caen Hill in good time. Fortunately, I had only a half hour to go before arriving at the first of them, which sits apart from the main flight. And joy of joys there was a team of two operating the lock gates and paddles. How odd that the part of the day most worrying me should prove the least troublesome.

"We're lock wardens," one of the two chaps said. "Volunteers."

"You mean you do this for fun?" I said with a little incredulity.

"And the exercise," the other said. "Gets you out of the house. Nice meeting people. Throw up the bow rope and we'll have you through."

"Not too late to get up the flight this afternoon, am I?"

"No. You'll be fine."

I am bemused. More than bemused. Quite possibly suffering from shock, but that is not what I meant. I had understood no one was manning the locks at Caen Hill but there were attendants at every lock, and I was soon on the main flight. Of course, it was still tiring throwing up and gathering ropes all the time and there was no chance of stopping even for a pee, but frankly, still not feeling myself after the bang on the head, I really don't think I could have coped by myself. Not that that mightn't have been so bad, given what happened next.

Ah. No time to finish. Bus is due. Back home to Avebury. Can't sleep possibly aboard the boat tonight.

AN ENCOUNTER

Bedtime; Avebury Trusloe

I am temporarily home. Mrs Pumphrey must have let Tusker out earlier. Boris is sound asleep. House quiet. Made myself a cup of tea and found biscuits and a bit of mousetrap in the fridge. No appetite to speak of.

Want to write this up before bed as I have an early start tomorrow.

The volunteer lockkeepers had seen me out at the top of the Caen Hill flight, and I was feeling rather pleased. A hard job had turned into something far easier than I feared. I had an evening meal at the Black Horse in mind (it's on CARP's list) and was making for a mooring near the café. The sun was at the horizon and the sky had a washed out look. I had just throttled back, ready to make the turn into the bank, when my free hand twitched as though it had touched a live wire. The pain travelled up my arm and I glanced down to shake it.

A child stood beside me in the stern, her pale face turned up to mine, her hand in mine. She was wet through, and her long hair fell across one eye.

"I need you to find Daddy."

It was the girl I had seen beside the burnt-out boat. The girl in the newspaper. The dead girl.

The pain was all over me now. My knees trembled and I could barely control the tiller.

"You... you shouldn't be here," I managed to say, though I could barely open my mouth.

"But I have to be here. Daddy needs me!"

"But your Daddy is... isn't he? Everyone knows what he did. You have to go to Heaven."

I said Heaven, as though I knew what happens when we die, as though I'm an authority. I don't know anymore than anyone else. I only have hope and trust in the mercy of our Lord.

The girl smiled; her pale face lit as if by a torch within.

"Don't be silly. Daddy wouldn't be mean. It was Mummy's other man."

"I don't want to help you. I'm not right for it."

"Yes you are. I always knew it was you."

I tried to turn the tiller to point the boat at the mooring, but the rudder resisted.

"Not yet," she said. "You have to find Daddy. I know he's here."

I shivered. The day had cooled but this was far more than an evening chill. The boat moved sluggishly towards the bank and then came the faintest of bumps, as though it had grounded. Next moment the propeller juddered and with a couple of horrendous bangs the engine stopped.

The girl had vanished.

Snipe was now adrift, still heading towards the bank but slowing quickly. I put the throttle in neutral and tried the engine. It turned but as soon as I let the clutch in it stalled.

"Hello!" I tried to raise someone in the moored boats. Snipe had a horn and I sounded it repeatedly as we drifted towards a boat.

"Hello! Help!"

I ran through the companionway to the bow, ready to fend off, but Snipe had too much momentum and thumped into the stern of a boat. Shouts came from within.

"What the devil!" A man appeared in the stern of the boat. He and I were separated by a yard of black water.

"So sorry," I said. "I'm adrift."

Fortunately, the chap had rather more grasp of the situation than I could manage, and he took my bow rope and helped me into a vacant mooring. He assured me there was no damage to his boat.

"Did it cut out?" he asked.

"What? Oh. No. Think it's the propeller."

"I'll have a look if you want."

I recalled Charlie's grim warning.

"It's perfectly okay. Besides, nearly dark. Get it sorted in the morning. Not going anywhere tonight."

I must have been in shock. Part of me thought everything was quite normal. The other part was barely coping.

The barely coping part took over after the chap returned to his boat leaving me to finish mooring. I was half supposing I would eat at the Black Horse, as planned, but as I stood in Snipe's saloon contemplating the evening ahead there was a faint knocking on the underside of the boat.

I barely even thought about things. I had my wash bag from the bathroom, my camera, and other valuables in a bag, inside five minutes, and was walking up the tow path towards the Black Horse in another five. I knew I had to telephone Charlie, and I knew I had to catch the bus home.

I heard the telephone ring for a good minute before Charlie answered. He was not impressed by the hour.

"Yes, I know," I said apologetically. "It is a bit late."

"So what's the problem?"

"Propeller. Think something has jammed. I remembered you saying not to try anything by myself."

"Good, good," he said. "Where are you?"

"The Black Horse in Devizes."

There was a long pause.

"I assume the boat isn't in there with you," he said.

"Ah. Sorry. The boat is on the canal. I mean near the lock. Beyond the last lock."

Charlie sighed. "Did you get the number of the lock?"

I didn't even know locks had numbers.

"The last lock. Top of the big staircase thing."

"Near the café?" he asked.

"Yes. Thank you, yes. Moored just past the café."

"Right. I'll see you at nine tomorrow. That's the earliest."

"Thank you. Oh yes. Thank you. Nine. I'll be there."

I rang off and sat down. My appetite had gone, and I didn't even want a pint. Horrible hollow feeling.

Someone's at the front door. God, I hope she hasn't followed me. Can't ignore it.

Postscriptum: Well, that takes the biscuit. Frightened out of my wits twice in one day. Three if you count being brained by the lock key.

"Who's there?" I called through the door.

"Nevil? That you?"

I opened the door to find Bill Pumphrey standing on the path. He had a torch and what I took to be a broom handle.

"You're back early," he said.

"Not exactly," I said. "Night at home. Boat's moored at Devizes. Anything wrong?"

"Wife heard noises and thought it might be a break-in. I popped round to give 'em a fright."

He waved the broom handle in the light of the torch, and it became a double-barrelled shotgun.

"Good Lord. Bit excessive," I said, taking a step back. I didn't fancy Mr Pumphrey letting off both barrels at some scallywags, even if they were robbing my house.

"Property rights, Nevil. Must defend what's ours."

My neighbour's politics were always on the farther fringes of the right, but this was alarming.

"Fortunately, no one is robbing me," I said. "But thank you and thank your wife for me. I'll be away again early tomorrow."

"Right you are. You managing on that boat?" he asked. "Only you're looking a bit grey round the gills."

"Ah. No, I'm fine." It was a barefaced lie as I felt awful, but I excused myself by saying I'd had a bump to the head, and it had been a long day. Bill went home, and I came in to finish my journal.

My head still throbs. Woman who gave me the elasto warned me to get it checked. Maybe tomorrow at Devizes Surgery. Of course, that means a delay and I feel like I've barely travelled anywhere. Which I haven't as I'm back where I started.

Can't stop seeing the girl's face. I let her down so badly. Nerve failed me.

A whisky will help get me to sleep.

29 May; Caen Hill Café

Reading may as well be Ithaca such are my trials and tribulations. It is now almost eleven and I have not moved one yard, save to walk to the café to wait while the ghastly business aboard Snipe is concluded.

My day began after breakfast with the bus to Devizes and a short wait for Charlie to arrive from Bath. He was prompt at nine. I had been waiting on the towpath.

"Morning. Soon have you on your way."

"Thank you. Thank you. Sorry for the inconvenience."

"No trouble. Enjoy your trip so far? Taken a bit of a knock, I see."

"Ah, yes. Lock key I'm afraid. Bash on the old noggin."

I explained that I had grown tired of the noise and lifted the pawl from the ratchet.

"I wouldn't do that again," he said.

"No fear. Don't want another bash, or to lose another lock key. I have two spares, but even so."

We had walked to Snipe. I boarded first, trying to hide my reluctance after the fright last evening. I had to unlock the stern door to enter. Charlie had a bag of tools with him.

"Let's see what it sounds like," he said and bent down to the engine panel just inside the door.

The switch turned in the ignition, but nothing happened.

"Is it the starter motor?" I said helpfully.

"Shouldn't be. Hang on. Battery's dead. What were you up to last night?"

"Last night? I wasn't here last night. I only live in Avebury. Went home rather than sleep here."

"Something's flattened it. I'll check the alternator while I'm here. Safer if I hang onto the keys while I'm messing about with the propeller."

He pocketed the keys and knelt down to remove the panel in the deck to expose the metal hatch.

"I was surprised to find lock keepers on this stretch," I

said. "Everyone has said I would be working the locks alone."

"They only work high season," he said. "You just made it. Started a week ago."

"I have had some luck then," I said. "Can't say I'm cut out for this."

"It's always a lot of work on your own."

He had the nuts off the panel and removed it.

"See down there. That's your propeller: or would be if the water were clear."

I could only see dark green water and a shadow. Charlie put rubber gloves on, and I remembered him saying about vile disease. He bent down, one hand thrust into the water.

"Blimey, feels like half a tree wrapped round it. Hang on—Oh, Jesus!"

He had come up from the hatch like a startled cat.

"Fuck me! It's afoot!"

"What's afoot?"

"A foot you bloody idiot. A fucking foot."

I leant forward, mystified, and caught a glimpse of something grey and swollen, just below the water. I recoiled but too late. It was a left foot, sole uppermost, toes pointing astern.

"Oh, Jesus. I dreaded this happening one day. Dead dog cut to pieces once. Now this."

"Should we call someone?" I asked.

"We could leave the poor bastard in the canal."

"I don't think..."

"It was a joke. Give me a minute will you. And yes, call the police."

"And an ambulance? What do you think?" I asked.

Charlie glanced up at me with a curious expression.

"I reckon he might be a bit far gone for an ambulance. Call the police. Jesus. What a morning."

I called the police from the café. I thought it best to keep my voice down to avoid startling the customers at breakfast.

"I'd like the police, please," I said down the line.

"Where are you calling from, sir?"

"The café by the canal locks."

"Can you be more precise, sir?"

"Ah. It's at the top of the hill. I mean where all the locks are. On the canal."

"The town sir, what town are you nearest?"

"Oh, this is Devizes."

Eventually she was happy with my location.

"And your reason for calling, sir?"

"We've found a body. I mean Charlie has. He's my friend. I mean not a friend. He works for the canal boat company. His foot's stuck in my propeller."

"Whose foot, sir?"

"The body."

"And the body belongs to Charlie?"

"Whatever gave you that idea? Charlie found the foot stuck in my propeller."

"And you are certain this person is dead?"

"Oh, I should jolly well think so. Been there since last night."

This went on for some time before the telephonist was satisfied. Meanwhile I think my voice must have risen slightly because when I hung up everyone in the café was staring.

"Nothing to worry about," I said cheerfully. "Ran over someone's foot last night. With my boat. Enjoy your breakfast."

Two policemen arrived at the boat some fifteen minutes later. One was young, clean shaven, the other a bit older. Charlie showed the policemen the foot.

"Blimey. Don't see that every day," the younger one said.

"Have you touched it, sir?" the elder one asked.

"Me! No fear," I protested.

"And you sir?"

"I tried to free the propeller," Charlie said. "Soon as I realised what it was I let go sharpish. Reckon it's well stuck. You can see where the propeller gouged across the heel. Shin must be jammed between the blades and the hull."

The older policeman leant closer.

"Bit of a mess," he said. "Been in the water a good while."

"Glad I was wearing gloves," Charlie said.

"Now you've seen it," I said, "I was hoping you might extract it from my propeller. I would really like to be away as soon as possible."

"I'm afraid it will be a while yet, sir," the elder policeman said. "We'll have to radio for back-up."

"Back-up?" I said. "But you're policemen. I assumed you would do policing."

Time was slipping away, and I was acutely aware I had many miles to go.

"This is a suspected crime scene, sir. We will need statements from both of you and assistance retrieving the body. Right, sonny," this to the younger policeman, "you go and radio the station: tell them unknown person found deceased in the canal. Body trapped. Diver requested. Off you go. Now sir, as you found the body I'd like your name and address."

Charlie replied and then the policeman turned to me.

"Actually," I interrupted. "If it's any help, I think I know who this is: I mean was..." I hesitated realising if I told the whole truth I would look a fool, or possibly mad.

"And who do you reckon it is, sir?"

"The father. I mean, the owner of the boat. The one who's supposed to have killed his daughter."

The policeman narrowed his eyes.

"And how do you arrive at that?"

"Isn't it obvious," I said hopefully.

I could tell what he was thinking. If I knew that then what else might I know and how might I know it? But it was too late to back down.

"Actually, sir, I don't think it's obvious at all. Name and address."

I have sat in the café for two hours. The place is deserted. The police have closed the canal and brought divers in. Out of guilt at the café's lost business I have ordered two pots of tea and three scones, two of which are uneaten. All I can think of is the girl asking me to find her Daddy.

Charlie has come in. Better close this. Might be incriminating.

Postscriptum: Charlie said the divers have freed the body. He's given the police a statement and they'll be along to ask me presently.

"How the fuck did you know who it was?" he asked.

"It occurred to me, that's all," I said. "Can't explain why."

"It's him though. Police identified him. What a bastard, eh?"

I didn't correct him, but my silence felt like a betrayal.

"I've fitted new batteries," he said. "Lucky for you they haven't impounded the boat. You should be able to get away before evening."

"Thank you. I'm sorry for an awful morning."

"Bound to happen one day."

Familiar surroundings

Afternoon; St Mary the Virgin, Bishops Cannings

I am in need of spiritual sustenance as much as lunch and have moored up near Bishops Cannings and walked into the village. I've always admired St Mary's and wanted a bit of peace and quiet to reflect. Plan to reach Wilcot by this evening which means four hours at the tiller. No more locks, thanks goodness. I have had my fill of locks.

My interview with the police was in the passenger seat of a police car parked behind the café. Youngish chap. Moustache. Said his name was Croup, or something like it. The radio bleeped throughout, and snatches of conversation kept interrupting us.

"Can I take your name, sir?"

"You already have my name. I gave it to the policeman who first attended."

"This is for your statement, sir. I have to ask you again."

"Very well. Nevil Warbrook."

"Can you spell that for me?"

He took my details and then got down to business.

"We have spoken to the boat mechanic, Charlie Brooks.

Can you confirm you hired the boat from Waterfowl Cruisers in Bath on Monday afternoon?"

"I can."

"And you're on holiday."

"Ah. No. Business trip for Canal and Riverside Publications. You can confirm with my agent: Desmond Catterick and Associates."

I handed him Desmond's card and he copied the details.

"And they can vouch for you?"

"Damn well hope so. He doesn't get commission for nothing. I have a week reviewing pubs and restaurants between Bath and Reading."

"Nice work," he said.

"It could have started better."

"Mr Brooks says you called him last evening to say an obstruction had fouled your propeller."

"Correct again."

"You didn't try to clear it yourself?"

"No. Charlie, I mean Mr Brooks, had given me instruction not to attempt it. The canal is full of vile disease."

"Vile?"

"That's what he said."

"Are you sure he didn't mean Weil's? It's spread by rats."

"Ah. Possibly. They do sound the same."

"And Mr Brooks came to you this morning to unblock your propeller. Can you describe what happened?"

I did, to the best of my memory right up until the arrival of the police.

"One detail. Mr Brooks claims you identified the body even though all you could see was the foot. Is that correct?"

"I wouldn't say I *identified* him. I knew a man was missing and put two and two together."

He was looking at me with a curious expression.

"I do hope this won't take too long," I said. "I really was hoping to get to Pewsey this evening."

"That depends, sir." He was flicking back through his notebook. "PC Nichols also heard you identify the man; he reports you saying: *I know who it is. It's the father. The one who's supposed to have killed his daughter.* That seems unusually precise."

I said nothing.

"Mr Warbrook, you are not under any suspicion, but I must warn you that withholding information helpful to our investigation may lead a charge of obstructing the police."

"Oh God."

"I understand it has been a difficult morning, but we do need your cooperation."

"More than you know. If I told you how I knew you will think I'm mad."

"Go on."

"The girl. The one who died on the boat. She asked me to find her daddy. This was last evening, you understand. She was suddenly there, on my boat. She held my hand. The boat turned and... I really did find her father."

The policeman had stopped writing.

"I said you wouldn't believe me."

"Can I ask, have you recently had a blow to the head? You have an elasto."

"Yes, I have. Yesterday in fact. Struck by a lock key. But don't tell me I was imagining her. Do I sound delusional?"

"What is hard to understand is why she would want to find her father, after what he did to her."

"Oh, he didn't do it." I was filled with elation as I suddenly knew what I had to pass on. I was like Mercury, the winged messenger. "She said..." I wracked my memory, for her exact words. "She said it was *Mummy's other man.* She was insistent. Her father didn't do it."

The policeman closed his notebook and stared at me. I felt like a criminal.

"I did say you wouldn't believe me."

"I'll ask you to wait here, sir. Won't be a moment. Best not touch anything. I need to speak to my superior officer."

I waited in the car. The windows were wound up and it was awfully warm while the radio kept up its unintelligible chatter. Admitting I had seen a ghost was like owning up to some terrible deed but what choice had I?

A shadow fell across the far side and the door opened.

"Mr Warbrook?"

"Yes."

The man joined me in the car. He was older, with a long coat that must have been too warm for the weather.

"I'm Inspector Donaldson. This won't take long."

"Jolly glad to hear it."

"Do you smoke, Mr Warbrook?"

"No. Gave it up years ago."

"Mind if I do? Helps me to think."

"No. Not at all."

He lit a cigarette, drew easily, then flipped open a notebook. It was the same one the younger officer had used.

"I'd like you to repeat what you just told my colleague."

"But you have what I said in that book."

"Humour me. It's rare a story is told the same way twice."

I repeated about seeing the girl last evening and her father's foot getting caught in the propeller.

"Did you know it was a foot last evening?"

"No. I had no idea. Though... I recall feeling very uneasy after I moored up. A chap on another boat helped me get into the mooring. Anyway, I didn't care to stay aboard last night so I got the bus home."

"You live in Avebury?"

"Yes. Avebury Trusloe. Just next door to the old village."

"I know it well. Avebury attracts a lot of people who believe in the supernatural."

"It does. I'm more Anglian Church. Nothing outlandish about my beliefs."

"But you saw a ghost."

"Yes. I believe so."

"Can you describe how she appeared?"

"Appeared? You mean did she manifest in some sort of blinding flash?"

"No. I'm asking what she looked like."

"Ah. Just an ordinary girl, except..."

I was trying to recall. There had been something strange about her appearance.

"It was dusk, so it was hard to tell, but she was there and not there at the same time. Like one of those old photographs where something has been painted on afterwards. I suppose that doesn't make sense."

"She shouldn't have been there at all," he said and wrote in the notebook. "And what was she wearing?"

"Nothing unusual. Jumper: I couldn't see the colour. Knee length dress—as though she had been at school. Except she was soaking wet."

"She had come to the boat from school the day she died."

It suddenly seemed so poignant. A young girl, straight from school. And then the horror of it all.

"You... forgive me for asking, but you believe me?"

"No one thinks you're mad, Mr Warbrook. Younger officers want to join the dots in a straight line; seeing a ghost doesn't fit with their way of thinking."

"But you think I did see her?"

"You saw something that appeared to be her. Can't say more than that. Though the body *is* that of her father. We identified it by a tattoo. I wouldn't take it so hard. Once you've seen a ghost or had some feeling that makes no sense but turns out to be true, you tend not to think other people in the same boat—pardon the pun—are mad. Otherwise, you'd have to doubt your own sanity, wouldn't you?"

I took a moment to absorb this.

"Do you mean what I think you mean?"

He nodded. "There comes a point when you accept that some things are beyond understanding. You confirm that the girl said her father was not responsible for her death."

"I do," I said with conviction. "She was very clear it was *Mummy's other man.* I don't know what happened, but she insisted it wasn't her father."

"Then we will be having a word with the girl's mother. Thank you, Mr Warbrook. That's all we need from you for now. We'll be in touch shortly to take a proper statement. I assume you'll be on the canal for a few more days."

"Aim to be home by the weekend."

"Then it will be sometime next week. Are you willing to testify what you just told me in court? I'd understand if you decline but it would make our job simpler."

"I'll testify," I said. "But I'll do it for her, not for you."

"Good man. We'll speak again, Mr Warbrook. Until then, *bon voyage*."

Evening; Blind Phoenician Sailor, Wilcot

It is strange that after more than two days travelling I have yet to sail beyond familiar haunts. Boating does curious things to one's sense of time and place. Cedric, keeper of the Blind Phoenician Sailor, greeted me familiarly as I entered.

"Evening; Nevil isn't it? Not dominoes tonight, is it?"

I reassured him it was not.

"Actually, I'm here to order food. Boating on the canal for a week."

"Best get your order in soon; we close the kitchen at nine. What can I get you?"

I said I would look at the menu first then choose something to go with dinner.

"One more thing, is there a telephone box in the village?"

"'Phone here you can use."

"Needs to be office hours. You won't be open till eleven."

"There's one on the far side of the green."

"Thank you."

I must telephone Dessie as I cannot possibly get to Reading by Friday. My only hope of completing the assignment is a day's extension or abandoning Snipe and finishing my reviews by motorcar at a later date. I have the excuse of losing half of today to the awful business in Devizes but even without that I doubt I could manage in the time al-lowed. It is the locks that delay one and I am not yet halfway.

Snipe is moored at what must have once been a busy little wharf east of Wilcot bridge. As I passed under it, the engine echoing off the arch, I recalled it was barely a week since I saw the poor girl in the road here as I drove Sid and Bert back to Avebury. Hope they're enjoying the match at The Red Lion tonight. If they lose badly in my absence I shall not hear the end of it.

It did not take long to choose off the menu. In truth, I was uncertain of my appetite, and I doubt many boaters are gourmands. Besides, one can only dine on stuffed plover once in a while. I returned to the bar to order.

"A large glass of merlot, and baked potato with bacon."

Cedric wrote a slip for the kitchen.

"With the trimmings?" He asked.

"Of course."

"Be fifteen minutes."

"I am in no hurry. Enjoying the sit down actually. Harder work than you might suppose piloting a canal boat."

"I wouldn't know," he said. "Didn't have those in the merchant navy. I was twenty years before the mast long before I settled down to running pubs."

I returned to my table to await dinner. I did not wait to start my wine and in fact had to order a second glass before food appeared. Jacket potato with smoky bacon filling drizzled with wild honey and a side-salad of diced celery, grated pecorino cheese, and walnuts tossed in walnut oil. Good wholesome food. The smokiness of the bacon mingling with the honey was close to divine.

It was near dusk when I had approached Wilcot. I passed several boats moored up for the night, their windows aglow with activity from within. The air was restful, like a body after an exhaled breath, and the sky pellucid. A handful of stars showed in the east while behind me the setting sun glazed the water of the canal. The only disturbance came from Snipe's passing. I can't say what caused me to glance behind—I am loath to say it was a sixth sense as I seem beset by strange feelings and senses lately—but I turned at just the right point where the winding of the canal brought the sun and water in line and for a second a vivid green path opened between my stern and the heart of the sun. It was extraordinary, despite only lasting a heartbeat before vanishing. A scent hung in the air and though I could not name it, it reminded me of some other time: lavender perhaps, or meadowsweet, or a perfume Edith once wore and whose memory has lodged deep and inaccessible in my thoughts. With that scent and the broken memory came a feeling that everything would come good, or had come good, and I took a great gulp of air, as though I had been starving myself of oxygen and the breath seemed to satisfy every part of me.

I cannot express it properly. It would take a poem to do so, and I have neither time nor energy, nor perhaps the talent. I did a good thing today, though it took a deal of prompting. If the right thing were always easy I suppose it would have no meaning.

The child has found her father, and his name will be cleared. All is well in their world and, for this evening, also in mine.

Postscriptum: two large glasses of merlot.

NOUVELLE-AQUITAINE

30 May; Pewsey Wharf

Knowing it would be useless to telephone Desmond before nine I cooked a leisurely breakfast aboard Snipe before walking into the village and finding the telephone box. It was the proper old-fashioned kind with iron-framed windows and a lamp on top.

I counted the change in my pocket before dialling. I should manage abut ten minutes before my coins ran short. If I went over they would have to call me back.

Pea answered.

"Hello Pea. It's Nevil."

"Oh, so glad it's you. Dessie asked me to ring you, but I kept getting your machine."

"Pea, I'm on a canal boat as arranged by Desmond. I can hardly be at home to answer the blasted telephone."

"Shilling, Nevil."

"If you're going to fine me for mild rudeness I can be considerably ruder. I had a dreadful day yesterday."

"I'll put the telephone down if you're rude again."

This was a clever tactic.

"Sorry, Pea. Look, I really do need to speak to Desmond. Bit of delay on this boat job. I need more time to finish the assignment."

"Dessie's not in the office. I can pass on a message. If it's a nice one."

"It's twenty past nine! Where on earth is he? Late night on the *Château Blotteau,* was it?"

"He's in Montmorillon."

"Where?"

"He's talking to Jean-Maxim le Cocq, the actor."

"Should the name mean anything to me?"

"Only if you know anything about films," she said. "He's awfully good-looking and very clever."

"I suppose if Dessie has gone to see him he must also be stinking rich."

"Probably. He wants to break into the English market, so Dessie is persuading him he needs a biography in English."

"If he's that famous surely he has a biography in French."

Pea giggled. "Dessie says we may not be ready for the full story of Jean-Maxim le Cocq, so it has to be a new version."

"I see. Nice work if you can get it."

"You don't want to do it?"

"Me? Surely this is more Dommy's thing."

"Dommy isn't in Dessie's good books any more. Dommy and Cecily have split up. Loads of tears. Awful."

"Oh dear. So, I really might be offered the assignment for *monsieur le Cocq.*"

"Dessie will have to ask someone to do it. But you'll have to stay in Montmorillon."

"And where is that, apart from in France?"

"Um, does Poitiers mean anything?"

"Vaguely. What région?"

"Wait a mo... Nouvelle-Aquitaine: does that help?"

"Ah, it does. Edith and I went there many years ago. Excellent wine, though it's France so it's hard to find bad wine: unless you drink the muck the locals make for themselves. If Desmond is after someone for the job, do put my name forward, there's a sweet pea."

She giggled again.

"Now, I need you to tell Desmond that there's been a slight delay on the canal. Completely unexpected and I was completely blameless, got that? If I am to get to Reading I shall need an extra day to do it in."

"Did you fall in?"

"Fall? No, nothing like that."

"Dessie was certain you would. He had a bet with me."

"Did he? Well, I haven't, so you're winning, so far, anyway. No. It was utterly ghastly, actually, but I'm not going to bore you with the details." Actually, Pea is such a sweet girl I didn't want to upset her. "Just ask Dessie to arrange an extra day's hire with the boat company. Got that? Or if he's handed the day-to-day stuff to you while he's away, you do it. Contract with the hire company is in Dessie's name so I don't think it's my responsibility."

I left it with her so hopefully all will be well in the next day or so. I have fond memories of Nouvelle-Aquitaine. It sounds a lot better than Reading.

Lunchtime; King George, Wootton Rivers

Alas, I passed the Crown and Trumpet in Pewsey far too early to call in—fortunately, it is not an establishment CARP insist I review—and have now moored up in Wootton Rivers for lunch at The King George having motored a whole five miles since telephoning Pea. The canal is still climbing as there's yet another lock beyond the bridge. It is the first of many this afternoon. My reviews for CARP will be scrupulously truthful but any bonhomie I muster for boating will be an invention. Three days aboard, not counting Tuesday night, and I am still scarcely an hour's drive from Bath.

Better order I suppose. What do they have? More to the

point, do I want to eat a full lunch here or have dinner later?

Ah. Just glanced at the map. Not going to make Bedwyn today and there's nothing on CARP's list between here and there. Looks like it's dinner aboard tonight. In that case, even though it's not long since breakfast I'd better eat now. Grilled pike. Don't see that very often. Today's special, locally caught. Nothing ventured.

Postscriptum: fish was bland and flabby, two stars; vegetables adequate but underseasoned, three stars; Pinot Grigio pleasant but too acidic, three stars; service polite and efficient, four stars; facilities immaculate, five stars.

PIKE'S REVENGE

Later; Summit Level

I have been violently ill and am recuperating below deck. Suspect this might be a symptom of delayed shock. One hears about that sort of thing.

Began to feel a bit poorly on way back from The King George but put it down to the unwelcome news that the pike had been caught in the canal. Given it's a carnivorous fish I was instantly reminded of what exactly had been lying in the canal for the last two weeks. It didn't help that immediately after leaving Wootton Rivers I had four locks to contend with and not a volunteer lockkeeper in sight. Meanwhile it had begun to drizzle and for the first time this trip I had to get my waterproof coat which meant I got far too warm shining up and down ladders and heaving on lock paddles and lock gates. Managed all the locks without mishap but my head was throbbing when I exited the last of them. It was then a large sign helpfully informed that I was at the summit of the canal, meaning it is all downhill from here to Reading. A smaller sign then warned that the water level was low, and I should beware of grounding. Ensuring the canal has water in it seems beyond the command of those in charge.

The drizzle worsened and the only respite from the weather was a short tunnel. Unfortunately, just as I had got used to not being rained on and had thrown off the hood of my coat a droplet fell from the tunnel roof and went straight down the back of my neck. Gave me quite a chill and what with the noise of the engine reverberating off the wall and the confined stink of the exhaust I began to feel rather woozy. Just managed to reach the end of the tunnel and pull in to the bank when my bowels rebelled, and the pike returned whence it came. That was half an hour ago and I have only now found the strength to write my journal. I have downgraded lunch at The King George to zero stars.

Will make a cup of tea and try to get my strength back. If I don't manage a few more miles this afternoon then I have no chance of reaching Reading before Sunday, and that's assuming Pea manages to get me an extra day.

Postscriptum: the saloon table is on the slant. Gave itself away when I put my cup down and tea slopped into the saucer. A tiny nudge sent it sliding across the table and I was lucky to catch it before it flew off the end. All is not well.

BUGGERING ABOUT ON BOATS
Evening; Great Bedwyn

A remarkable afternoon and I have scarcely deserved my luck, both good and bad. Much to my surprise, Snipe is moored at the wharf in Great Bedwyn. Calculated, so far as I am capable, that if I start at dawn tomorrow, finish at sunset and start again at dawn on Saturday, I should make Reading by Saturday evening.

Quite how I am to satisfy CARP is another matter as there are five establishments to review between Bedwyn and Reading.

I arrived on deck to find Snipe aground by the bows. Either I took her into the bank a little too enthusiastically when I fell ill, or the water level had dropped in the last hour. The rain had settled in and there was not another boat to be seen along the grey expanse of water. The guidebook had a chapter at the end on common misadventures and it included running aground. The first suggestion was using the engine to reverse off. I tried that but all it achieved was a lot of muddy frothing. The next suggestion was to get everyone aboard to stand at the floating end and jump up and down. Unhappily, there was only me and I was in no condition to do more than gently flex my knees and even that left me light-headed. Then it suggested taking a rope from the free end to the opposite bank and pull the boat free. The book helpfully suggested one could do that via a bridge, but the only bridge was a narrow wooden walkway across the lock gates and that was too far for my rope to reach. However, I reckoned that my stern rope was long enough to reach to the far bank if only I could get it there. I could then cross via the wooden walkway, gather up the rope, and hopefully pull Snipe off.

This was all assuming my feeble health lasted the course.

I coiled the stern rope around my arm and flung it as far as I could. The strain was too much, and my tummy rebelled again. After I had recovered I saw the rope floating a yard short of the bank and hauled it in. I tried again, this time without further sickness, but the rope, now wet through, fell far short. It was simply too heavy to be thrown any distance.

Meanwhile, there was still no sign of an approaching boat, and the rain was beating down.

What I needed was something I could throw that would carry the rope to the far bank and I remembered the boathook. This, I reasoned, could function as a harpoon.

I managed to stab the hooked end of the pole through the weave of the rope, and then launched it, tail first, as hard as I could. To my astonishment it landed upright in a clump of bulrushes on the far bank.

Fearful it would fall back into the canal I quickly got along the tow path and over the walkway to the far bank, then down to where the boathook nestled in the bulrushes.

It was tantalisingly out of reach.

I returned to Snipe, hauled in the rope with the boat-hook still attached and tried again. This time I got the throw completely wrong, and it finished in the middle of the canal. The third time the boathook cleared the bulrushes, and I had my chance.

The boathook had toppled forward as it landed, bringing it just within reach, and I soon had it and the rope in my hands. Now all I had to do was pull Snipe free and I could be on my way.

I was, I suspect, more than a little light-headed as I would not usually be quite so optimistic and might even have considered what could go wrong with my scheme. But in my enfeebled condition, I leant back on the rope and pulled. Nothing happened except Snipe's stern swung across the canal towards me. I walked back towards the lock until I was almost at the very end of the rope, and pulled again, thinking if I were inline with the bow I would be pulling more directly.

The bow stayed firm upon the farther bank, and I tried again, digging in my heels and straining my back. My stomach churned and then my feet slipped from under me. At least I managed to roll onto my front before my cup of tea came back up.

I remained on all fours for half a minute before muttering a 'God give me strength' rather more forcefully than one ought when calling on the Almighty and clambered to my feet. To my horror, Snipe was floating serenely midstream with the stern rope trailing in the water.

Try as I might, I could not reach the rope with the boathook, so I returned to the other bank and tried from there, but with the same result. Meanwhile the wind was gently taking Snipe downstream. I followed on the towpath, hoping for a bend or anything that might bring the boat to one side or the other, but there was nothing. Eventually I found a bench and sat down for a rest. My insides were hollow, as though I had been gutted, and I soon began shivering uncontrollably. Snipe continued to drift.

I was roused by noise of an approaching engine and just as I looked round a voice called out.

"Halloo. Anyone aboard?"

Snipe was a considerable distance downstream and had been joined by a second boat. A chap stood in its stern, and another was in the bows with a boat hook.

"I can get the rope, Jim."

"Right ho. See anyone?"

"Not a soul aboard."

I was on my feet. "Ah, hello. I wonder if you might help."

"Is this your boat?" said the chap at the stern.

"It is, yes. Ran aground. Bit of a mishap getting her off."

A violent stomach cramp gripped me, and I bent over and retched. Nothing came up.

"Are you feeling all right?"

"Touch of food poisoning. Look, don't suppose you could get me aboard."

Jim, the chap in the bows, had grabbed Snipe's stern rope and quickly stepped onto her. Together, they got Snipe secure to their boat and then brought it into the bank. Jim dropped the gangplank for me, and I crossed gingerly aboard Snipe.

"Thank you so much. Blessed relief. Thought I'd be here all afternoon."

"Are you boating far?" Jim's friend asked.

"Reading," I said. "Hopefully by the end of Saturday."

"You've got a fair way to go," Jim said.

"Don't I know it. I don't suppose I could tag along with you chaps for a bit? Feeling a bit queasy. Name's Nevil Warbrook."

"Warbrook?" Jim asked. "No relation to Tom Warbrook, I suppose?"

"My father, actually."

"Then it will be a pleasure. Tell you what. You go inside and get warm, and we'll see to it."

Some people are angels sent to earth to help fools. Jim and his friend, who I soon discovered was Algy, were good as their word. I lost count of the number of locks, but I suppose it was as easy with two boats as with one. They set me down here around seven and then motored into the twilight. They're making for Lunden.

At last, I have managed to keep some food down. Evening has turned chilly, and the gas fire is roaring away. A week in Montmorillon sounds jolly pleasant right now.

Midnight; as previous

Woke a short while ago to a horrible scream. Utterly desolate sound. Reminded me of Captain Wolfe hearing William's death cry. It was probably a water bird, albeit of the eldritch kind. Lay in bed for a few minutes listening to the night before a call of nature took me to the lavatory. Fortunately, I have not been ill again but am now thoroughly purged. Have set the alarm for five.

Up with the birds

31 May; Great Bedwyn

Woken by the alarm. Lay in bed in a state of catatonia before the increasing noise, and my desire for it to stop overcame inertia, whereon a flailing arm awakened my senses.

This close to midsummer the day is well advanced even at this hour and a glance out the porthole showed blue sky and sun sparkling on the waters. A covey of ducks dabbled in the shallows and swallows arrowed overhead catching insects with balletic skill. I, like them, was migratory and I had not set the alarm only to ignore it. Moreover, I was famished having kept down almost nothing the day before.

Breakfasted on toast and scrambled eggs, with a pot of coffee. Tempted by bacon but am still uncertain how strong my constitution is so thought it best to do without. CARP will still expect reviews of pubs and restaurants and I can hardly oblige on a weak stomach.

Curious interruption as I was finishing the last slice of toast. Caught a movement at the lower edge of the window and glanced up to see a swan looking back at me. I stood, the better to admire the creature, whereon it stretched its neck and spread its wings in a great unfurling. After vigorous flapping, it tucked everything in place and resumed staring, first with one eye and then with the other.

Anxious not to disturb the creature, I slid open the window and said hello.

Its eyes, first one, then the other, studied my toast.

"Ah, so you too are peckish," I said.

The bird dipped its head.

"If you wait there I might have something."

I pealed a slice of bread from the loaf and brought it to the window. I know white bread isn't the best thing for birds but other than bacon it was all I had and I'm certain bacon is bad for swans.

Shredded the bread and scattered a few pieces through the window. The swan dabbled and picked them up before resuming its curious head-turning stare. I scattered more bread and two ducks set out from the far bank towards me. I told the swan it had competition and it turned and bent its neck low and hissed. The ducks sidled away and out of pity I threw a few crumbs their way. The swan hissed at me, obviously annoyed at my generosity. I told it off but then a second swan joined followed by more ducks and a timid moorhen. Several more slices of bread followed before I decided my fellowship with God's feathered creations must end or I would have no toast for tomorrow's breakfast.

Closed the window and have spent ten minutes tidying the galley and washing dishes. I should be off by quarter past six. Powerfully moved to pray but I might do that once underway. Snipe's stern is somewhat like a pulpit.

Late morning; Hungerford Wharf

I have moored by a pleasant café for morning coffee and a chance to telephone Pea. Of course, if I had decided to forego elevenses I might have lain in bed another half hour, but I simply must find out if I have been granted an extra day. If I have not then I will telephone Charlie and say I will have to abandon Snipe twenty-five miles short of their boatyard in Reading. He will not be best pleased.

But that can wait while I sip my coffee and bite into a slice of Dundee Cake.

Already pleasantly warm in the sunshine. A blessed relief after yesterday's misery. Indeed, if yesterday was my *dies horribilis* then today is its opposite for I at last had proper view of a kingfisher. This was not a gleam of azure in the distance before it takes flight in a dazzle of wings, but the greeting of equals: both of us creatures of the waterway. As soon as I saw it I expected it to flee, as all others have, before Snipe, but the bird remained perched on a reed above the water and watched me pass with apparent indifference. I suppose had I exclaimed, or even so much as reached for my camera, it would have been off, but I took the precaution of remaining utterly still until it had slipped behind.

Then, having corrected Snipe's course before she buried her prow in the towpath, I continued in a state of elation. Was yesterday a trial, which having passed, I am now rewarded for? I know it is foolish to see life as a series of ordeals and examinations but at times I do feel tested, and reward is rare.

My one disappointment is this journal will be the only record of my encounter and who will read it? Let alone believe me when I tell them. It is like those rare moments when I sense Him beyond the veil; powerfully present, yet whose presence is always incommunicable to others.

I must make my telephone call, though not without reluctance. The morning may yet end in rancour after so promising a beginning.

DISASTER AVERTED

Lunchtime; The Bluebell, Kintbury

Never heard of Kintbury but The Bluebell is a 'must review' on CARP's list of hostelries. Mixed news from Pea but I am reconciled to it. Blasted bad luck Dessie being away.

She answered within a minute which is as good as it gets for Desmond Catterick and Associates.

"Hello Pea, Nevil here. Have you managed to speak to Dessie or the chap at Waterfowl Cruisers?"

"Oh, good. I mean good you called. I was going to 'phone you."

"Pea, I rather doubt you could have telephoned me as I am on the canal. Being on the canal, or rather staying on it a bit longer than I intended, is the reason I called you."

I may have sounded testy which was a shame on my part

as the day had been lovely so far. Pea seemed to take an age replying.

"You can sound quite cross at times," she said.

"I am not cross. But as I am on a canal boat I have no means of receiving telephone calls. It's rather unfortunate actually as my cat is poorly and Mummy, well I could get a call at anytime from the nursing home. In fact, I will jolly well telephone them right after speaking to you."

"That doesn't sound like an apology," said Pea.

For the sake of efficiency I apologised, gave her the number of the telephone box, and asked her to call me back.

Frustratingly, I had no sooner put the receiver down ready to receive her call than someone rapped on the door.

"Have you done?" asked a spotty youth.

"Not really. Waiting for a call."

The novelty of standing in a telephone box waiting for it to ring appeared to be outside his experience.

"Only I've been waiting," he said.

"I'm waiting too," I said. "For the telephone to ring."

"You have to put money in it," he said as though talking to an imbecile.

"I have put money in it, and I have asked the person I spoke to to return the call. It really will ring any moment."

Except the telephone remained silent and after a few more minutes I had to make way for the surly boy-man. I lingered, just out of obvious earshot but close enough to observe when he would leave. His conversation appeared to be a lengthy and imaginative account of what he would do to, what I assumed was a young lady at the other end of the line and what she would do to him. Fortunately, his descriptive powers ended when he ran out of change, and I was on the scene in an instant in case he asked his correspondent to return his call.

"Did you enjoy that?" he said with a smirk as he sauntered away. "Saw you listening, you perv."

"I'll have you know I'm happily married."

"Oh yeah? Where is she then?"

"Lout! I hope the girl's mother knows what you intend."

He said something to the effect that if the girl's mother joined in he wouldn't mind a bit.

Once inside I had a distinct aversion to touching anything and carefully wiped the receiver with my handkerchief before telephoning Pea with my last sixpence.

"Pea? Nevil again. Telephone me back immediately."

This time I only had to wait a minute before she called.

"You sound even more cross," she said.

"But not with you," I said. "Someone insisted it was their turn to use the telephone. I had to wait. Now, have you news from Dessie or the boatyard chap?"

She had, but it was something of a mixed bag. Dessie understands but is powerless while out of the country. There is a surcharge of one-hundred and fifty crowns for unauthorised late return of a boat. This is rather more than Pea can authorise without Dessie's signature. The most she can sign for is seventy-five crowns. Charlie has agreed to an extra day's hire for seventy-five provided I pay up the extra on arrival at Reading. Given that I left my Rover in Waterfowl Cruisers' care they have considerable leverage, so I had no choice but to agree or risk CARP deciding I had not fulfilled the contract.

Speaking of which, lunch is arriving.

Postscriptum: prawns wrapped in wafer-thin slices of lemon with capers and pasta ribbons, four stars; raspberry sorbet with sloe gin sauce, five stars; chilled Chablis, four stars; facilities, first class, five stars.

Slight risk with seafood after yesterday's trouble with pike but at least I know they've been nowhere near the canal.

Early evening; Thatcham Wharf

Earlier this afternoon I passed a watercolourist. She was sitting on a little chair perched on the towpath, easel before her and brush in hand. Slim, strawberry blonde, with a straw hat to keep the sun off and one of those floaty pastel dresses: pretty as a picture.

Seeing her reminded me that the Avebury Society of Painters were convening at about that hour in the New Barn School, and I was absent.

Naturally, I had given my apologies last week but when I mentioned the cause of my absence Angela Spendlove insisted I take my painting materials in case "Inspiration should strike" and as I have made good time today, thanks to taking the last six locks in tandem with another boat, and the day is drawing into a long and bright ending I brought Snipe into the nearest decent mooring and set up my easel.

It was not quite the joy I had hoped for as the canal wharf seemed to gather the breeze which ruffled my paper more than I would have liked, but I have made a passable job of the old wharf and its rusty crane. Something to show Angela next Friday as proof I have not wasted the week merely earning a crust.

I would have liked to try my hand at the sunset as it was building into a splendid drama, but I have a dinner-date at The Lohengrin. The place is under new management and specialises in vegetarian cuisine (was it too much to expect swan?) and according to CARP meatless dining will soon be popular. Not with me I suspect but one must keep an open mind.

Left my masterpiece on the table in the galley. Still a bit damp but will hopefully dry flat. CARP mentions The Lohengrin has a dress code so I must go and smarten myself up. Didn't bother to shave this morning and these battered corduroys will not do at all. Hope dinner is something splendid but not too surprising.

Had a good day today, which is to say a thoroughly ordinary day which has been excellent because nothing appalling has happened. Caught myself wondering while dabbling paint if anyone in the history of boating has had quite such a horrid journey as yours truly. Only name I could think of was Odysseus and he had a wife to go home to.

Dinner; Lohengrin, Thatcham

The Lohengrin has seen better days; as have the three stuffed swans suspended, wings akimbo, from the beams of the dining room ceiling. They are, at close quarters, surprisingly large birds: far larger than one supposes when they glide upon the water.

I enquired of the maître d', an Italian from Lugarno, and he explained the décor belonged to the previous owner, an enthusiastic hunter and wildfowler now departed this earth, and they would be renovating in the autumn.

Not a moment too soon, I thought. Can't imagine what effect the swans have on those who abjure meat, but they left me hunch-shouldered and sympathising with those cowering in their cellars during the Zeppelin Raids.

"Our cuizine," the maître d' then informed me with obvious delight, "Iz entairely a la mode: venizohn, pfft! Pickled 'aire, breast of wild gooze, alzo pfft! If, zir, I mey recommend ze artichoke wiz buttairre zauce, or perhapz ze asparaguz rizotto wiz grilled muzz."

I assumed I had misheard muzz for something else but as I waited for grilled aubergine with peppers and pesto the couple next to me were served oily blackened chunks of something usually found on the roof. It did not look appetising. Meanwhile I was thinking the swans might be worth it if I could exchange my aubergine for venison.

I was already thinking of my CARP review and glancing about for other signs of shabbiness when I spotted something small and brown on the tablecloth. My first thought was mouse droppings, which was appalling enough, but when I flapped the napkin at it I was astonished to see it curl into a ball.

This was tricky. CARP's guidelines on reviewing state that if one is too pernickety about minor matters the establishments may rumble that one is a reviewer. On the other hand, a laissez-faire attitude to the extraordinary has the same risk.

Uncertain if this was minor or extraordinary, I got out

my journal as cover while I found my reading glasses. Then, while apparently studying the page, I observed the creature.

It was half the length of the nail on my little finger, proportioned like a sausage, and covered in reddish brown hairs. In motion it was like a caterpillar; halting its foreparts, then compressing its middle parts to proceed in a series of small loops. It was quite fascinating if mildly repellent. I was still distracted by it when my grilled aubergine arrived.

"Just my book," I said. "Record of my trip. Thank you. I was wondering; I spotted a small creature on the tablecloth. Could you please...?"

"Ah, but of course. Allow me."

The maître d' flicked the creature from the table with a serving cloth.

"What was it?" I asked.

"Ooo noze," the man shrugged. "Ze live on ze svarnz. Ze dine, ve dine. *Così è la vita.*" And he ground the toe of his shoe into the carpet and left.

I ate my slab of grilled aubergine decorated with peppers and fresh pesto sauce. It was excessively greasy and a little acidic. The side salad had wilted from exhaustion.

How odd that my first vegetarian meal in living memory should be marked by my active participation in the destruction of animal life. The tiny creature had done me no harm and I had even been charmed by its determined progress across the expanse of linen. I felt redeemed when another ball of fuzz dropped from overhead onto a disused side plate. Without waiting to observe it I picked up the plate and flicked the creature towards the skirting board where it might find refuge.

I suspect that last comment will not go into my review.

Ended dinner with flambéed camembert on French toast: not bad but I had lost most of my appetite by then.

Food, two stars; ambience, one star—begrudgingly; service, three stars—the maître d' did not have to be so flamboyantly murderous; wine, an indifferent Italian Pinot Grigio, two stars; facilities, not yet checked.

1 June; Thatcham Wharf

I'm writing this sitting up in bed, or berth, as Wildfowl Cruisers insist on calling it. Headache this morning. Might have got a little too much sun yesterday. Bad night's sleep as well and I'm out of sorts. It's as though I have forgotten something terribly important, and everything is coasting on like an aeroplane with no fuel. My last day aboard Snipe. Back home by late tonight. Can't say I'll go boating again in a hurry. Yesterday was the best of the lot and even that ended… well, let me finish off my notes on last night first, then I can get up and see if today is any better.

The facilities at The Lohengrin proved as appalling as everything else on offer. They were outside under a plastic awning. The dramatic sunset from earlier proved to be gathering rain clouds and the weather had closed in. Rain made an awful sound on the awning. It was like being attacked by noise. If I had wished earlier for venison then my appetite vanished when I saw a stuffed stag's head on the lintel over the door to the gents. It quite gave me a turn as the eyes at first glance appeared to be alive. A second glance, now through my reading glasses, left me nauseous. The eyes were indeed alive with more of those reddish-brown grubs. Any sympathy I had with the creature I had rescued evaporated, and I could cheerfully have taken the stag's head off the wall and thrown it in the fire. Bad enough someone had shot the animal but to mount its head above the gents and then let it be eaten by vermin revolted me.

Did my business within and left with alacrity: no stars.

I did not have an umbrella with me. Perhaps I could not have used it anyway as the rain was squally. Wisely, I had on my coat—which I still have not replaced despite earmarking it as no longer fit for use as far back as my Glastonbury trip—and I buttoned it up thoroughly and marched into the night for the half mile back to the boat. I had decided I would have a cup of tea before writing up my dining notes and was looking forward to getting into the dry when I came to the canal bridge. This arrived a bit earlier than I had expected, but I walked down the curving approach—gently sloping to allow the horses to ascend and cross the road without breaking their tow on the boats—and arrived at the towpath. Snipe, I recalled, lay west of the bridge but the way was blocked as there was no towpath beneath the arch.

This worried me as I distinctly remembered passing through the bridge to ascend to the road.

I backtracked, crossed over the canal by the bridge and took the curved approach on that side. I was now west of the bridge but there was still no sign of Snipe. Nor could I have walked beneath the bridge to reach the approach path, for this side was also blocked by the arch of the bridge.

I regained the road and stood in the middle of the bridge. Lights were scant but I had my torch and shone it first east along the canal and then west. There were no boats.

Eventually, given there was no Snipe and, moreover, no way of descending from the bridge to where I was convinced I had left her, I deduced this was not the bridge I had moored beside. I retraced my steps towards The Lohengrin and found the fork in the road I had missed. At once I began passing shops and premises I vaguely recognised from earlier and moved on with relief even though I was now chilled and damp. After anther twenty minutes of hunched walking into the weather I refound the canal, descended by a bridge whose geometry was almost the opposite of that which had confused me, and boarded Snipe.

I made tea as I had promised myself but could not get warm again and my journal—this journal—where I intended completing my notes lay unopened.

It seemed a shame to end, what had been an enjoyable day, cold, miserable, and wet-through, but I should not have expected fortune to last. Still have a queer sense of having forgotten something. Had hoped my journal would remind me of it but no luck. Eight o'clock already and many miles to go. Someone is up earlier than me though. I can hear shouting and that horn is awfully close. Wonder what the matter is...

Late morning; Lock Café, Woolhampton

I am the victim of a wicked prank. The noisy horn came from a boat whose prow was only yards from my bedroom window. I could not see who was shouting—presumably, it was the steersman—but the bows were occupied by a boy of perhaps twelve who on seeing me gestured with hands wide apart.

I stared back, not comprehending why his boat should choose to ram Snipe or why the horn was sounding as though to force me to give way. It was only when I realised I could see both banks of the canal from the one window that I grasped the problem and waved to the child to convey my willingness to do something about it.

I suppose that was rather a lot to convey with a single hand movement and the horn continued until I had found my slippers and dressing gown and emerged onto Snipe's stern.

I now had view of the steersman; a middle aged chap with a floppy hat and a red face.

"Move your bloody boat," he yelled, "You're blocking the canal."

This last observation was rather unnecessary. Frankly, the speed one can do on a boat is so low one hardly wastes more time standing still than one does underway, but I didn't discuss the matter.

"Ah. Sorry. I was moored. The bank. Last night."

The gentleman's boat moved a little closer. The child angled a boat hook towards Snipe's midriff like a harpooner to a whale.

"Wait a mo. Just need to. Keys. Engine."

My ability to talk in complete sentences was temporarily scrambled. As, I now discovered, was my recollection of the boat keys. I had returned from The Lohengrin last evening in something of a mood and had, apparently, flung them down on entering. After much searching I found the keys in a teacup on a shelf above the stove. A glance through the window revealed the boat's prow almost upon me and I had visions of being cut in two. I dashed back to the stern.

"Keys!" I said hopefully. "Just a jiffy."

I got the engine going and returned to the tiller. Someone was shouting about a rope.

"Sorry?" I called.

"Stern rope. Water!"

It was the steersman again. He gestured at me and jabbed his hand downwards. I stared at my feet but could see nothing wrong, other than my slippers.

"Rope's in the water," joined in the boy.

I glanced overboard. Snipe's mooring rope had drifted around her stern.

"Ah! Yes. Jolly good thing. Thank you. Just..."

I managed to pull the rope up and got smelly canal water all over my pyjama bottoms. Had I put the engine in gear I should have sucked the rope around my propeller and that would have been that. Not likely to persuade Charlie to release me a second time after what happened at Devizes.

Finally, after much toing and froing, Snipe lay against the bank once more and the gentleman on the other boat motored past with a valedictory admonishment.

"Bad mooring," he said. "Always check your ropes last thing at night."

I am quite certain Snipe was secure yesterday evening and some childish prankster has untied my ropes and cast me off in the night but there was no sense trying to explain. Anyway, I had still to get the gangplank ashore and then tie Snipe up securely so I could attend ablutions and breakfast.

As a start to my final day, it does not bode well but at least I shall spend tonight in a proper bed.

Lock Café is drab and rather soulless. The coffee is tasteless, and the sweet pastry is from yesterday or the day before. I will not be recommending it to CARP readers.

Wonder if there is a bank here. Need to cash a cheque so I can pay off Waterfowl Cruisers later. Damned liberty having to use my own money but if I don't keep them happy they may not return my motorcar.

Lunchtime; Butty Inn, Aldermaston

The manager at the Lock Café in Woolhampton gave me directions to a branch of the Wiltshire Bank and I cashed a cheque for two hundred. Suspect funds are low but there's a Creative Haven in Pembrokeshire week after next and I should be able to get Dessie to pay me back for the additional costs of the boat hire. CARP need their article and even then they'll be a month or two paying.

Cast off shortly after eleven-thirty knowing it was only a few miles and one or two locks to Aldermaston. Had hoped to pair up with another boat to make life easier but ended up alone and had a bit of an accident at the second lock as I was coming into the town. Quite forgotten how many locks I have climbed in and out of this week and perhaps I was taking matters for granted on the way down to Snipe's stern to drive her out of the lock and onwards. Suffice to say, the rungs were even more slippery than usual and as I shimmied down my left foot slid forward off the rung and jammed behind the ladder while my right foot slid the opposite way. It happened so quickly I had no time to react. My right hand let go and I was swinging sideways into space with Snipe's stern and the evil gap between her stern and the lock gates yawning beneath me. As I swung the lock key dangling from my jacket pocket slipped loose, bounced off Snipe's stern and into the water. I am now down to my last lock key.

After a few seconds swinging wildly with my shin jammed against the wall of the lock I managed to extricate myself. Nasty bruise on the back of my calf but surprisingly the knee is undamaged.

Occurs to me that 'falling in' is the only misfortune I have avoided. Hope it's not too soon to say that.

Ordered the Bargee's Lunch. Pretends to be the traditional fare of canal folk, though I rather doubt they would recognise it, or afford it. Pint of Butty Bitter will wash it down. It's a decent drop of ale with a mellow aftertaste. One could get very used to it, though I would have been perfectly happy to stay aboard with a sandwich and a cup of tea. Alas,

CARP would not be happy with my opinion of *déjeuner chez* Snipe so I must make small talk with a bored waiter and find something on the menu that will awaken my jaded palate.

This was inevitable, I suppose. Lucky to get this far before my appetite wore off and certainly my encounter with the pike and last night at The Lohengrin haven't helped.

Notes: The Butty Inn is named after a kind of barge and nothing to do with sandwiches. Nice enough place and if I were a chap or chapess eager for a canalside lunch it would be more than adequate—there is a modest wine list and a touch of the daring to the cuisine, but if you've spent the last five days dining out it's a different matter. My Bargee's Lunch turned out to be a boat-shaped pie with a filling of ground meat and potato served in a basket of hay. I asked the waitress if the hay was intended to keep the pastry warm, but she said it was what the bargee's horse ate for lunch. Mustering some wit, I asked if I were expected to eat it too and she said I could if I wanted.

Pie, four stars; service, four stars for eccentricity; ambience, three stars; facilities satisfactory, three stars.

KEY

Evening; The Ostrich, Reading

Something of a false start from Aldermaston. I had only been motoring ten minutes when I came to another lock and discovered my spare lock key did not fit the mechanism. Where the mechanism had a square spigot to wind the paddles my key was meant for a spigot with five faces.

Had to moor up as there was no room to turn the boat and walk back to the main town bridge in search of a replacement. Weather had turned again and there was distinct chill as I climbed the brick steps to the road. Noticed rope-worn grooves in the stone coping left by decades of horses pulling canal boats.

Aldermaston did not impress. Dismal looking High Street and nothing that immediately looked like the sort of place one might buy a replacement lock key. Forced to hail a chap and ask for directions.

"A lock key?" he replied to my question.

"Yes. For a lock."

He pondered this.

"I mean," he said, "depends what sort of lock it is. One of them modern locks you can probably get it in Dengies. They do that sort of thing. If it's an older key, a special key, then reckon you need the ironmongers."

"Ironmongers? I want to buy a lock key. I don't expect them to make one."

"Course," he said, "for a com'nation you don't need a key. Just remem—."

"Ah, no," I said, realisation dawning. "I don't mean that sort of key. Or rather that sort of lock. It's for the canal. A key for a canal lock. I'm on a boat."

"Oh, whyn't you say so. Reckon you can get that in Dengies an' all."

"Thank you. Thank you. And?"

"Top of High Street; alleyway next to the Baptist House. Down there."

Dengies was one of those places that have at least one of everything if one knows where to find it. Fortunately, the chap at the counter did and directed me to a small chandlery section. Unlike the box of tarnished and worn metal at the chandlery next to Caen Hill Café, these were bright and shiny and individually packaged at twenty crowns each. I winced, trusted even I could not lose another key in the course of a single afternoon, and bought one.

"Twenty-two crowns and ten shillings," he said.

"But?" I pointed at the price tag.

"Tax," he replied.

Grudgingly, I handed over a fifty crown note took my change and left. The weather had worsened, and I returned to Snipe in a steady drizzle. Inclined to a second cup of tea but am still a long way from Reading, in canal terms, so changed into my boating gear, removed the key from its plastic wrapping—how much packaging does steel need?—and wound up the paddles to let the lock fill so I might enter.

All in all, I left Aldermaston ninety minutes later than intended and put the throttle well-forward to make it to Reading before the office at Waterfowl Cruisers closed.

It was a curious, almost anticlimactic end to my trip. There were fields and patches of woodland on either bank, and you wouldn't have known a large town lay ahead. Then, on the last few miles or so, the fields gave way to a watery landscape of lakes and meandering rivers with the canal cutting through them. It was rather haunting and would have been pretty but for the persistent drizzle.

I had before leaving Aldermaston glanced at the guidebook and when I saw the sign for Waterfowl Cruisers on a bridge I knew to make for the left-most arch and found myself on a backwater. In a few yards I had drawn into the bank where a young man helped me moor.

"We were expecting you back yesterday," he said without the formality of introducing himself.

"Someone will have called your office," I said. "I believe I owe you for the extra day."

He confirmed the sum of seventy-five crowns.

"Single-manning?" he said.

"Yes. Took longer than planned."

I decided against telling him the true reason and paid up. He showed me where they had parked my Rover and I drove it closer to the boat and moved my things off Snipe. It was strange saying goodbye to the boat. Despite my misadventures she had been steadfast throughout. I won't go boating again but I think I shall miss being on a boat. Despite the weariness of the locks and the constant noise of the engine there have been many moments of utter peace.

I stopped in the canal office before driving off and asked where I might get a decent meal. He suggested The Ostrich and it isn't too bad. Gone for a simple pie and chips. Had enough of fine dining and this won't go into CARP's review. All that leaves is the drive home in the dark.

Night; Avebury Trusloe

Arrived home about ten. The week has taken its toll, and I am exhausted. Rain is tipping down and half my things are still in the car. Vase of lilies in the kitchen with a note from Mrs Pumphrey asking me to call round.

No sign of the cats but found only one half-eaten bowl of Kitty Nibbles in the kitchen. I fear I have lost Boris.

BORIS R.I.P.

2 June; Avebury Trusloe

Woke feeling dreadful. Suspect I have caught a chill in yesterday's drizzle. Came down for breakfast in my pyjamas and dressing gown. No eggs or bacon as I've been away so made do with toast and marmalade. Tusker was waiting outside the door. Let him in and refreshed his bowl of Kitty Nibbles. Barely acknowledged me before scoffing the lot and curling on his cushion. Lilies looked ridiculous and the smell is dreadful. Mrs Pumphrey means well.

Having shaved and dressed I called on my neighbours.

"Oh, Nevil. I didn't know what to do. Please come in. Would you like a cup of tea?" I declined. "My Bill has gone for his constitutional. I'm on my own."

She said this last almost with a wink. Felt desperately out of place. Reminded me of those times with Mummy when I had been found out and it was only a matter of time before a charge would be laid on me followed by punishment. This might take the form of a sad stare and silence from Mummy or, for really bad offences, a comment that my father would have to know.

"I saw your note. Thank you for the lilies. Very thoughtful. Tell me please, was it..." I stumbled. Something seemed to be wrong with my tongue. "I assume the worst."

"It was the Wednesday," she said as she plugged in the kettle. "He had been very quiet, like you said he was. But he started shaking and wouldn't stop. It was dreadful. I persuaded Bill—you know he's none too fond of cats—to take me into the vets in Devizes. Boris was on the back seat. He cried the whole time. I wish I could say he didn't suffer..."

I've sometimes felt Mrs Pumphrey were almost trying to adopt my cats but hearing her struggle to get the words out I felt a wave of sympathy for her.

"The vet said nothing could be done except to stop him suffering. It was very quick. I hope you understand."

"Of course, yes."

"The vet who seen to it, he was a lovely man; he said he would wait a week while you decide what to do."

"Do?"

"With the remains. This is their number. If you give them a call."

Mrs Pumphrey gave me a business card.

"If you would prefer, they can cremate him. Or you could have a casket. Some people like to bury their pet. My Bill buried Charlie in the garden."

That was half an hour ago and I've barely recovered. Got home from next door and picked up Boris's old cushion. I intended to put it in the bin, but I buried my face in it and blubbed like a baby. Smell was horrible. Shortly heading to Communion. Can one pray for the soul of a cat? Do cats have souls? Are there cats in Heaven? It seems unlikely. I've never known a cat to come when it's called so perhaps they sit outside the gate driving Saint Peter mad. Unless God has Kitty Nibbles, I suppose.

Plenty of dogs, though. Can't imagine dogs ever leaving Him alone. Depressing thought.

CHURCHLY DUTIES

Lunchtime; Red Lion, Avebury

Left home later than I wanted but arrived at church in what I hoped was the nick of time. Soon as I saw Sophia Mudge in the porch I remembered I was down to be welcomer today and actually half an hour late.

"Dreadfully sorry. Awful morning," I grovelled.

"Now that you're here you may as well go straight in," she said and handed me the order of service.

"I've lost my cat," I said.

"Again?"

Sophia Mudge has the face of a hammer and the same way of dealing with things.

"Sorry? Ah. I mean he died last week."

"I can't see how that should matter," she said, with a look that would have soured milk. "My Ronald was a staff to me but when I lost him I was at church the next day, prompt. It's what he would have wanted."

Not sure Boris had any opinion on my churchgoing. Ronald Mudge was a twerp, but Sophia never fails to mention how great a loss he was. She was a stalwart of the PCC until his death. Gave up the office because "One can't trust the streets at night." Avebury only has the one street, so her concern seemed excessive.

I went in, clutching the order of service, and took my usual pew with nods and grimaces to everyone I knew.

Peter started us off with "Lord thy bounty is merciful and wise," played at a rattling pace by Paul Durdle on the organ. Left the rest of us gasping in his wake. Buggered if I can see what's merciful and wise about taking poor Boris. He was only six and that's no age for a cat. Sermon was something about the long bright days of summer being no time for idle hands. Don't recall much brightness about yesterday. Definitely caught a snivel.

Molly made a beeline for me over tea and biscuits.

"Was that you in the Messenger?"

"What?"

"The Devizes Messenger. About the body in the canal. Only there was a photograph and I thought it was you."

"Ah. Probably. My boat ran over the poor chap. His..." I stopped myself going into more detail and asked Molly what the paper had said. Probably should have thought to buy a copy last week but never mind.

"Only that he'd been found by police divers."

"Ah, well, they didn't exactly find him. I did. Anyway, at least we know he was innocent."

"Do we?"

That was a tricky moment and I had to bluff. Didn't want to say how I knew.

"The police took a statement off me. They seem to have ruled him out. Another suspect. Can't say anything."

"But you just have," Molly said perceptively.

"Then I shouldn't have. Sorry. Only been home since last night and had a dreadful shock. Boris died while I was away. My neighbour, Mrs Pumphrey, took him to the vets, but they couldn't do anything."

"Oh, I'm so sorry. It's hard when our furry friends pass away. What will you do?"

"Bury him in the garden, I suppose. Don't like the idea of cremation."

"No, I mean will you get another cat?"

"Gosh, no. Tusker would tear it to pieces. No. I am a one cat person from now on. But how have you been?"

Molly has been well, but business is slow. Her mother is doing better—I didn't know she was doing badly: must pay more attention—and said that if I changed my mind about another cat that Manor Farm always had kittens for sale.

"I don't know if you're around mid-week, but we're gathering on Thursday afternoon to tidy up the churchyard."

"I hope it doesn't involve actual gardening," I said. "Not my forte."

"I'm sure we'll keep you busy."

Agreed to turn up providing it wasn't raining.

Soon after Peter Chadwick came across, beaming like Buddha—the early athletic version—and asked if he might have a word. Molly took her leave.

"And take care," she said. "You and Tusker."

"Tusker?" Chadwick asked.

"My cat. Lost his brother a few days ago. Not a good time."

"We shall be reunited in Heaven with all that loved us," Chadwick said.

I'm not sure if Boris loved me. Tolerated is a better word.

"Paul played well," I said but Chadwick wasn't after small talk.

"My sermon on the bright days of summer," he said as though I were to intuit some purpose from it.

"Yes. Rained rather a lot yesterday," I said.

"How was the canal? Did you fall in?"

"I did not," I said with some dignity. "And my boat arrived safe and sound in Reading."

I did not add that they were almost the only things that had gone to plan.

"Good. Good. Wanted a word about Midsummer's Eve," he continued. "The village will be home to a night of revelry, music, dance, and celebration. Sid Morris may call them *wicket folk*, but we know better, don't we."

I wasn't sure if this was a question or a rhetorical device. I muttered something about Sid's old-fashioned values.

"I was impressed by your Easter talks," Chadwick said. "I thought they captured the true spirit of the Passion. Lucy thought so too."

He was adding to the blackmail.

"We, that is the dean and I, would like to bring the revellers and the village closer together and I mentioned that in your Easter Pieces you had bridged the divide between church and land, between the divine and the landscape and that you were writing something for the Solstice. He was very enthusiastic, and I said that I'd ask if you would be interested in writing something suitable for the diocese. It's not that different for writing for the parish magazine, is it?"

"The diocese?" I asked.

"The Salisbury Diocese. The bishop has approved the idea."

"Gosh. I see."

The diocese covered almost the whole county and most of Dorset. It was quite a lot different from writing for the parish magazine. An order or two of magnitude different.

"The Bishop wants to see spiritual outreach embracing those with alternative beliefs," Chadwick said.

"Even after what happened to Paul?" I said, reminding him of Paul's bloodied nose.

"I am sure you have more diplomacy. Besides, you only have to report what you see."

"Sort of fly on the wall. Or fly on the stones," I said.

Chadwick looked blank.

"But for the Bishop I can hardly refuse," I added. "Especially when I have already been, so it seems, volunteered."

Chadwick smiled. "I knew I could be sure of you. Do try to blend in."

"Blend in?"

"Dress for the night. Don't wear your Sunday best."

"Oh, I see. Not sure I have anything that will blend in. No kaftan. And certainly, no horns or drums."

"Just don't look like a mourner at a wedding."

Chadwick had that awful self-satisfied face he pulls when he thinks he's been droll. Wonder what he meant by *mourner at a wedding*. Does he think I'm a misery guts?

Sorely tempted by a second pint and spot of lunch. Dining in pubs is becoming a bad habit but there's bugger all at home until I go shopping tomorrow.

Late afternoon; Longstones, Avebury Trusloe

Tried settling down to editing once I got home but couldn't concentrate. Tusker was acting very odd: kept rubbing his back against my calves but if I bent to pet him he hissed at me. Wonder if he's lonely without his brother.

Unable to work, I looked through the refrigerator and kitchen cupboards and made a list for shopping tomorrow. Electric bill arrived while I was away last week so I can take that in and pay it at the bank, assuming I have sufficient credit. Speak to Dessie tomorrow, assuming he's back from France. Need him to pay the extra hire costs for the boat. Begin writing up my notes for CARP as well. Always like to give my thoughts a day's rest before I press keys to paper.

Did a better job of it than editing *This Iron Race* but I still couldn't settle. Eventually I put on my walking shoes and went out for fresh air. Perhaps my week on Snipe, much of it standing in the stern, has given me a taste for the outdoors. I took the bridleway across the field behind the house. Didn't intend going far but even so I didn't expect to be sitting with my back against one of the Longstones still in sight of my house. I think this is Eve but I'm never too sure. Ground's damp from yesterday's rain but the sun has warmed the stone nicely. Looking at my house I can almost imagine the curved avenue of long-gone stones connecting to the circle. Don't believe Sid's story that the avenue runs under my house. Surely the builders would have noticed something like that.

Do I really seem like a misery guts? Chadwick's comment bothers me. Suppose it would help to blend in at the Solstice if I'm not in my usual jacket and brogues. Not that I have anything that looks like a Wiccan reveller. Only thing remotely outlandish is my kilt. Still, how often will you get the chance to wear it?

Skylark overhead. Just make out the flutter of wings. Extraordinarily loud. Not what you'd call a tune, but listenable. Better than whoever it is I can hear laughing. Must be on the road behind the hedge as I can't see anyone. Inane giggling. Really irritating.

Wondering whether to head home or continue along the footpath to Windmill Hill. Thinking the latter as it will keep me out of the house longer. Will feel settled after I bury Boris. Already have a plot in mind.

Really is very damp underfoot, or rather under bum.

Evening; Avebury Trusloe

Managed half a dozen pages of editing MacGregor after tea. Bribed myself with a stiff measure of Owl Service. Slipped up lately and stopped keeping account of my drinking. Dr Saunders will not be happy.

Telephone the vets in the morning. Off to bed.

Postscriptum: pint of Cropwell's Bitter at lunch; stiff measure malt whisky before bed.

3 June; Avebury Trusloe

I'm sitting down to a second cup of tea before I head off to Devizes. Telephoned Snood and McWatters (that's the vets) after breakfast. Gave my name and address and Boris's name. Complete consternation from the receptionist.

"I'm sorry. We have no record in that name."

"But the cat is definitely Boris. Was Boris, I mean."

"Has the cat subsequently deceased?"

"What? No. You killed it. I mean, you put it to sleep."

"We don't keep our records under the name of the pet. It would be confusing. We have no record for Mr Warbrook."

"It may be under my neighbour's name. Do you have anything under Pumphrey?"

I spelled out the name. There was a pause.

"Would that be an examination, diagnosis, recommendation of euthanasia and a kindness injection?" she asked.

"I thought that was obvious from what I just said."

"Can you confirm, sir?"

"Yes. I can confirm."

"And how will you be settling your bill?"

"Bill? Oh, I see. In person I expect. I would like to collect my cat's remains."

"Of course. There is an additional charge for cremation."

"You've cremated him? I say that's a bit much. I wanted to bury him."

"No, sir. Only cremation is more usual."

"Boris was an unusual cat and I would like to collect him as he is."

"Of course, sir. Would you like a casket?"

"Is that necessary?"

"We really do recommend some kind of container."

"And how much is a casket?"

"Our prices go up to three hundred crowns for the deluxe model with black lacquered ash wood with brass handles: there's an additional cost if you want a brass plaque with more than nine letters."

"His name was Boris, which is five letters; and no, I think

the deluxe is excessive. Boris…" I looked for the right words. "Black lacquer wasn't his style. I think something simpler would be better. Cardboard would be perfectly fine. When he was a kitten he loved playing in cardboard boxes. Nearly lost him in the refuse lorry the first Christmas."

The memory caught me by surprise, and I had to blink away a tear.

"Our budget casket is forty crowns. Is that suitable?"

It still seemed rather a lot to bury in the garden.

"The only other service we offer is the bio-bag. It's transparent but quite effective."

I couldn't face collecting Boris in a plastic bag so ordered the budget casket. She warned me not to delay burying him.

"We keep remains in cold storage but don't recommend you do that at home."

"I have no intention of putting him in the refrigerator. When may I collect him?"

"Anytime sir. We are open till five this afternoon."

"Thank you."

Not too bad in the end. Better take my chequebook with me. Hadn't given any thought to a bill but I can't complain. I'm sure Mrs Pumphrey did what she thought best.

REMAINS

Lunchtime; Market Street Tearooms, Devizes

I am utterly bemused and considerably poorer than I was this morning. I shall have to tell Mr Pumphrey that whoever ran over that rat-brained Jack Russell of his did him a favour. Three-hundred and twenty-eight crowns! 'Painless,' my arse. Painless to Boris, perhaps. That's a quarter of last week's earnings and all I have is a cardboard box and a dead cat. The box has a best-before date printed on the side. Twenty-four hours to bury him. Just as well I intend doing it this evening.

But the cost isn't the reason I am bemused. Realising Boris had been declining after his week missing I asked the girl on reception if they had diagnosed his ailment. If I'm honest, I wanted to reassure myself nothing would have been different if I had acted sooner.

"If you wait here," she said. "I'll ask the assistant vet who was on duty that day. Won't be a moment."

I had already paid—through gritted teeth and without protest—so the receptionist was happy to leave me at the desk with Boris's casket while she went into the surgery room. I overheard conversation and after a few minutes an older woman emerged.

"Mr Warbrook, isn't it?"

"Yes, that's me. To be honest, I wasn't able to get Boris in to see you as soon as I hoped. Away on business for a week. Tell me, was there anything that could have been done?"

"We all have to let go eventually, Mr Warbrook. It would have been cruel otherwise. I'm sure he had a good life."

"A good life? I suppose he had a good life, but it wasn't as long as one would hope."

"He was an elderly cat, Mr Warbrook."

"He was only six. Hardly any age for a cat. He has a brother, Tusker. Perfectly good health."

"I'm sorry, the cat we treated was much older than that."

"That's absurd."

"Are you sure it was your cat? The lady who brought him in mentioned he had been missing for a while shortly before he fell ill."

"Yes. He went missing. But he was my cat. He recognised me!"

I was most insistent about that point.

Meanwhile the receptionist had been looking at the log book where they write in the admittance times of patients.

"In that case," the older woman continued, "I have no explanation. As I say, the cat we examined and recommended for euthanasia was at least fifteen. You say," she glanced at the lid of the box where a pasted-on label bore his name, "Boris has a brother."

"Indeed. Tusker."

"Did you have them from kittens?"

"They had just been weaned. Yes. Look, I'm sorry. This is a bit distressing."

A tear was growing, and I hate blubbing in public. I felt as though I was on trial for having let poor Boris down.

"I understand, Mr Warbrook. But I assure you there was nothing you could have done that would have made a difference. Is that all, Sophie?"

The last she directed to the receptionist.

"Thank you, yes. If Mr Warbrook is satisfied."

"Satisfied isn't the word I would use," I said. "Mystified better describes it."

The older woman went back to the surgery.

"But thank you for your help," I said to the receptionist. "I'm sorry if I made a scene."

"Not at all. Actually..." She glanced towards the surgery door. "I shouldn't say this as they're a bit stuffy here."

"Yes?"

I had my handkerchief out and made a show of blowing my nose while wiping away a tear.

"The woman who brought Boris in." The receptionist was looking at the log book. "Mrs Pumphrey?"

"Yes. My neighbour."

"It's just that, you're in Avebury."

I listened, doing my best to take her seriously as she said, with frequent glances at the surgery door, that they see a lot of peculiar cases from Avebury: dogs that bark at nothing; hens that are always broody but never lay; and cows whose udders are full one moment and empty the next. Quite a list.

"But you're certain the cat that returned was your cat."

"As I said, he recognised me. He was just poorly."

"But according to our surgery, much older than before."

"It is a puzzle," I said.

"Don't tell anyone I gave you this." She wrote a name and number on a Snood and McWatters business card. "Call her and explain everything. She may be able to help."

"Gosh! I mean. I know her."

"Cool. She's good."

"Thank you. It completely mystifies me but thank you."

Feeling rather puzzled I left Snood and McWatters for Market Street, intending a sit down and a gathering of thoughts over a cup of tea, for the name and telephone number belongs to Angela Spendlove.

Postscriptum: while I was enjoying tea and toasted muffins a lady with a small dog sat down at the next table. I had to move some of my things to give her room, including the bag with the casket. Immediately the dog growled and leapt at the bag. Fortunately, its lead restrained it.

"Down, Buster. Get down. Naughty dog."

The dog leant forward on its back legs, front paws clawing the air. I shifted my bags away from it.

"I'm dreadfully sorry," she said. "He's usually well behaved. Buster! Down!"

I couldn't see what the woman did, but suddenly the horrid little dog leapt into the air as though it had been kicked and ran round the back of its owner's chair. Didn't so much as squeak after that. Remembered on way back to my motorcar that it's Mummy's birthday on Saturday. Called at W B Jones for a card and will post it closer to time.

Late afternoon; Avebury Trusloe

It was as dignified as I could manage, once I'd extricated the spade from the garden shed. That bit was less than orderly. Astonishing what gathers in a garden shed even when one hardly ever opens it.

Spade was rusty but I don't think that matters. Haven't used it in two years and unlikely to do so again in the near future. I suppose Mr Pumphrey would think that deplorable and would have it polished like a silver spoon.

It dug the hole for Boris and that's all that matters. A yard deep, the instructions said, and a yard it is. Don't want the foxes getting at him. He's been through enough.

Tusker was nowhere to be seen. Foolish to think he might have said goodbye to his brother.

I set the spade aside and gently lowered the casket into

the hole. I then stood for a moment looking over the hedge into the field beyond. The wind was just enough to ripple the barley. The Longstones at the far side like islands in the waves.

I had my thumb hooked in the pages of the Prayer Book. Didn't care if the page got a bit of dirt on it from my damp fingers. Then I opened it and spoke over the casket.

"We who are living yet know death, let us pray for those we loved."

Loved might be pushing it. So might reading the Prayer Book for a cat, but Boris was my cat and it's my prayer book. God can choose not to hear. I think He often chooses not to hear.

"For even as we walk in the sun, death is our constant shadow and at the setting of the sun he shall have dominion."

Then I read aloud from Daddy's "Verses for Practical Cats," having chosen 'Percival Pedigree' as the cat who, of all Daddy's creations, best described Boris.

"Percival Pedigree, King of the Cats,

Lorded it on his comfortable mats..."

Suddenly aware of a spy in the camp, I glanced up and saw Mr Pumphrey watching. He had a pair of garden sheers.

"Please, don't let me interrupt," he said.

But the moment was broken, and I closed Daddy's book.

"I had finished," I lied. "Just need to cover him over. He was a good cat, you know. A good companion."

"I know what it's like," he said. "After I buried Charlie I couldn't step in the garden for a week. He's under that rose."

Mr Pumphrey pointed into the corner of his garden. In life he had often cursed the dog for digging up his plants. Now it was helping them grow.

"Don't mind if I say something," he said. "Only you might want to know."

"Go on," I said, thinking it unlikely I would stop him.

"Where you've put him is where the faeries run."

"The... Well, not that I believe in the faeries, but if it is they can jolly well go round him."

Late evening; Avebury Trusloe

Lost myself for a few hours editing *This Iron Race*. Away next week and am expecting O'Brien to visit soon after. Must confirm that with Dessie. Can't quite see Boris's grave from the kitchen window, which is good. Don't want it in my line of sight whenever I'm at the sink. Bedroom window is another matter. Noticed while changing from my outdoor things that I'd managed to put him plumb in line with the Longstones so maybe Mr Pumphrey is right. What am I saying? Of course he isn't.

Considering getting some kind of grave marker. Don't suppose I'll always be living here and can't bear the thought of someone digging him up by accident. Have to let Edith know he's gone. But not this evening. Can't face anything more today.

Bad news

4 June; Avebury Trusloe

If I didn't get on with it first thing I knew I would prevaricate all day, so I telephoned Edith straight after breakfast.

"Glendale Stables. Edith speaking."

"Edith, Nevil here. Good morning."

"Nevil, I'm still in bed. It's only..." There were muffled noises. "It's nine. Later than I thought. Bit of a lie in."

"Err. He isn't there, is he?"

"If you mean Rupert, no."

"Ah. Good. I mean, wanted to speak to you..."

"Is it Boris?" she interrupted. "You said you would call if you had news."

"Yes. Afraid it is."

"What did the vets say? If it's an operation..."

I let her finish speaking. I hadn't realised how keen she was to help. It seemed such an awful shame.

"I'm afraid it's very bad news. He passed away last week. I was on assignment. On a canal boat. Mrs Pumphrey was looking after the cats. Got back Saturday night to find a vase of lilies and a note. I'm afraid he's gone."

Edith paused before answering. I'd done my best to smooth out the story, but I was never very good at hiding anything.

"What are you not saying?"

"He was taken ill last week. Very ill. Mrs Pumphrey took him to the vets in Devizes. Anyway, the vets couldn't do anything, so they put him to sleep."

"And she didn't tell you until after?"

Edith, however sleepy she had been, was now wide awake.

"She couldn't reach me. I was on a boat. The whole week."

"But surely you telephoned them to find out how he was?"

"Err. No."

"Oh, Nevil. But why didn't she call me then?"

"I don't suppose she has your number."

"You might have given it to her. In case this happened. You knew he wasn't his usual self. You said as much."

She was right of course. I was so absorbed in the canal trip I never thought of it.

"Did the vets say what it was?"

"They weren't sure. He really hadn't been himself since he went missing for a week. Very lethargic. Looked thinner as well."

"Are you sure it was our Boris?"

I wish she hadn't said 'Our Boris.' Yes, we had bought him and Tusker for the two of us but the last three years he had really been mine. Or so I thought. It was as though Edith was claiming part of her life back, her life with me. I was still wondering why she and Rupert had separate bedrooms. Perhaps it's just the luxury of having a large house.

I said I was sure it was Boris.

"He recognised me, I'm certain of it. When he returned he ran straight up to me."

"Cats will befriend anyone who feeds them," Edith said.

I thought she was rather clutching at straws.

"I'm as sure as I can be," I said. "I went in yesterday and

picked up his body. Buried him in the back garden. They gave him a sort of coffin. Only cardboard, but it was all done properly. I thought you'd want to know that."

"Was it expensive?"

"It's paid for, Edith. I took care of it."

I expected her to argue for me to accept her money, but she didn't. Instead, she asked if she could visit to see where I'd buried him.

"It's only in the back garden. Near the hedge," I said. "There's nothing really to see."

"I would still like to visit. He really was my cat as well. The only photo you had of him was lying across my legs."

"True. But only because he would have scratched mine to pieces."

"I'll call you and let you know when I'm popping round," she said. "How's Tusker?"

"Oh, he's fine. Bit more friendly now as well. Rubs his back up against my leg."

"He's lonely."

"You think so? Hadn't thought of it like that. Perhaps you're right. I'm away next week in Wales so if you do call it will have to be this week or the week after next."

"Thank you. I'd better go. There's a call waiting. Bye, Nevil."

"Bye."

The telephone clicked. I stared at the table for a moment before clearing the breakfast things.

Evening; Avebury Trusloe

Managed a full day's editing on *This Iron Race* today. Reasonably confident of finishing the text within the next few weeks, assuming no nasty surprises. Need to know from Dessie when O'Brien is visiting. If I haven't heard by Thursday I'll give Dessie a call. Also remind him I'm still owed for the extra day's boat hire.

Still very uncertain whether to continue beyond volume three. I shall assess the waters when O'Brien visits.

Settling down to watch the television tonight. The film channel is showing Deedee's *Calypso and Wine* at ten o'clock and I wouldn't mind a bit of light entertainment to take my mind off the last week. Even poured myself a glass of wine for company.

Postscriptum: three-quarters of a bottle of Merlot.

LE COCQ

5 June; Avebury Trusloe

Had settled down to editing this morning when Dessie telephoned to inform me O'Brien wishes to collect the manuscript for *This Iron Race* on June 21st. No explanation why that date instead of another but I said that I didn't foresee any difficulties.

"Actually, I was hoping you might call," I said. "Any chance of payment for the extra day's boat hire. I trust Pea explained everything."

"Cheque's in the post, old boy. Signed it yesterday."

This was uncommonly efficient of him. I had expected needing to ask twice for it.

"What delayed you, anyway? Overdid research for the pub reviews?"

"Certainly not. If you must know, I became an unwitting part in a police investigation. Found a body in the canal. Most unfortunate."

I decided against too much detail, mainly because I did not want to go through it all again.

"I hope you'll put it in the article for CARP."

"I will certainly not. It was far too grim. Pea mentioned you were in France with a famous actor."

"Jean-Maxim le Cocq. Frankly, a bit of a bore after a while but he's keen. Very keen. Written a novel and wants to break into the literary scene. Roman-á-clef, of course, about a brilliant actor no one takes seriously. Anyway, soon as I mentioned your name; son of the famous etcetera, etcetera, he practically bit my hand off."

"So, you want me to do it?"

"I'm certainly not giving it to that arse, Dominic Manners. Still all a bit up in the air. I'll have news for definite within the month. Fabulous house. Montmorillon. Heard of it?"

"Pea mentioned it was in Nouvelle-Aquitaine."

"That's it. Chap loves country living. Acts like he's the local squire, or whatever a squire is in France."

"You had better keep me informed."

"Oh, not likely to slip my mind. Le Cocq's loaded. Morals of a skunk, mind you. Wouldn't let him near my daughter. Bad enough with Dominic. Look, phone's ringing. Got to go. Speak soon."

Dessie rang off. Only hope he remembers I'm starting work at Belshade in October.

Back to editing MacGregor.

Lunchtime; Avebury Trusloe

Put a load of laundry on during my break for mid-morning coffee. A few of my things got a bit damp last week and I shall need a change of wardrobe for next week's trip to Wales. Anyway, I was out in the garden hanging the washing when Mrs Pumphrey appeared at the hedge.

"How is Tusker taking to being an only child?" she asked.

"He seems to have adjusted," I said. "Actually, I was going to ask about Boris. You didn't notice anything odd about him last week? Before he was ill, that is."

"He was quiet. Not really his old self."

"That's the very phrase I used. 'Not his old self'. Thing is, Snood and McWatters said he died of old age. Claimed Boris was at least fifteen. That's ridiculous as he was only six, the same age as Tusker. I'm wondering if I took in an impostor."

"Oh, it was definitely him," Mrs Pumphrey said.

"Are you sure?"

"Oh, yes. He had a little scar on his nose."

"Scar?"

"Tiny pink scar on the left side. I'd know his face anywhere."

"Ah. Now you mention it, I remember Boris cutting himself quite badly one time. Got his head stuck in a pilchard tin. Or sardines, can't recall. Vet had to put stitches in. Boris wasn't impressed; took a chunk out of the vet's thumb soon as the anaesthetic wore off."

"He was such a character, wasn't he."

That's one way of putting it. But I am still completely at a loss to explain it.

Late; Avebury Trusloe

Dominoes this evening at The Red Lion against the Green Dragon from Marlborough. Had hoped for a quiet night but one of the Marlborough players had recognised my face in the Devizes Messenger.

"Must have given you a bit of a turn," he said.

"Yes, it did rather."

"Put him off his lunch for, oh, at least half an hour," Sid said gracelessly. "What was it? Lemon sole? Pig's trotters?"

"It was quite appalling and had you been there you wouldn't be making light of it."

"Reckon he got what he deserved, though," said the Marlborough chap.

I didn't reply. The truth would come out soon enough and there was no need for me to leap to his defence. It left a nasty taste in my mouth all the same.

Dismal match. I drew one and lost two. Sid and Bert did rather better, but we still lost by four games to five.

Postscriptum: two pints of Cropwell's Bitter and a whisky nightcap.

6 June; Avebury Trusloe

I received a telephone call from Inspector Donaldson this morning. He requires a formal statement concerning my discovery of the body and wanted to arrange a convenient time. Said I was in Wales next week and would it wait.

"We would prefer to take a statement while events are fresh in your memory, Mr Warbrook."

"I really don't think I'm going to forget in a hurry."

"Perhaps not, but are you available tomorrow?" he asked. "I know it's short notice, but we're stretched at the moment."

I didn't see how I could say no. Hateful trying to deal with so many things at once: There's Stackpole to prepare for and of course there are still my doubts about Boris. Anyway, Inspector Donaldson is calling tomorrow morning. While he was there on the line, I asked if they'd found the man the girl had identified.

"I'm afraid I can't reveal any details while we are actively investigating," he said. I took that as a no.

Will attempt a few hours of editing before lunch. Due at St James this afternoon for gardening duties. Weather is delightful so I can hardly weasel out of it. Call at the pub after.

Postscriptum: weighed myself this morning: fifteen stone, two. My trousers are baggy and I'm tightening my belt an extra notch.

WEEDS

Late afternoon; Red Lion, Avebury

Horrid afternoon. My ears are buzzing and everything itches. Turned up at St James expecting a civilised spot of weeding and instead was handed a contraption called a buzzwhip. It has a small petrol engine—hellishly noisy—and a short whip which spins round and severs anything in its way. Unfortunately, the whip was constantly snapping or tangling around stuff and stalling the motor. Even when working properly it sent up a spray of thrashed weeds which settled on everything within three yards, including me! I smell like a compost heap and am certain to get a rash. It also meant any social aspect of gardening at the church was lost as no one could hear anything I said, and I couldn't hear them. Only came in here as I was desperately thirsty and the only thing on offer at church was tea. Honestly, it must be eighty degrees outside. Exceptional for the time of year but not welcome when one is buzzwhipping. Bath soon as I get home.

There was one brief break from the torture when Molly

arranged a tea break for everyone. Good to see Fred Thirsk back at the church, though he was on light duties after his recent heart troubles. I had already observed that all those who had turned out to work on this glorious afternoon were on the traditional wing of the PCC and was keen to find out if Ruby Miller, Fred's replacement as Captain of the Tower, would be sympathetic to us.

"Oh, Nevil, we can't talk 'shop' on an afternoon like this," Molly protested.

"But it's our only opportunity to learn about our new council member before we meet," I said.

"I don't mind," Fred said. "Be happy to see continuity."

"Continuity! Ah, that sounds promising," I said.

"Same old same old is as good," Sid said.

"A little negative, Sid. Besides, when the church is under siege same-old-same-old is all for which we can hope. Eventually the enemy will leave the gate."

"I hardly think Peter is the enemy," Molly reprimanded me.

"The last few weeks have brought me round to thinking our reverend has a point," Fred said. "Focuses the mind when Old Grimm sticks his fork in you."

"None of us are getting younger," Sid said. "None of us here are under fifty, sorry to say when a lady's present, but that's the truth of it."

"There's the Trees," I said. "Redwood is younger than any of us and his three girls are active in the church. I'm not as gloomy as you."

"Apple's starting college in Norwich come October,' said Fred. "She won't be here term time. Perhaps not in the holidays either. Can't see May or Elder staying more than a year or two."

"Fair point," I admitted.

"Swindon doesn't offer 'em much," Sid said. "The youngsters want more than we had, and I don't blame them."

"And remember you saw a bit of the world before you settled here," Fred said to me. "Oxford and the like."

"All true," I admitted. "Speaking of which, I may have difficulty getting to council meetings in the autumn. I'll be working in Oxford. Lecturing at one of the colleges. Only three days a week so I'll do my best to get back for Thursday evenings, but I can't see making Tuesdays or Wednesdays."

"Pays well?" Sid asked.

"Reasonable. Main thing is it's regular."

"We will miss your support," Molly said.

"I couldn't turn it down," I said.

"So, it's unfair to criticise the young for leaving if you're leaving too," Fred said.

"I didn't intend to criticise anyone," I said. "I hope the Tree sisters get on in life. Lovely girls. But to get back to my question, can we rely on Ruby?"

"She's got her head screwed on," Fred said. "Swears like a trooper, so that will upset Prudence and Paul, and takes no nonsense. Unlike them, she has one or two relatives here in this turf, so she has a personal investment in the old place."

"Good to hear it," I said.

"How have you been?" Molly asked Fred.

"So-so. Very iffy for a bit. But mending. Can't do what I was, but Doc reckons I shouldn't have been doing it anyway. Enjoyed today, though. Not done much but done a bit."

"For which we are grateful," said Sid with rare grace.

"Do they know what brought it on?" Molly asked.

"Doc asked me how old I am, then asked me what I thought might be the trouble. It's age, Molly. Getting old. Queer thing was, I knew the exact moment I started feeling poorly. Doesn't always happen, Doc said. It can creep up on you and that's the most dangerous because you don't sense it till it's too late. But I was walking up to the shop for my newspaper and fags when I saw this baboon standing at the end of the road."

"A baboon?" Sid said. "Y'mean like a big monkey."

"A bloody big monkey with a red arse, that's a baboon. And when this bugger saw me coming it ran down the road towards me. Just managed to get myself into The Henge

Shop, of all places, before I keeled over. Luckily, Apple Tree is a smart girl, and she called an ambulance."

I was remembering the queer animal I saw painted on the side of the white van outside The Henge Shop, but I'd be hard-pressed to call it a baboon.

"Not heard of any baboon sightings," Sid said.

"Don't suppose you will," Fred said. "Reckoned it had come for me and me only. Bloody queer though. Not seen one since I was a lad. Dad was stationed out in Gambia with Mum and me on the camp. You'd see them everywhere. Bold buggers they are."

"Were you born out there?" Molly asked.

"I was, as it happens. Bit of Africa in my veins."

I didn't tell Fred what I was thinking but I am wondering about that white horse I saw at Easter.

Home shortly and a long soak.

Postscriptum: two pints of Cropwell's Bitter this afternoon. Decent bit of editing done later but better check it in the morning as I was feeling a little fuzzy at the time.

Witness

7 June; Avebury Trusloe

Inspector Donaldson called shortly after ten. He was alone. Can't say why that surprised me. Perhaps I thought policemen always worked in twos, like they do on television. Not that I watch many of those shows. His car was quite ordinary but even so I couldn't help glancing up and down the road as I welcomed him inside. Too many gossips about.

"Sorry for the short notice, Mr Warbrook. Hope I'm not keeping you from anything."

"I'm working from home this week. Really no trouble. Have a chair."

I had invited him into the front parlour. I don't use it very often, but it has the best furniture. It was also more formal. Less as though I were inviting him fully into the house. Perhaps he sensed this.

"You keep the place tidy, Mr Warbrook. Is it just you?"

"Unfortunately, yes. My wife and I divorced a few years ago. She still lives locally but we hardly ever see each other. I have a son... He's in Borneo. Hardly ever see him either."

Inspector Donaldson had sat down and produced a notebook and pen.

"Understandably, you may feel a bit nervous, Mr Warbrook. But you are only a witness. Despite the... unconventional nature of what you told me at Devizes you have nothing to worry about."

"Thank you. It's not so much saying what I saw, and heard of course, so much as seeing and hearing it in the first place. It rather invades one's sense of right and wrong."

"Stranger things have I known than thou canst conceive," he said cryptically.

"Really? Are you, as they say, psychic?"

"It was a quote, Mr Warbrook. I understood you were a literary man."

"Sorry. I didn't recognise it."

"The hermit says it in Lidyard's *Freeman Rides.* Thirteenth century. But I have seen things I can't explain, which is why I was sympathetic to your report at Devizes. Can you tell me how you arrived at the scene?"

I explained about the locks and bringing the boat through the last stretch of water as I looked for a mooring near the café. Then I described the girl.

"And you're quite certain she couldn't have jumped aboard from the bank, or been hiding inside the boat?"

"Quite certain. I was several yards from the bank and looking straight ahead. It would also have been quite impossible for her to climb up from the cabin without me seeing her. And..."

I had shivered as I recalled everything that had happened.

"Go on, Mr Warbrook."

"It was my hand. Like getting a shock, an electric shock. There's research suggesting ghosts manifest as electromagnetic fields. That they have no actual substance."

"And this *field* is what you think you felt?"

"Perhaps. Also, I recognised her from the newspaper report. I knew it was the same girl."

I decided not to mention that I had seen the girl, or rather her ghost, beside the boat a few weeks previously. It would have muddied the waters.

"In any event," I continued, "she insisted that she needed me to find her father, she called him Daddy. And I suppose that's what I did."

"That is compelling, I admit." Inspector Donaldson said.

"I remember something else she said. Just after. It was, I forget the exact words, but she was very clear that she had to find her father. It was why she was there."

Donaldson smiled, though it was a weary smile.

"Ghosts have a reason for being ghosts. You might call it unfinished business."

I agreed with him, then broached something that had troubled me more than anything else since seeing the girl.

"Do you know why the dead choose one person and not another? There must have been hundreds of boats pass by before mine."

I suppose it was disingenuous of me. I knew the girl had seen me the first time I saw her, but she could have appeared to many others.

"I do not," Inspector Donaldson said and again came that weary smile. "If I knew I should ask every one of them to join the police force as their skills would be invaluable."

"Ah, yes," I said. "I suppose the only difficulty would be persuading the public your methods were reliable."

"True," he agreed. "But I know this: the dead choose who they communicate with. They're like cats in that respect; fussy who they acknowledge."

No idea why he should mention cats: it's something of a touchy subject. Obviously, he was very interested in my statement about the mother's 'other man' and I insisted I had heard the girl perfectly.

"I wrote them down actually. This is my journal. She said 'Daddy wouldn't be mean. It was Mummy's other man'."

"She didn't say how she identified this other man?"

"Sorry, afraid not. I suppose the mother was having an affair."

"Let's not leap to conclusions, just yet," the inspector said.

"Of course not. Though..."

"Yes, Mr Warbrook?"

"I suppose if she were there for a purpose that would be it. Clearing her father's name would be 'unfinished business' would it not?"

"You and I might think so. The jury would need convincing."

Inspector Donaldson left shortly after, having reassured me he would be in touch should I be needed, and I made a cup of tea and settled down to write up my journal. Off to painting this afternoon. Hope to have a word with Angela about the business at the vet. No idea why I should have been given her telephone number, but I mean to find out.

MEMORIES

Late afternoon; Antiquities Trust tearoom, Avebury

The part-time serving staff, which includes the middle member (should that be branch or sapling?) of the Tree sisters, are clearing up around me as I scribble away. Suggested to Angela that we might talk at The Red Lion, but she said her late husband died an alcoholic and she would prefer not to be in the presence of the demon drink. Not her exact words but that was the message. Anyway, she suggested the tea room and for the first time ever, I believe, I have sat down in Avebury with a cup of expensive coffee rather than a glass of beer or whisky.

The view across the duck pond is, I admit, prettier than anything in The Red Lion and the late sun is pleasant. The coffee is one of those modern frothy confections and not really me but never mind. I won't be repeating the occasion.

Today's lesson was all about style, or as Angela called it, "The artist's vision." I'll come to the main reason I am sitting here scribbling away in a moment, but I think this is pertinent as it says something about how Angela sees the world.

"You recall last week's lesson," she began this afternoon.

I put my hand up.

"We are not formal, Nevil. I do remember you were not here last week."

"Err, no," I said. "Unavoidably. On the canal. Working. I mean writing. Restaurants. But what I mean is, obviously I don't know what everyone did last week."

"As I was about to explain for those who were absent," Angela continued with a smile somewhere between amusement and exasperation, "We looked at memory and attempted to create a scene from the past as it might be now."

I went to put my hand up again, but then stopped myself and merely caught her eye.

"Yes, Nevil?"

"I was wondering, were we, I mean everyone here, except me. Were they blindfolded like before?"

"No. That was a different exercise. If you have any more questions perhaps you could ask me afterwards?"

"Yes, yes of course."

Angela continued, describing how this week we were to summon a memory from the past, of a person or place, or, if we were feeling adventurous, an event and paint it in such a way that it described how we felt.

"You mean like in sepia for something long ago," someone said.

"Yes," Angela agreed, "though perhaps that is a cliché."

"Or as though the paint was tears," Apple said.

"Yes, that's it exactly," Angela said.

Oh, Lord. I am not one for dwelling on the past if I can at all help it, but just then every memory I could think of was unhappy until, of all things, I remembered Mummy's tartan travel rug. I didn't quite trust the memory as it seemed so trivial, but that rug had been in the background of so much of my childhood and it was a sort of safe ground, rather like the Warbrook flag marking out our territory.

Tricky trying to remember the colours, particularly as I have trouble with reds and greens, but I hoped even I could manage to paint something that looked like tartan.

We had been painting about twenty minutes when Angela approached my shoulder on her rounds.

"The colours are vivid," she said. "Is the memory recent?"

"Hardly," I said. "I'd say it's fifty years old. Belonged to my mother. I still have it. Bit battered and faded now."

"The memory must be very strong," she said.

I would have agreed but she had already moved on.

It was only when class had finished that I approached Angela. I had the vet's business card in my hand.

"Angela, I couldn't have a word, could I?"

"That rather depends, Nevil."

"It's nothing untoward, or unseemly," I said perhaps too effusively. "You recall one of my cats went missing..." She acknowledged she did remember. "Anyway, he came back but wasn't his old self at all. And then last week he died. Rather, the vets put him to sleep."

Angela had, I think, become more attentive. Certainly, she had slowed packing away her things and I entertained hope there really was a good reason the receptionist had given me Angela's number.

"Thing is, the vets seem to think Boris, if it was Boris, was far older than I know him to be and when I mentioned this the receptionist gave me your number and said you might be able to help. She actually said, and it was quite a long speech, that Avebury has a bit of a record when it comes to strange events and animals."

"Do you believe it was your cat?" she asked.

"It seemed like Boris in some ways," I said. "My neighbour is Mrs Pumphrey and she looks after my cats when I'm away; she thought it was him. But I'm not certain. And what the vet said, well that makes no sense. Boris was six not fifteen. Edith and I bought him as a kitten!"

"There are ways to find out," she said. "But you have to accept that not everything is as you suppose."

I could have told her I already had good reason to know that but decided against. After agreeing on a venue, we sat here for half an hour over our coffees while I told her everything I could recall about Boris going missing; how Tusker had behaved; the odd sightings of a cat that may have been Boris; and then his return and how he had changed.

At one point Angela took out her sketch pad and began writing but I couldn't see what she had written.

"I'll have to talk to some friends," she said. "But I can't make any promises. Would you be able to unbury Boris and bring him to my cottage?"

"Gosh. Yes, I suppose so. Might be a bit whiffy. Vets warned me not to delay burying him."

"I'm sure we can survive," she said. "Can't say when, as I need to arrange everything first."

"Oh, I'm away next week. Working in Pembrokeshire."

"The week after," she said. "I'll call you."

So, there we are. Somehow I am to know, or probably know, if Boris is really Boris.

Must pack up my things as the girls have cleared every table but mine.

8 June; Avebury Trusloe

Today is Mummy's birthday: her eightieth, no less. Crossstones always put on a good occasion for any resident marking a special day—though I suppose they get more eightieth birthdays than most—so no need for me to call today. Anyway, I popped the card in the post a few days ago so Mummy will not think I've forgotten her. Plan on dropping in on her the week after next, assuming I survive reporting on the solstice celebrations.

Happy surprise in this morning's post: cheque from Desmond for the seventy-five crowns I paid to Waterfowl Cruisers. It's signed by Pea, of course. I do hope Dessie never takes up his threat to sack her. Mind you, I won't actually be able to bank the damn thing until I'm back from Wales, unless I get the chance to drop into Tenby one afternoon.

The cheque came with a hand-written note from Dessie and a press-pack devoted to Jean-Maxim le Cocq and his works. Can't say any of his films have entered my consciousness but I suppose *Homme du Destin*, *Le Prince et la Grenade* and *Sous le Nuage Noir* must have their following, judging by the prominence given them. Most of it is in French which will tax my patience. Few photographs of his house in Montmorillon cut out of a magazine, also French. Very plush, I must say. Jean-Maxim is something of a catch for Dessie. The note ends with the dates 29th and 30th July and a question mark. Not entirely sure what he intends by that. Will try and telephone next week and find out.

Intend several hours editing today. Must crack on as I'm out this evening. Kronus, the people taking over the Black brothers' antique shop, are putting on a goodwill evening at the village hall. Suspect they might be in for a bit of a surprise. Heard a few rumblings of displeasure during the socials after church and May Tree mentioned when she cleared my table at the teashop that The Henge Shop is not best pleased.

KRONUS

Later; Red Lion, Avebury

It was quite busy outside the village hall when I arrived just before seven. I had bumped into Sid and Bert who had been in The Red Lion, and we joined the queue to enter.

"Suppose they have a crowd in," Bert said.

"They can get us in quicker than this," Sid said. "What's keepin' 'em?"

I recognised Paul Durdle in the line ahead. He would be here representing Christian opposition. Redwood Tree was with his wife, Rowan, and their eldest. The evening was warm, so it wasn't a hardship to wait. Kronus had tied a banner above the doorway saying that they welcomed Avebury. I mentioned it to Bert.

"Shouldn't that be other round," he said. "Avebury welcomes whoever they are."

"Not that we bloody do," Sid said.

"So long as there's a bit of grub," Bert said.

The queue shuffled forwards but it was some minutes before we reached the porch. There was some sort of inspection at the door, like you get at an airport, which was holding us up. I couldn't see past Bert, but Sid was complaining.

"'Ere! You'll not wave that at me!"

Bert chuckled and I glanced round him to see a dowser attempting to wrestle a hazel stick from Sid.

"It's to harmonise our vibrations," the dowser protested.

"You leave my buggering vibrations alone!"

There was a crack and Sid victoriously waved a stub of twig before darting into the hall. Bert and I swiftly followed.

"Bloody nerve of it," Sid said.

The rest of the queue entered quickly, presumably unharmonised. The dowser had his eyes shut as he chanted over his broken stick. He reminded me of Glastonbury.

Kronus had arranged a table at the far end of the hall with a screen above and a projector but as I was glancing at this I noticed a petite and well-preserved blonde staring at me with a wry smile and a raised eyebrow.

"Good God," I muttered.

"Hold up," Sid said. "We might need to invoke the Almighty later but best keep our powder dry."

"It's my wife," I hissed.

"I think you'll find it isn't," Bert said.

"Ex-wife, then. Front row. What's she doing here?"

"Same as us, shouldn't wonder," Bert said. "Don't reckon she'll bite you. Not as if you're still married."

"Not the point."

I couldn't admit that every time I see Edith I get a pang of regret. Not in front of Sid and Bert.

Once everyone was sitting down a chap started the meeting by introducing another chap and then there was a short film about Kronus, the Greek god, which mercifully cut back on the infanticide and his murder by Zeus, before looking at the growth of the New-Age industry and tourism.

Afterwards the first chap asked for audience questions.

Apple was the quickest to get her hand up and I suppose having a pretty face helped the chap pick her first.

"Hi. Apple Tree," she said. To his credit, the chap didn't even smile. "I work at The Henge Shop and really I just see you as the big bad enemy, but what I wanted to say is that no one here will ever go into your shop because no one here ever uses The Henge Shop. It's just not for local people."

She sat down and Prudence Turnstone, who I recognised by voice, jumped in and said what the village really needed was a proper greengrocer.

"We have a proper greengrocer," Molly said from the back. "The village shop is a proper greengrocer."

"Hear, hear," someone agreed.

"Some of the produce could be fresher," Prudence said.

This led to some choice words before the chap at the front tried to restore order.

"Let me assure you all, Kronus is not in the greengrocer business and our business model is not in direct competition with any existing shops in Avebury."

This brought a protest from Apple who was taking her Henge Shop representative duties very seriously.

After that there was more to-ing and fro-ing with the chap from Kronus getting no support from the audience.

"You see what I don't see?" Bert said cryptically.

"No, what don't you see?"

"Any grub. Bloody skinflints."

What there was on show were several tables of products Kronus intended to sell in their new shop. Apple had swiftly identified quite a lot of material sold at The Henge Shop.

"It's just ripped off," she said. "Look. It's all cheap."

I hadn't spotted Edith sidling up behind me.

"Hello stranger," she said by way of introduction.

"Ah. Hello. Saw you earlier. I... you're looking lovely. I mean well. You're looking well."

"You look... thinner. Have you lost weight?"

"Yes, actually. Doctor advised I did something about it. So, I have."

"You look better for it. I don't think these Kronus people quite know what they've taken on."

"Rather a lamb to the slaughter, but I suspect it won't make any difference. As Apple said, we're not their customers. I'm surprised it interests you. Not your sort of thing."

"I'm here with Eurydice."

"Ah. Rupert isn't here, is he?"

"No. Too busy. He's often too busy. You didn't help Eurydice with her project."

"No, sorry. I suggested some books. I was too busy. Suppose that makes two of us, Rupert, I mean, and me. Where is she?"

"Over by all the knick-knacks. Unlike me she is interested. How is Tusker without his brother?"

"Seems to be okay. Not pining, anyway."

"I do want to drop by and see where you've buried him. I know that sounds odd, but he was our cat."

"Not odd at all," I said. "Week after next, perhaps. Off to Wales on Monday. Writing week."

"You're still with Creative Havens?"

"Yes. They still pay me, so I still work for them. It's a useful arrangement."

My attempt at levity fell flat.

"I suppose you want to see where Boris is buried so you can check I've done it right."

"Of course not. You will have done it perfectly. There's Eurydice. Over with Angela Spendlove and Jenny Atkins. I'd better do my *in loco parentis* thing."

I could see Angela and Jenny talking to the chap from Kronus but the young woman with them had her back to me. Very tall and gracile. Somehow Angela seemed far older in comparison, but I suppose the light was unflattering.

Edith left to join them, and I was swiftly joined by Paul Durdle. He was not the happiest of company.

"Good turnout for the PCC. Fighting the evil among us."

"I think that is overstating it," I said.

"Come and see these," he said.

He took me to one of the tables showing off Kronus's wares and indicated some pewter crosses.

"I can't really see what you object to," I said. "Celtic crosses are common in Eireland and the north of England."

"Even with those marks on them?"

I took a closer look. They were runes, or Ogham.

"I can't read them; but you can find crosses with such markings. Pope Gregory said the church shouldn't seek to destroy the old religions but incorporate them."

"We are not papists," he said darkly.

I wonder if Paul Durdle is entirely happy in our church.

Postscriptum: pint of Cropwell's Bitter. Only the one as I am driving home.

POLYPHONY

Whitsuntide; Avebury Trusloe

Our Reverend's sense of occasion is rather wasted on us. Arrived in good time for Communion and found Sid on welcoming duties in the porch.

"One for you," he said leafing through several sheets of paper.

"One what?" I asked.

"He's buggering about again," he said sotto voce so Mrs Mudge wouldn't hear. She was standing just inside the door to the church. "Here you go."

The page was from *Acts of the Apostles*, chapter two, verses one to twenty-one, written in Ancient Greek.

"Am I supposed to read this?"

"That's the idea. You're not alone. Be a cacophony when we gets goin'."

"How many are there?"

"'Bout a dozen, including me."

"You? Didn't think you could speak anything other than native Wiltshire."

"An' tha's wha oi'll be spaykin'," he said.

The oddest thing was, once everyone started reciting after "And they were all filled with the Holy Ghost: and they began to speak with divers tongues, as the Holy Ghost gave them to speak," delivered by Redwood Tree in Danish, it wasn't cacophony at all but truly rather wonderful; really captured the sense of the same spoken many ways at once. Jolly glad that my Greek text included a Latin alphabet version, or I'd have been floundering.

Fred Thirsk recited in what I assume was some African language. Paul Durdle in Russian. Prudence in excellent French. Elder Tree in Spanish. Sid hammed his rendition up no end, and I don't suppose any Wiltshireman has sounded like that since the twelfth century. Molly's version was a bit of a mystery, and I approached her during tea and biscuits.

"Swahili," she said.

"I had no idea you'd ever been to Africa."

"We have chapters of our lives that have gone and are often quite useless," she said. "My first husband worked for a mining company in Botswana. We lived there. What were you speaking?"

"Ancient Greek, I hope. I doubt Mr Baker of Ripon Prep would have approved."

"It was beautiful, though. I mean all of it."

"It was... affecting," I said.

Everyone seemed in a good mood and after Peter's sermon on the plight of refugees in India I went round with the collection plate and gathered a decent twenty crowns, four shillings.

The Red Lion has run out of my favourite tipple and in the spirit of international relations I have a cognac. Speaking of which, I've worked out the dates on Dessie's note must be when he wants me to fly out to Le Cocq. Presumably, it's only an initial meeting as the work for the biography will require at least a week.

Wonder if I can get the video on my television set working. Might be able to borrow a copy of 'The Prince and the Pomegranate' from the library.

Postscriptum: glass of Buonoparte's finest.

Later; Avebury Trusloe

I am packed for tomorrow. Remembered the Pumphreys are away, and Molly will be popping round to look in on Tusker next week. Ruminated on this morning's Communion. For all that we suffer from Chadwick's modernising tendencies, I suppose from his viewpoint we are hopelessly fuddy-duddy. There was a real sense of celebration at church this morning. One felt elated afterwards and that doesn't happen often. Doesn't change my mind about the church pews though: they will stay where they are. What might change are the congregation and perhaps for the better.

Off to bed with a glass of whisky.

Arrival

10 June; Stackpole Retreat Centre

Why is it when you plan something to the nth degree people always assume you have forgotten some crucial detail? There I was, all set to leave home at eight this morning, when Mrs Pumphrey calls round.

"Morning Nevil. Saw you packing last evening. Is it one of your trips?"

I agreed it was.

"Only I thought I'd remind you Bill and I are on holiday this week. We're off shortly."

"Yes. I recall you mentioned it. Do you need anything?"

"Oh, no. Bill is very prepared. Only we won't be here to look after Boris and—oh I am sorry. I mean Tusker while you're away."

"All taken care of. But thank you anyway. Molly Poppins is going to call round. You know Molly, from the Linden Tree?"

"Oh. I'm sure she'll be perfect. Better go. Enjoy... wherever you're going."

It wasn't so much the duration of the conversation that delayed me—it was all of five minutes—but the woman left me discombobulated. She seemed put out that I had made alternative arrangements for Tusker. No idea what she expected me to do: I can hardly leave him to fend for himself and I can't take him with me.

Wrote a note for Molly telling her where everything is kept and left at eighty-twenty. Roads reasonable and stopped for a cup of tea and bathroom break at Chepstow. Always like to stop there as having crossed the Severn and left England it feels one is getting somewhere, even if there is still all of Wales to traverse.

Arrived at Stackpole just before midday. Elfa had been there for hours, but found Bernadette Mulvey hobbling on crutches in the car park.

"Whatever have you done to yourself?" I asked with what I hope was the right degree of concerned support.

"Fell off my bike," she said. "Hit a pothole. Bike one way: me the other. Leathers are ruined and I broke a leg."

"Ah, well, if you will do dangerous sports," I said.

"Sports? I was on my way to work."

Good grief. Bernadette must be fifty! Still, confirms my thoughts on motorbikes. Nasty, dangerous things.

"I can get about and the 'car's an automatic," she continued, "but gutted I won't make the walk on Wednesday."

"Oh. Do you know where we're going?"

"The lily ponds and along the beach," she said. "We always go there. Only I can't use these bloody things on sand." She waved her crutches in the air for emphasis like a deranged windmill and the young chap helping unpack her things had to duck smartly or risk losing an eye.

The lily ponds are spectacular this time of year and one really can't expect everyone to miss them on account of Bernadette. I sympathised but agreed there was no solution. Would have offered to help carry her things, but that was already in hand, so I got my bags inside and made myself comfortable. It's the same room as last year so I know what to expect.

Lunch will be called shortly. First chance to meet the Castaways. Must thank Elfa for her journal encouragement at last year's Exmoor Haven as it clearly worked.

Postscriptum: weight this morning fifteen stone, four.

ICELANDERS DO THINGS DIFFERENTLY

Later; Stackpole Retreat Centre

I had forgotten how excellent the food is at Stackpole: proper fish soup for lunch—fresh from the quay at Tenby—with crusty bread and a dry Riesling. Only the one glass allowed as we are straight into the first session this afternoon.

Elfa surprised me by refusing even a sip of wine then surprised me even more.

"I am having a baby," she said, as though its arrival was imminent. She was as slim as ever, so one wouldn't know.

"Gosh. Forgive me. I had no idea you were married."

Elfa gave me a disapproving look.

"There is no man; I vished for child so I am having child. Is it so hard?"

Call me old-fashioned but I do think it is perfectly reasonable to assume a woman expecting a child is married.

"Well," I persevered, sensing that somehow I could only make matters more awkward but determined nonetheless, "there must have *been* a man."

"No *man*," she insisted. "Clinic. How do you say it?"

"A sperm donor?" Bernadette said helpfully.

"Já," Elfa said. "Man in bottle. Bottle in me."

I think something was lost in the translation, but my thoughts were leaping ahead.

"But surely you know his name?" I asked.

"Why? I do not know if it boy or girl."

"I mean the father's name."

"No father," Elfa said. "I vish for child. Not man."

I decided to give up. Elfa is much younger and perhaps Icelanders do things differently, but to grow up not knowing your father beggars belief.

Paid only scant attention to the Castaways. More women than men, as usual. No familiar faces, which is always good as second-timers arrive expecting more than they got the previous time and become agitated if they think they are treading the same ground—wonder what they expect as most of the Castaways will be new to the course? No matter.

Not an issue this week. No obvious 'bards', which is a relief. Usually get one or two who think they're a reincarnation of Taliesin or Llywarch Hen.

Better go. Need to have a word with Elfa before the afternoon session. It will be mostly introductions and admin, but we should get them writing after the break.

RUSSIA

Late afternoon; Stackpole Retreat Centre

Session dragged on a bit. Three hours, even with a break, is too much after a long drive. Fortunately, Elfa was on fine form having only driven from Cardiff Aerodrome. Have to buck up, though, as I have them tomorrow morning for "What is a story?" Brush up later on the course notes for *The Odyssey* and *Don Quixote*. I can probably get away without revisiting Edgar Salvage's *Prometheus*. Students are still only a vague mass at the moment. Two or three are more engaged than the rest but none have obvious talent or eccentricities.

Afterwards I retired to my room for a lie down before dinner, but Bernadette knocked with an invitation.

"Fancy a walk? Gloriously sunny out here. Wander down to the lily ponds? Also, I need to ask you something."

"Actually, I was hoping for a rest. Long drive earlier."

"You can rest when you're dead," she said. "Besides, a walk will invigorate you."

I rather doubted that but seeing Bernie on her crutches made me too ashamed to refuse.

"Is Elfa not about?" I asked.

"She has tutorials. Three of them."

"So soon? We hardly know their names let alone what they're writing."

"And you wouldn't let a poor crippled woman be off by herself now, would you? Besides, like I said, I've a favour to ask so get your shoes on."

"Then as we're walking, you can step outside while I change into something more comfortable."

"I'll be waiting," she said.

Presently I met her in the car park.

"How difficult is it to use those things?" I asked of the crutches.

"Not difficult but bloody annoying," she said. "That's another reason I asked you and not Elfa. She walks too damn fast at the best of times."

The favour-asking was delayed while we started down the path to the lily ponds. I was now looking forward to the walk as the lilies are glorious and their flowering only lasts a few weeks.

"What happened to you at Glastonbury?" Bernie asked.

"What did you hear?"

"Deedee said you fainted. Airlifted off the Tor. Bloody envious about the helicopter. All I got for my leg was a ride in the back of a truck."

"Can't recall anything about the helicopter. Rather out of it. Some sort of ear-infection seems to be the verdict."

I simplified matters as I didn't want a long conversation on something I was rather hazy about.

"Deedee was very supportive afterwards. As was Józef Mazur despite..."

Wasn't sure if Bernie was compos regarding Józef's illness so didn't finish what I was saying.

"Anyway, that wasn't the end of it; C.H. booked me into a health farm at Malvern to give me the once over. Interesting week. Survived it, and been well since."

The path had dropped down to skirt the first of the ponds. I say ponds, but really they are sizeable lakes. Shallow, though, which explains why lilies are so numerous. Like brilliant white crystals on the water.

"Thank you for dragging me out," I said. "It really is very pretty."

"It was Józef I was going to ask you about," Bernie said.

"Ah. Why's that?" I asked, wary not to break Deedee's confidence.

"You don't know?"

"I know some things, but I'm sworn to secrecy."

"Deedee said she told you."

"Ah, yes, I do know. Poor chap. Have you read *Dead Sun*?"

"Three times."

That struck me as excessive.

"Deedee told me when we were at Glastonbury. That was four months ago so I don't know anything more recent. I assume Józef is still with us. Only I would have thought the company would make an announcement."

"You would, wouldn't you? They've not said a thing. Heard all this from Roman."

That would be Roman Bold, our devout Catholic and ex-Foreign Legion (allegedly), thriller writer and sometime co-tutor.

"Józef was a silly old fool and flew back to Moscow to see his son and granddaughter. The son reckons Józef was given reassurances by the Kremlin but as soon as he landed they arrested him. He's under house arrest pending trial for bringing the state into disrepute."

"Good Lord."

"I mean, Christ-on-a-bike; could he do anything to bring those bastards into more disrepute than they already are?"

"It's deplorable."

I had run out of words to describe Józef's circumstances when the conversation took a surreal turn.

"We have to get him out of there," Bernie said.

"What?"

"We have to get him out. Will you help?"

"Help? What are we going to do? Invade Russia?"

"Oh, yeah. That would work," she said bitterly. "You could talk the guards to death while I whisk him away on my fucking crutches. Or maybe our Icelandic goddess 'll fling him over a shoulder and carry him out."

"I don't think Elfa is quite up to that," I said. "I mean, she is expecting."

"Lucky for her. Fuck. Jeez. Sorry."

Bernie stopped walking. She looked ill.

"Not going too fast am I?"

"No. Only these are knackering. Guess I'll have to forget about seeing the sea this evening. Sorry for what I said about Elfa and you, and everything."

"I don't think she'd mind," I said. "I know I didn't."

That wasn't strictly true. I can talk people into a stupor, but one doesn't care to be reminded of it. Bernadette had still not moved.

"She's just too damn gorgeous, don't you think? Too successful, too wonderful, and just too damn nice about it. She wants a child, so she has a child. Just like that."

"Ah."

I remembered that Bernadette had no children. I suppose I never thought about it before, but there must have been reasons. Gerald isn't the most attentive of sons but to not have children at all must be... lonely I suppose. Where is the sense in having no one to pass things on to?

"So..." I said. "You don't want me to invade Russia."

"No. You're no Buonoparte and even he fucked it up. I want you to write a letter to Boris Malinovsky."

"And who is he?"

"Russian foreign minister. It's him we need to convince. You need to do it because he's a huge fan of your boy, Tam MacGregor; so, your opinion will count more than that of a dried up poet or a hack from Italy."

"I wouldn't exactly say Roman is from Italy," I said. "And you're hardly dried up."

"I've not written anything decent in five years," she said. "Well ran dry. But don't mind me. Will you do it?"

"Of course. Not that I really know what to say or the address or anything."

"We can get it to him. You find the right words."

"I think you have too much trust in me. But I'll do my best."

I've written some rum things in my time, but a plea to a Russian foreign minister may be the rummest of them all.

Dinner bell is sounding. Better go.

Bedtime; Stackpole Retreat Centre

Dinner was a quiet affair, though that may have just been me. It's been a day of odd revelations: first Elfa, then Bernie and poor Józef. At least Elfa's is good news, in a way. I mean, happy for her, even if I still think the child will miss having a father in his or her life.

And Józef. Tall order writing a plea to some Russian you've never heard of. Have to learn a bit about him. Fan of MacGregor? It's a connection of sorts. Would a signed copy of *This Iron Race, volume one* help? Sounds like a daft idea, but you never know. Can hardly make things worse. That's not the attitude; Józef needs me to do something better than not make things worse. I suppose he's getting the care he needs. I mean, he must be on some kind of treatment.

And Bernie thinks she's a dried-up has-been. Perhaps she is. It happens to the best of us. Daddy hardly wrote anything in his last year. Mind, he was desperately ill.

One bit of good news. I had settled down to an hour's reading of a few short stories from the Castaways ready for the tutorials tomorrow when someone quietly knocked at my door.

"Who is it?" I called from the desk.

"Elfa." Her voice was quiet; as though she was anxious not to be overheard.

I opened the door to find her kneeling at the keyhole.

"Spying on me?"

"Secrecy," she said. "Need a man. Big strong man. I thought of you."

She grinned impishly and looked ridiculously pretty. Elfa will be one of those women who are radiant during pregnancy. Not like Edith. She barely survived Gerald and swore never again.

"I am neither big nor particularly strong," I said.

"But no one else here and can't ask Castaways: so, you."

"Thank you for the flattery. But hadn't you decided to have nothing to do with men?"

"They have their uses. It's for Bernie. She can't get on vork to beach."

"I know. We went for a little walk this afternoon, but it was too hard for her. Shame as the lilies are lovely."

"But I find answer. Need your help."

"Ah. Big strong man help?"

"Yes. My doctor said no strong lifting."

"Oh. Then of course. One moment."

I returned to the desk, closed my journal, and put on my walking shoes.

"Now. Where are we going?"

"Shush," she protested. "Don't vant Bernie hearing. She angry vith me."

"Hardly," I said. "I mean why would she be angry?"

"Voman can tell. You know she lost bebby ven she vos young?"

I didn't know.

"I shouldn't have been so proud at lunch. Made her jealous. My bad. Ve make up to her."

Elfa led me outside into the yard between the buildings. A security light came on so we could see the way. Moths swiftly gathered round the naked bulb.

"In here," she said.

'Here' was an outbuilding at the end of the row of arts centre rooms. Elfa opened the door. Inside was a black chair with a steel frame. There was a cloth thrown over it and cardboard boxes piled on top.

"Is that what I think it is?" I asked.

"Think so. Got to get it out see if it verks."

"Should be a light switch somewhere," I said and reached round the doorframe.

"Ah. There."

The light was feeble but rather better than before.

"Better close the door so we're not discovered," I said, warming to the task.

Everything was covered in dust and soon I was working in a musty cloud, but none of the boxes were heavy. Once free, I pulled the wheelchair into the centre of the room. It was filthy and needed oiling, but all the wheels turned.

"It verks?" Elfa asked.

"I think it does."

And on that happy note it is time for bed.

11 June; Stackpole Retreat Centre

Grabbing a few minutes after breakfast and before the first session starts with the Castaways. Short lecture on what is a story and then I hope to get them writing after the mid-morning coffee break. Might take a cup in with me, actually. Headache this morning. Think I have an allergy to the dust in that storeroom.

Speaking of which, I have doubts about Elfa's plan. Need to go down to the lily ponds later to be certain. Otherwise, tomorrow's walk could end sooner than we hope. Have to be after the tutorials, but I am free most of the afternoon: Elfa has them for Character Creation and Bernie will be reading from 'Moonspinner Summer.' Still her best work and it's twenty years old. Wonder if she's right about drying up?

Breakfasted on poached duck eggs and Pembroke Kippers. Not as good as an Arbroath Smokie but not bad. Elfa turned her nose up at the eggs and had some kind of cereal mix. No wonder she's so slim: it wouldn't have fed a decent rabbit. Still, she went out of her way to be nice to Bernie and any ill-feeling seems to have gone. Can't go on too long as time's passing and I need to get my books together: Cervantes, Homer, and Edgar Salvage. The Don unchanged, except by death; Odysseus returned to Ithaca and still in his pomp; and poor old Prometheus chained to a rock and yet defiant: heroes all. It's bollocks, of course, but I'm just the messenger. Real heroes are changed by the story; they're not boulders a story washes over but leaves unaltered.

That's rather good. I might sneak it in this morning. A real hero must lose something in the strife. And not just his liver, like Prometheus.

WRITERS

Afternoon; lily ponds, Stackpole Retreat Centre

I was right to have doubts. The wooden walkway is built on pilings and some two feet wide with a single handrail. I suppose the wheelchair might just fit but the slightest mistake and Bernie's in the water.

No need to hurry back just yet. Bench to sit on and it is delightful just here. Hordes of damselflies, like turquoise nymphs dazzling over the water.

The lecture went well, up to a point. Always frustrating when someone in the group knows more about a subject than I do. Didn't even know Edgar Salvage had a fan club; man's been dead fifty years.

Think the chap's name was Donald. Or Ronald. Something like that. Perhaps I should have brushed up on *Prometheus* last night. He insisted the 'fire' Prometheus steals from the gods is a metaphor for divine wisdom. Complete poppycock: why can't things just be as they appear?

Lunch was excellent. If only all Creative Havens were this well run. Grilled Caerphilly cheese—the proper local stuff not the rubbish you get in Budgitts—with fresh tomatoes that have never seen the inside of a refrigerator. Utter bliss. Indulged in two glasses of chilled Pinot Grigio as I'm off duty this afternoon.

Do believe someone is coming. Better put this away.

Postscriptum: to my surprise, the intruder into my postprandial rest was Bernadette Mulvey.

"Not disturbing you?" she asked as she swung into view, literally as she was planting both crutches on the ground and swinging between them like a gibbon.

"Not at all," I said.

"Thought I saw you writing."

"Just my journal; nothing of consequence. I say, you've improved your technique. Only yesterday you could barely manage a hundred yards."

"Elfa gave me lessons. She was a gymnast, wasn't she."

"Olympic level, so someone told me. Injured a wrist and

couldn't compete after that."

"I take back what I said. She may be a goddess, but she's our feckin goddess. Mind if I join you?"

"Be my guest."

Bernie sat and leant her crutches on the bench.

"These are still no use on the beach so I'm out of tomorrow's walk. Shame, as I reckon I could get a good head of speed along that boardwalk."

"Better chance of falling in," I said.

"Worth a try," she said. "What do you reckon of them?"

"The Castaways? Not much. One did his best to upstage me this morning. Knew more about Edgar Salvage than I did and wanted everyone to know it."

"Is that Donald Williamson?"

"Possibly. Haven't got all their names yet."

"He's a decent poet; the rest are too damn quiet. We need to bring them out of themselves."

"Never understood that. It's costing them enough to be here; you'd think they'd make a go of it."

Bernie was quiet for at least a minute, but I could sense her mulling over her reply. That awful feeling I have when I've put my foot in it was creeping over me.

"I sense your disapproval," I said.

"They're nervous as fuck. That's why they're quiet."

"But what are they nervous about? When I arrived at the Glastonbury Haven in February I met a Castaway unpacking three boxes of wine from her car. Three boxes! She must have assumed I was in the group because she said it was the only way she thought she'd cope."

"Nevil, did it ever occur to you that you weren't gonna be a writer? Did you expect to work in a bank, or some manager in an office?"

"Now you mention it, no. Daddy... I mean, my father was a writer and I think he assumed I would be too. Or if not I'd join a college and teach somewhere."

"My da was a builder's mate. Not a builder, the mate of a builder. My ma took in laundry to make ends meet. The idea that I might be a feckin *poet* would've been as mad to them as me sayin' I was gonna fly to the moon."

"And your point?" I said. "I can't help it if I was born into a life of privilege!"

I admit Bernie had touched a nerve. It is the very fact I am my father's son that leaves me guilty of not living up to the opportunity he gave me.

"I didn't *know* I was a writer," she continued. "Nor do these poor feckers. They're quiet because they don't want to find out they're *not* writers, some of them anyways. Others are terrified they'll find out they are, and they'll spend the rest of their lives typing stuff no one will ever read because there's so much crap out there already. It's a mug's game, but ye have to do it. I don't blame ye for your daddy or the feckin silver spoon in your gob, but have some sympathy for those who've neither."

"I see."

"I doubt y'do," Bernadette got to her feet and onto her crutches. "But at least y'could pretend y'do. I'm getting back. Got my second wind. Hey." She bent down and kissed the top of my head.

"You're full of shite, but ye've a good heart. See you."

Bernadette left me in a thoroughly bad mood. The saying 'don't shoot the messenger' says nothing about kicking away their damn crutches. Won't feel so bad telling Elfa about the wheelchair.

After dinner; St Govan's Inn, Bosherston

Despite what I wrote earlier, there is another change of plan. If the wheelchair cannot get to the beach by the lily ponds it must get to the beach another way.

This was Elfa's suggestion; I had merely given the news it was too wide for the walkway and assumed that was the end of it. I was, I admit, still cross with Bernadette, though am somewhat calmer now. That may be an effect of the pint of Old Abbot at my elbow but no matter. Tomorrow lunch-time Elfa and I drive to Broad Haven separately in our motorcars, with the wheelchair in my Rover. I leave the Rover in the car park at the beach and return with Elfa. Bernie can then join us on the walk as far as the beach where we can retrieve the wheelchair and push her across the sand. It all seems complicated, but Elfa is certain it is the right thing to do.

Astonishing the amount of daylight at this time of year. Can't believe I began this journal in February when the nights began before five in the afternoon. It is half past eight and the sun is still shining. Of course, the sea amplifies the light, but even so. Days almost last forever.

Before settling here, I drove down to the beach to refresh my memory. Plenty of parking but a steep drop to the sand. Stayed a while getting some air and watching the surfers. Had the beach café been open I would have sat down with tea and cake, but its shutters were down. So when I bored of watching people enjoying the sea I left and called at the inn.

Williamson sat next to me at dinner and apologised for monopolising class this morning.

"Don't often get a chance to talk about Great Uncle Edgar," he said. "I got carried away."

"Your uncle?"

"Great uncle. On my mother's side. Only real writer in the family. Lot to live up to. Even if he doesn't get the attention nowadays."

"I don't suppose you knew him?" I asked.

"Only when I was very young. I knew his son, though; he was my uncle so hard not to. Dedalus Salvage."

"Ah. What did happen to him? I mean to your uncle."

"He tried to follow in Edgar's footsteps. Even wrote a sequel to Prometheus: *Prometheus Unbound.* Unfortunately, Uncle Dedalus fell, badly: a broken marriage and then drink. He died when I was twelve."

"I'm sorry to hear that. And I'm sorry if I was a little irritable this morning. Not often the tutor is upstaged by the student; unless the student is Mozart, I suppose."

"Not sure I understand," Williamson said.

"Mozart. He upstaged his tutor, Salieri. You must know that."

Williamson shook his head. "Not my scene," he said. "Prefer jazz and swing."

Ah well. So that's what happened to Dedalus Salvage. How dreadfully ordinary. I didn't tell Williamson my connection to his uncle as no point dragging his family laundry through the dirt. Dedalus was a friend of my father's at Oxford. Got involved with Lester Rookwood and, according to Daddy, was never quite right afterwards. I'll ask Williamson tomorrow if Dedalus ever published.

Dinner was excellent again. Seafood and rice; Spanish I think, with those wonderful large prawns. Forget what they're called. But my pint is a little too wet without something to nibble so I need a packet of nuts.

Postscriptum: bumped into Williamson as I was returning to the Retreat Centre. Dedalus did publish but only in a limited edition. Seems his father's old publisher rejected *Prometheus Unbound* as too sordid. Williamson was surprised at my interest, but I said I was always interested in what the sons of famous writers got up to. Not sure he got my meaning. Is he really as good a poet as Bernie claims? Strikes me as a bit slow on the uptake.

Off to bed as tomorrow will be a busy day what with wheelchair duties.

Post-Postscriptum: thought of a reply to Bernadette's jibe about silver spoons. Thing is, if one is born with advantages then people, especially one's parents, jolly well expect you to make the most of them.

12 June; Stackpole Retreat Centre

Day began with devilled Welsh lamb's kidneys and scrambled eggs followed by toast and Welsh honey. Elfa then told the Castaways about this afternoon's inspirational walk down to the beach and along the cliffs to the chapel. The weather, we had been assured, would be excellent and there was the usual advice about comfortable shoes and taking plenty of water.

The Castaways then dispersed back to their rooms to get ready for the first session of the day, which will be led by me.

"Ve have a surprise," Elfa said to Bernie, who had sat patiently listening to Elfa's talk; "Nevil and I sorted it. This vey."

Elfa led Bernie and me into the courtyard where, glinting in the sun, stood the wheelchair.

"Elfa found it and I helped get it out and clean it up a bit," I said. "We think it will do fine across the beach so if you can manage the path by the lake and the boardwalk across the lake you can join us this afternoon."

"I've never used one in my life," Bernie said.

"Easy. Ve take to beach. You sit. Ve push."

"That's my job at lunchtime," I said. "It's all worked out."

"I'm blown away. You two are stars."

"I'd better get ready for the first session," I said. "I'll meet you before lunch," I added to Elfa.

Now, have I everything for this morning? Tackling 'The Fictive Dream,' which is the posh way of saying: keep the bloody reader reading and don't do anything to stop them.

Nice to see Bernie looking so grateful. With any luck I'll get some sort of apology later. Now, off to class.

ICES BY THE SEA

After lunch; Stackpole Retreat Centre

Elfa and I met as agreed before lunch and loaded the wheelchair in my Rover. I then drove down to the beach by way of Bosherston with Elfa following.

Unfortunately, the scene at the beach was much changed from last evening. The café was open and doing good trade and the car park was full—I drove round twice to be sure—and there were even cars parked down on the beach.

Elfa flagged me down before I began a third circuit.

"Surfers," she said.

I hadn't the foggiest what she meant until she pointed to the sea. It was full of people bobbing about or balancing on surfboards.

"Competition," she said. "See. Surfing competition."

There was an advertising board beside the café. Some sort of surfing jamboree and of course everyone had parked where I wanted to park. The only space left was on the beach below us.

"Don't suppose we could wheel it down to the beach and leave it," I said. "It looks rather steep."

"It vill be stolen. Or pushed in sea. They manage."

Four motorcars had indeed made it to the bottom of the track and presumably their owners had every expectation of getting up again.

"I suppose. My Rover is a bit old for this sort of thing."

"Old car; good car," Elfa said. "I come vith you."

Elfa left her hire car in the corner of the car park—it really is a tiny thing—and joined me in the Rover.

"Go. Go. Pronto," she said. "I'm hungry."

We needed to get back before lunch was served at the retreat centre, so I pointed the Rover at the top of the track and inched my way forwards and down. Apart from one or two lurches it coped well, and we soon arrived at the bottom and after a bit of squirming around on the sand we were parked. A sign warned that all cars must be off the beach by high tide but that wasn't until seven this evening and we would be long-gone by then.

"I suppose here will do," I said, relieved to turn off the engine.

"Is good," Elfa agreed. "Race you up."

She set off up the slope—whatever happened to pregnant women taking things easy—while I toiled after her. The day had turned very warm indeed and halfway up I stopped to remove my jacket. My shirt was dripping, and I almost tied a handkerchief around my head like Daddy used to do.

"You too slow," Elfa said unfeelingly when I gained the car park.

"Me too old," I said. "Do you mind? Only, the café. I really need something to drink."

"Ach. If you then I too. Get me ice cream."

I queued while Elfa waited in her car. The lady in the café wanted to know what type of ice-cream and I hadn't a clue and it would take ages signalling across the car park to Elfa. I bought her the most expensive one because she found the wheelchair and I am a gentleman. In a moment of devilry I had rum 'n' raisin.

"Vá! Is big," Elfa said when I joined her.

It had seemed quite modest in the café lady's hand but in Elfa's it was enormous.

"Ve sit here. Eat. Or ice cream everyhere," she said.

So, we sat, like children at the seaside, eating ice-cream and watching people swimming, bobbing, and surfing in the sea below.

"A shame," I said. "Sometimes this beach is so peaceful."

"But people enjoy. Is good. You done that?"

"Surfed? Not likely. Don't even like boats much. I mean boats at sea. All that rolling about. Mind you, I've gone off all boats lately. Haven't told you about my canal adventures."

"Eat ice-cream so ve go."

Lunch was actually less fun than eating ice-cream in Elfa's car. It was fish soup again and the weather is far too hot for soup. Better stop as we are meeting in reception for the walk. I'm feeling rather proud of our little plan. Though I suppose it's more Elfa's than mine, even if I have done most of the work.

Shock

Early evening; Stackpole Retreat Centre

I am sitting up in bed recuperating. Bernadette's idea as she thinks I may have thermal shock. Confess I am not feeling too well, though that's probably from drinking pond water.

It had all gone swimmingly—oh dear: such a ghastly pun and wholly unintended—with Elfa leading and Bernie and I bringing up the rear. I must say Bernie was doing excellently and could easily keep up with everyone on her crutches. I was pushed to keep up with her, though as I reminded myself

I had received my daily exercise climbing back from the beach earlier.

The weather was wonderful.

"Do ve vant to see the lilies, or ve go straight to beach?" Elfa called from the head of the procession. We had reached a fork in the path where a short-cut led across a grassy bank between two of the lily ponds and thence directly to the sea.

"The lilies," Bernie called.

"Are you sure?"

"Yes, go on, go on. I can keep up."

"Nevil, vhat about you?"

"Oh, I'm fine," I said.

To be honest, I wouldn't have minded the shortcut as I had seen the lilies twice now. I think this was Bernie's first time at Stackpole so it would be a shame for her to miss out. Elfa continued beyond the short-cut to take the path around a headland between two arms of water and we were soon at the walkway across the lake.

"This was the part that was too narrow for the wheelchair," I said to Bernie. "Worried we might tip you over the side."

"Looks okay to me," she said. "Yeah, be a help if you took one of my crutches. Then I can hang onto the rail."

"Of course. Ah. Gosh. It's much lighter than I thought."

"You reckon so? Heavy enough after a while. Don't drop it."

"No. Of course not."

It was an awkward thing to carry and ended up holding it against my chest, like a ceremonial mace.

"Off you go," I said and followed Bernie onto the walkway.

With the whole group on it the walkway was shaking a fair bit, but it all went well until about halfway across when someone yelled "Otter!" No idea who it was but the whole group stopped dead with lots of pointing and shouting. I suspect the otter had dived at the first cry but that didn't stop everyone trying to see it.

"There," Bernie said. "I saw it."

I turned and as I did the crutch caught between my legs and knocked me off balance. Oddest thing is, as I fell I had a distinct vision of an ottery face looking up at me.

It was horribly cold, and I was immediately trapped by the thick stems of the water lilies. They seemed to pin my arms and legs down. I struggled to get my head up but only succeeded in raising a massive lily pad, so I thrashed about and sank down again.

Meanwhile there were other noises. Lots of shouting and then a splash followed by more shouting, but much nearer now. Then a hand grabbed my arm and pulled, and I briefly bobbed into the air again and managed a gasp of breath.

"Stand up! Stand up Nevvie. It not deep."

Elfa had hold of my arm and with my head clear of the water I managed to get my legs clear of the lilies and found I could stand upright.

"What happened?" she asked."

"I. Um. The crutch. It. Um."

Fortunately, Bernadette's crutch was hollow and hadn't sunk so we retrieved it. Then Elfa and Williamson helped me onto the walkway.

"Excuse me. Don't feel—oh dear."

I managed to lean over the railing before being ill.

"You svallow vater?" Elfa asked.

"'Fraid..."

I was ill again, and Bernie said I ought to sit down. I did so gladly and slumped against the upright of the railing.

Most of the group had made it to the far side of the walkway and were standing there hopeful of carrying on. Unfortunately, I was in no condition to do so.

"You should help Nevil back to the house," Bernie said. "I can carry on and lead the walk."

"You need vheelchair," Elfa said. "In Nevil's car at beach."

"Wait," I said. "Easy matter. Take my keys. Wheelchair's in the boot. Wait a mo."

I got a hand in my pocket. All I found was a sodden five crown note and a shilling.

"Other pocket," I said.

That was empty.

"Ah, perhaps."

My shirt pocket was also empty. I had left my jacket behind but knew I had the car keys with me. I just knew it.

"They were in my pocket," I said dismally. "I think they fell out. All that thrashing about. Bugger."

Without the wheelchair Bernie stood no chance of crossing the beach. Nor could she help me get back to the centre as frankly I needed someone to lean on as my head was all woozy.

"Dreadfully sorry," I said. "Rather buggered it up."

So here we are. Inspirational walk ruined. Glastonbury all over again. At least I'm not in hospital this time. And I definitely didn't faint. Tripped myself up, that's all. Could have happened...

Oh Lord! The Rover's still on the beach. What time was high tide? Certain I wrote it down. Seven o'clock. Oh hell. Oh, bloody hell!

Evening; St Govan's Inn, Bosherston

This is my headquarters for the evening. Elfa drove me here after I telephoned a garage in Tenby. The mechanic is down on the beach with Elfa trying to get the Rover started. Situation does not look good as there's a "swell running." Mechanic suspects it's ruined the electrics and has radioed for a tow truck. Whether the truck can get down to the beach is another matter.

Only hope they can get it out tonight as the next high tide is eight in the morning.

Feeling rather shivery and probably should have heeded Bernadette's advice.

"You stay here," she said. "Elfa knows what she's doing."

"But she doesn't know my Rover. It's temperamental."

"You had a shock and you swallowed pond water."

All that is true, and it may well be a waste of effort unless by some miracle they get it started and off the beach.

To think I managed a week on a boat without serious mishap—well, one or two mishaps, but nothing major—only to fall in a pond and drown my motorcar on the same day.

Only hope the insurance pays up.

Meanwhile I shall sit here with a glass of brandy and await news from the beach.

Bedtime; Stackpole Retreat Centre

The truck eventually arrived and dragged the Rover from the beach to the car park by the café. After a brief inspection, the truck towed it to a garage in Tenby.

I can drop in after ten in the morning, by which time they will have inspected the damage. Only hope there's no delay repairing it as I'm due home on Friday evening.

Bernadette has just come in.

"I brought you hot milk," she said.

"Very thoughtful," I said.

"Thanks for the wheelchair. It was a great thought."

"You didn't get to use it," I said.

"Doesn't matter. There'll be other times."

"For some," I said. "I may start thinking of retirement."

"You!"

"And why not?" I asked.

Why not indeed.

ALLER

13 June; Glendower Café, Tenby

Elfa has the Castaways this morning, but Bernadette offered to drive me into Tenby in her automatic. Unfortunately, she had to get back to Stackpole as she is reading from 'The Blind Ermine' later during Elfa's session, so we agreed she would drop me at the garage, and I would telephone if I needed a lift back. The plan was to hear the news on the Rover and confirm my R.A.A. insurance covers the repair. Called in here for tea and a slice of bara brith before heading back. Nice to have a sea view but it reminds me that I shan't get to see St Govan's Chapel this year. Can't be helped.

The garage was two large, corrugated iron sheds in shades of tar and rust, but I recognised the tow truck from last night parked in the forecourt and as the roller-shutter door was up I went in. The aroma of oil reminded me of my father as he was forever tinkering with motorcars. There were noises of activity, but I couldn't see anyone.

"Hello? Anyone here? You rescued my motorcar from the beach last night. Hello?"

A chap wheeled himself out on a trolley from beneath a van.

"Ah, Good morning. You said I could call after ten."

"Oh yes. Oh yes. What name was it?"

"Warbrook," I said. "Nevil Warbrook. Is it just you here?"

"There's Sally in the office. Name's Owen. Owner." He indicated everything around him. "Taffy should be here by now, but..." he let the words trail off.

"Taffy?" I said.

"On account of him being Welsh."

"Oh, I see. Only I thought..."

"He's Welsh. I'm from Pembroke, see. We're more English than the English. He's from Taffyland."

"Ah. I see."

I didn't. Not really.

"About my car."

"Washing the salt out of it," he said and led me into the yard behind the garage. The Rover sat in a large puddle fed by three hoses poked into various parts of its anatomy.

"I was hoping it might be drying out," I said.

"Bad news if it was. Need to wash the salt through or the bottom will rust out before Christmas."

"Have you had a chance to see what's what?"

"I have that. Could be worse, could be worse. Most of the electrics need replacing. New battery as this one's a goner. Carpet's ruined, but I expect you guessed that."

"Err. Not really. Never drowned my 'car before."

"We took them out so we can get the salt off the metalwork. That's the worry."

"Rather hoping to have it back for the weekend?"

Mr Owen gave me what I suspect was a pitying look reserved for those ignorant about motorcars.

"On holiday?" he asked.

"Working at the Stackpole Retreat Centre. Back home tomorrow."

"Home?"

"Wiltshire," I said. "England England."

"Insured with the R.A.A. are you?"

"I am. Bit concerned about my cover. Not sure if the tide counts as an Act of God or not."

"You should be all right. You're not the first to get stuck at Broad Haven. Have a word with Sally and she'll do the paperwork for a courtesy car... Oh, bugger."

"Anything wrong?"

"Yes and no, see. We got two out at the moment. Only leaves... Don't mind an older car, do you?"

"Well, my Rover is hardly youthful."

"That's what I thought. And it seems looked after. Only spare car I got is my Aller. More of a hobby car, but I put it through the books as a courtesy car. You'd better take a look at it."

"An Aller?" I said.

"Aller Quatre."

"Gosh. My father had one in eggshell blue. Don't see many about."

"What number was it?"

"I was too young to care. It had dark blue seats."

"Sounds like a Deux," he said.

The Aller was in the corner of the yard and covered by a tarpaulin. It was bright yellow and glowed in the sun.

"It's like new," I said.

"Spent enough on it. Found it in a barn near Bordeaux. We'll get your car done next week. I'll give you a ring and deliver it to you."

"That would be very convenient, thank you. So long as everything is covered."

"Sally can sort you out," he said.

Sally was a plump young woman with a Welsh valley's sing-song voice. Fortunately, my insurance papers had been in the glove locker and survived last night intact. Not only was the damage covered but I was entitled to a courtesy car, so all was in order. Then Mr Owen instructed me in the eccentricities of the Aller before letting me go. I rather fancy he was reluctant to let me have it but eventually I escaped and dropped by here.

Ought to get back as it will be lunch soon.

Later; Stackpole Retreat Centre

First thing I did when I got back to the retreat centre was open the Aller's rear door and sit where I used to sit as a child. Of course, it was nothing like it seemed as a child. Everything was much smaller, and the colours were all wrong and it wasn't the right model of Aller. The only thing exactly as I remembered it was the steering wheel with the flying 'A' in the hub.

As I was getting out I saw Elfa looking at me from the entrance.

"Rover won't be fixed till next week," I said. "Meanwhile I have this to run about in."

"It's tiny, like toy," she said.

"It was a very good car for its day. They raced them at Monte Carlo."

"You can drive it from back," she said. "I think that's vhat you vere doing."

"As it happens, my father had one very much like it when I was a boy. You caught me revisiting my childhood."

"It's sveet," she said. "Like colour."

Lunch was excellent, though the bara brith had taken the edge off my appetite. Afterwards I retired to a tutorial room and read the submitted work before the students entered. Donald Williamson was on my list, and I admit his poetry shows promise, though as he's at least sixty it's arrived late. The other two Castaways were ghastly. I was at my most diplomatic, but there is really nothing useful you can say to someone who has the desire to write but no talent for writing.

Afterwards, I helped Elfa with her talk on character development and plotting which involved a bit of acting, which I always enjoy. Having the group together gave me a chance to apologise for ruining yesterday's walk. That was followed by a suggestion that we try again that evening.

"It's daylight until almost ten so there's plenty of time," a young woman said.

"If enough vish to valk, I can lead them," Elfa said.

It was agreed that Elfa would take them off immediately after dinner and just before the session ended Elfa asked me if I wanted to join them.

"I'd rather not, if I'm honest. Yesterday rather knocked me back."

"You can keep Bernie company," she said.

"That is a good idea. I can drive Bernie to the café by the beach and meet you all there."

It was agreed. Elfa is getting some torches for the group as there's every chance we will call at St Govan's Inn and finish the walk in the dark. Anyone feeling a bit footsore at that point can join Bernie and me in the Aller.

Better get down for dinner.

MORTALITY

Bedtime; Stackpole Retreat Centre

Dinner was rushed as everyone was keen to go walking. It was a shame as the chef had done something interesting with lobster and caramelised tomatoes. Haven't eaten this well on a Creative Haven since Aix-en-Provence and that was March last year. Mind you, next month I'm off to Rocamadour so that will be excellent, assuming it isn't too hot in which case I won't have an appetite for anything.

To this evening.

After seeing everyone off towards the lily ponds, Bernie and I got in the Aller and drove to the quay. The café was closed, and the car park deserted, save for a campervan and a motorcycle. No one seemed in attendance with either.

"I suppose we should get out and admire the view," I said. "Elfa and the others will be a while yet."

"I'm not sitting looking through the glass," Bernie said. "Pass me my crutches."

We got out and leant on the railing at the end of the car park where it overlooked the water. The wind had a cool, damp feel, contrasting with the warmth of the day.

"It's the sea," Bernie said after a moment.

"What is?"

"Why it's so cold. Sea's barely begun to warm up."

"Ah. Yes. Too cold for a swim. As I found out."

"Any aches and shivers since?"

"Few last night. Woke up in the small hours feeling none too good. Told myself I was worrying about my motorcar."

"And were you?"

"Of course. Though I admit it shook me up."

I didn't mention to her that I had seen something in the water as I was falling.

"Did anyone actually see the otter?" I asked.

"Someone must have. I didn't. Mind you, I was distracted by you in the water."

"I imagine I was a sight."

"I thought you'd collapsed or something."

"Actually, I tripped on your crutch. Got it caught between my legs."

Bernie didn't reply. I hadn't intended her to think I was blaming her because I wasn't. It was my foolishness after all.

"That's what comes of being distracted," I said. "Entirely my fault."

It was almost nine and the sun was low over the higher ground to the north-west. I didn't see how I would get to St Govan's chapel this year. Perhaps because it's so isolated and exposed, it feels especially close to God. One feels a prayer there is more likely to be heard. Last day tomorrow and won't want to hang around after the last tutorials. Long way home and I suspect the Aller will be even slower than my Rover. The chapel will be here next year. Assuming I am booked for the Stackpole Haven. Assuming Poseidon Travel haven't closed us down. Assuming I'm still here.

Why was I so maudlin? Beautiful sunset, Bernie for company, onshore breeze and the high tide filling the bay and there was I pondering... mortality, I suppose.

"Is that them?" Bernie asked.

"Hard to tell," I said.

The lower edge of the sun had slipped below the horizon. Shafts of light beamed up and lit the underside of the clouds. The beach below was already in shadow.

"I can see a few torches," Bernie said. "It must be them."

It was. Several of the Castaways wandered down to the waves while the rest picked their way across the soft sand at the top of the beach. Elfa had to call everyone together before leading them up to the car park. All seemed happy with the sunset walk, as they called it.

"How far is the pub?" someone called.

"Two miles," I replied. "About forty minutes walk."

"We've room for three if anyone's footsore," Bernie said.

From my experience sitting in the back earlier I thought Bernie was optimistic.

"Was it worth an evening ramble?" I asked Elfa.

"It vos beautiful. Ve should do it alvays at this time."

"We could really smell the lilies," someone said.

I spent an hour in the shower yesterday trying to get rid of the smell, so did not reciprocate the feeling.

"And we're certain we saw the otter," someone said.

If otter it was, I thought.

Plans to drop into the pub came to nothing. Most wanted to get back before it was dark, and I suppose I can't blame them on a narrow and unfamiliar lane. Bernie suggested getting the centre's minibus and driving everyone, but they elected to walk. I drove Bernie back along with two others who claimed to have blisters. I was in the meeting room when Elfa returned with everyone else. Bernie had gone to bed.

Elfa made a herbal tea and joined me. We were alone.

"Did you see an otter?" I asked.

"Ve saw something. Maybe it vas otter. Who knows?"

"Everyone seemed happy about it."

"It vos good to finish vot vos started."

"That reminds me. You recall at Exmoor last year you suggested I keep a journal."

"Because your father died at the age you are?"

"That's the one. I've got it here. Started it in February; just before my birthday."

I had brought it down with me intending to write up the conclusion to the evening. Ended up talking to Elfa instead and have been writing this in bed.

"Have you learned anything from writing?" she asked.

"Learned? Can't say I've thought of it like that."

"But surely you discover something."

"Well. I was ill at Glastonbury, got well at Malvern—CH paid for a week in a health farm—had a couple of odd encounters in Edenborough, a dreadful week on the canal, and now this week. Oh, and one of my cats died."

"I'm sorry."

I fell silent for a moment. There had been something very odd about poor Boris's demise, but I wasn't about to bore Elfa with it. That reminds me; Angela's supposed to be telephoning next week; wants me to disinter him. What a horrid business.

Then I mentioned to Elfa that I had a position at Belshade College.

"Three days a week in Oxford."

"Oh. So, you give up retreats?"

"I hope not. Nice little earners and usually good fun. I'll fit them in during the holidays and half term."

"Everyone vould miss you," Elfa said.

"It's sweet of you to say. But I'm sure you, Philip, Deedee, Clarissa and Roman would cope. Not that it should come to that."

"Roman is bore. You not bore. Philip vant to fuck me."

"Really?"

"Já. He alveys try it on. You are gentleman."

"Of course," I said.

The reason I don't 'try it on' with Elfa is I'm old enough to be her father. If I were Philip's age... well, best not think about that. After all I couldn't get Madeleine into bed, and she practically threw herself at me. I suppose that might be one thing I have learned from keeping this journal: I am still in love with Edith.

Gosh. I'm yawning my head off and have a long drive tomorrow. Wanted to say more, not least that Elfa also has plans, but will have to leave that until the morning.

14 June; Stackpole Retreat Centre

Breakfast of poached egg on toast with anchovies. Weather is miserable with heavy grey skies and driving rain. Hardly seems like summer. Heard a few comments agreeing it was just as well they had the walk last evening rather than leaving it until today.

Got a few minutes between breakfast and the start of this morning's session and am catching up on yesterday.

Thing is, Elfa will be leaving Creative Havens on maternity leave and there's no guarantee she'll return. At least, she is very unclear whether she will come back, and I suppose I am uncertain whether it will work out for me once I start at Belshade. It's all very raw and silly, but as we were talking I realised I might never see her again and would miss her terribly. I think I must have written that I find her fiction too macabre, but as a person she is so agreeably level-headed and personable. Her finding the wheelchair is only the latest example of her thoughtfulness and practicality. Her news left me glum and out of sorts and I didn't sleep at all well last night. Usually on the last day of a retreat I'm only too happy to say goodbye and go home, but not this time.

Not long before I'm needed in the lecture hall. Elfa and I have two hours to explore genre traits. Then the Castaways have an hour to compose a piece combining two or more genres. Of course, practically every novel worth reading combines two or more genres, but try telling that to an agent and see where it gets you. I digress. Creative Havens aren't keen on the tutors telling the Castaways how damn hard it is selling anything outside the 'rules'.

I'd like to get Elfa some kind of goodbye present but don't see when I'll get the chance before we go our separate ways.

Coffee break; Stackpole Retreat Centre

Left the Castaways scribbling away or tapping their portable typewriters. They have the rest of this morning's session plus whatever time they can get at lunch with the work to be looked at in tutorials this afternoon.

Elfa was going to join me, but she was called away by a telephone call. Instead, I found Bernie with her bags in reception and dropping off her room key. I offered to carry her things to her car.

"Would you? That would be great."

"No trouble. Long drive?"

"Lunden."

"Long enough."

"Thanks for what you said the other night."

"Said? When was that?"

"Not so much what you said. The lily pond on Tuesday. It was more you letting me rant."

"Ah. Something about a silver spoon."

"Yeah. Sorry for that. You got a spoon, and I got a feckin' rock on my back. You reminded me of it."

"Is that good?"

"I'd sooner know it was still there than not. It's time I got back to writing; writing something to be proud of, don't you think?"

"I do. Not that I think you haven't. Lately, I mean."

"Yeah, you do. Everyone does. You'll write that letter for Józef, won't you?"

"Of course. Dear Boris Malinovsky: I haven't forgotten."

"I knew you hadn't."

We had reached her car and I helped stow her bags in the boot and crutches on the back seat.

"Safe journey," I said.

"You too. Shame we never got to that chapel."

"St Govan's," I said. "There's always next year."

"Maybe," she said. "Say goodbye to Elfa for me."

I said I would be happy to and watched her drive away. Returning through reception I caught a glimpse of Elfa on the telephone. She was talking heatedly in Icelandic. Not seen her since and think she's gone to her room. She's probably packing.

It is a shame not to get to the chapel. Almost tempted to delay leaving for a couple of hours and walk along the cliff tops then get a bite to eat at the pub in Bosherston before driving home. Later on the roads will be quieter as well.

After lunch; Stackpole Retreat Centre

I shall get to see the chapel and in company as well. After saying goodbye to Bernie, I finished my coffee and then rejoined the class for the last fifteen minutes. Elfa was there but I knew something was wrong. Her eyes were unusually bright, but not with happiness, and her cheeks were flushed. I supposed it had something to do with the telephone call, and I was right, but learning the cause had to wait until after lunch and I'm scribbling away in the twenty minutes before the start of the last tranche of tutorials.

"Is everything all right?" I asked her when we had a few minutes alone.

"I've asked reception to let me stay another night," she said.

"They agreed?"

"Yes. But..."

She didn't finish speaking. I had put two and two together and for once made four.

"I saw you on the telephone," I said. "You were upset. If you want me to take some extra tutorials this afternoon I'd be happy to."

Actually, I was very unwilling as I dislike tutorials immensely—it's my least favourite aspect of Havens—but what else could I offer?

"No. Is okay. You hear me talking to my sister."

"Is she unwell?"

"No. My mother's in hospital."

"Oh. I'm so sorry. Is it serious?"

"Yes. No. Maybe. It's not the first time. Von't be the last. She drinks too much."

"Look. I'd planned to take a walk down to the sea before leaving, but I can easily delay driving home till tomorrow. Not as if my cats, I mean my cat, singular, will miss me for an extra day. That is if you'd like some company. It will be awfully quiet here this evening."

She smiled but it wasn't her usual broad and impish smile. This was fragile and wary. Whatever she was telling me was only part of what was worrying her.

"You don't have to," she said. "I'll fly to Reykjavík from Cardiff tomorrow. It's only vun night."

"I didn't offer because I thought I had to. If you do pack it in because of the baby it might be the last time I see you and I'd sooner not say goodbye with you unhappy."

Her smile was firmer this time.

"I genuinely had planned to walk to the chapel, and I'd be very happy if you joined me. Afterwards we can have dinner at the pub."

"Thank you. That vould be nice. There's no food here. They tell me at reception."

"Have you told your mother about the baby? I'm sure it would make her happy, even, well, even if you don't know who the father is."

"No. She von't take it vell, and not for vy you say. She hates getting old. Dress too young, act too young. Von't like being grandmamma."

"Oh, dear. I suppose you will have to tell her, eventually."

Elfa shrugged. "Like I have choice?" She mimed being pregnant. "She's a drunk but not blind."

"How awful. Must admit, I always thought Icelanders were sensible people. Not the sort to hang onto their youth and all that sort of thing."

"You think? How many Icelanders do you know?"

"Well, there's you, and what I've seen on television."

"Ha!" She actually laughed. Though it was more a snort of derision, it was enough of a laugh to buoy me up a little. "TV only show the drunks in Reykjavík and the crazies making veird-shit music. Ve're as fucked up as you English, except there's six months darkness in vinter to think about it and six months in summer ven ve can't sleep."

"Surely Iceland isn't that far n..."

"I vas joking," she said. "But you vill stay tonight?"

"Of course. And don't thank me. It will be a pleasure."

Better get going or I'll be late for the tutorials. Just noticed that apart from Williamson I haven't mentioned any of the Castaways all week. Truth is none of them have really stuck in my memory. How awful is that?

Evening; St Govan's Inn, Bosherston

I, Elfa Jonsdottír am helping Nevvie write his journal as my idea he write.

Actually, it was your idea but really I began it when my doctor told me to record my weight and my drinking.

Bad Nevvie

Thank you. When did I get to be Nevvie?

Always I think of you as Nevvie. You mind?

No. It's rather nice. I mean, it's nice from you. If Philip Strutt called me 'Nevvie' I'd be miffed.

Miffed?

Means annoyed.

Ah. Miffed is good word. Don't like Strutt. Told you why. You read his books?

I tried. Couldn't get into it. Like waiting for a train.

Funny, yes. *Paris, Trains* boring. You read mine?

No. But they're not boring. I'm just squeamish.

Ha! Já, I know. Readers want, readers get. This is fun.

More fun when you're a little drunk.

You drunk?

Probably. Think the sea air has left me light-headed. And seeing the Green Ray. Or the Green Road.

Já. Saw too. But not green. In Iceland call sólstafir.

Sol?

Like staffs. Pillars. Pillars of the sun. Holding up sun.

Ah. No. This is different. The Green Road is a reflection off the sea marking the path the soul takes into the next world.

Oh. Did not see that.

Surely you must have.

No, only sólstafir. I think I drive us back to bed if you drunk and seeing things.

That is probably a good idea. I hope tomorrow isn't too awful for you.

Nevvie. Will you stay with me tonight?

I'm certainly not driving home like this.

No. I mean with me.

Oh. Crikey. Are you sure? I mean, I'm flattered. You're very lovely. Always thought so.

Not mean that. Not like what Strutt wants. Just share with me. Don't want to be alone.

Of course. And I swear on my honour as a member of the Boy's Adventure Corps. Haven't forgotten what you said about no men.

Ha, ha, ha. You make me laugh. Nevvie, I'm not a fucking lesbian!

~~I didn't~~ I mean I never thought you were.

We should go. This not drinking and watching you drink drive me crazy.

Now that I understand. Lent was bad enough. Nine whole without a drink doesn't bear thinking about. Do you want to write anything more?

No. We go now.

Elfa

15 June; Stackpole Retreat Centre

Quod non scriptum est non historia est

Green Lane

Late Morning; Evans the Tea, Aberdare

Elfa and I left Stackpole within minutes of each other but Mr Owen's old Aller was no match for her hire car, and she had an aeroplane to catch and could not dilly-dally. Hope all goes well for her. Or at least, I hope her day goes less badly than it might do. Very much hope I shall see her again. Very much indeed.

Mustn't dwell on things. It is what it is. Elfa is having a child and that must come first. I, meanwhile, must resume life at Avebury and I'm taking a detour along the Heads-of-the-Valleys road. Not by choice, for, though it's scenically superior, this road is much slower than the Expressway. However, in Mr Owen's Aller I think it will be far less nerve-wracking. We did fine on the roads near Tenby but once on the Expressway near Llanelli I could barely keep up even in the slow lane and every time a lorry overtook us the Aller skittered about like a frightened kitten. Won't be home until late afternoon at this rate but at least I shall arrive physically and nervously intact.

I don't know the road at all well and Evans the Tea is simply a pit-stop for the lavatories and a cuppa—served in a proper china cup with a saucer and lace doily: it really is like stepping back into my childhood and it's not the first time that's happened in the last few days—and I've scarcely even glanced at the pastries. Not that I am hungry as it's only a few hours since breakfast, which Elfa and I rustled up between us as the staff had the weekend off, but I'm also mindful that Elfa said some kind things about my recent loss of weight, and I will endeavour to continue. Speaking of which, I have an appointment with Dr Saunders on Monday. I hope she also is impressed.

Haven't written anything about last evening. Not *Quod*

non scriptum est non historia est, I don't mean that. But earlier, before Elfa and I arrived at the pub.

Elfa drove down to the end of the road beyond Bosherston and parked in a lay-by. We had a view of the sky, cropped grass, and gorse bushes but Elfa was unimpressed.

"Ve can't see the sea," she protested.

"We shall in a little while. The path drops down to the shore."

In fact, it was barely a walk at all as the road ends close to the chapel, and I suppose at one time that was the road's purpose as it's the only point of interest on this mile of coast. The wind was into our faces, but we were soon walking down the slope towards the cliff edge with the sea spread out like a silver plain below. Dark clouds hung over the horizon lit from right to left by the sun.

Elfa wore a clingy yellow dress with a cotton jacket. There was absolutely no sign she was expecting but though she tried to button it up the jacket wouldn't quite fit across her tummy and bust.

"Is it too cold?"

"It's the vind."

"I thought Icelanders were used to the wind."

"This isn't Iceland," she said cryptically.

"You can borrow my jacket."

"Then you freeze."

"I'll be fine. We'll be out of it soon enough."

Of course, it was bloody freezing—or as freezing as June gets—without my jacket, but we were soon walking down a steep defile in the cliff with the stone chapel ahead and tucked in between the rocks, as though sheltering from the weather.

"Is it still used?" Elfa asked.

"Not likely. It was abandoned centuries ago. Someone's put the roof back, that's all. Antiquities Trust, probably."

But the doors and narrow windows were unrestored and inside it was one empty space from the back of the chapel where we entered to the front overlooking the sea. Once there had been a small quay serving the chapel, but it had been dashed to pieces centuries ago. In the distant past the sea connected, not divided communities.

"Better out of vind," Elfa said. "But loud!"

The noise was the sea. It echoed through the chapel, and one sensed the ground shaking under its onslaught. The tops of the waves caught the sun, turning the white spume a golden yellow, while the front of the waves remained bottle-green in the shadow.

There was a plaque on one wall describing the history of the chapel. I had seen it before, but Elfa stood and read it patiently.

"They lived here?" she said.

"They died here too. Some are buried on the cliffs."

"Look!" Elfa had moved to the window. I leant out to follow her gaze. The sun rode over a bank of cloud. Beneath it, columns of light fanned over the sea. The effect only lasted a moment before the cloud swallowed the sun.

"I try to visit here every time I'm at Stackpole."

"Vhy? It's beautiful, yes, but sad also."

"It feels holy to me. There's a sense that all the prayers are stored up in the stones. I suppose it's a Christian thing."

How else to explain it? I am a Christian, but I admit I find the same sense of holiness on the Downs above Avebury and in the barrow at West Kennet; even at times in the circle at Avebury, though usually it's too crowded to feel anything. God is everywhere, isn't He?

Elfa shivered and I too was mindful it was cold in the chapel. The pub would be warmer, and I was ready to suggest we go when something caught my eye. It was a shift in the colour of the sea. On the horizon below the sun was a point of vivid green, and as the sun emerged below the cloud the point swelled and then lanced towards me bridging the wave tops with a broad swathe of emerald.

It was the Green Road. I had never seen it before but knew it instantly. All that stopped it reaching my feet was a line of rocks at the entrance to the cove below the chapel.

I waved to Elfa, and she also leant out the window to see.

Except she didn't see it. What did she call them...? Sun pillars. Yes. She saw those, but not the Green Road. How odd. Perhaps it needed someone to stand at exactly the right position and she, at a different window, was out by a degree.

Perhaps it was as well. Expectant women are prone to all manner of troubles and the Green Road must bring ill-luck to some.

It was remiss not to have my camera with me.

HOME

Evening; Avebury Trusloe

House was deathly quiet when I arrived home. Molly had left a note saying Tusker was eating well and apologised for the state of the back garden. She thinks some deer got in and made a bit of a mess. I shall check in the morning but fancy it may be another visit from the faeries, or whatever they are. Deer sounds a great deal more likely. Molly left my post on the breakfast table. Only thing of interest is an invite from KJU but don't want to go into that now.

I've let Tusker out for the night—he barely acknowledged me, which as I am away so much is probably fair—and I've been playing Handel on the gramophone. What on earth made me choose his "Water Music"? Only noticed the connection when it was halfway through.

Mr Owen's Aller survived the journey, but it was making a strange noise once past Bristol. Perhaps it dislikes being outside Wales. Will need it on Monday to go to Devizes and may drive to church in the morning, depending on weather.

Bed shortly. Given in to temptation and had a whisky.

Postscriptum: nightcap of malt whisky.

Post-Postscriptum: can't recall what I had last night but it was far too much. Really shouldn't have let Elfa be so generous.

16 June; Red Lion, Avebury

Not much in the refrigerator so called here for lunch: ordered the smoked mackerel with salad, which Dr Saunders should approve off, and washing it down with a half bottle of Pinot Grigio, which she won't. Left Mr Owen's Aller at home as it's a warm day and pleasant walking. Suspect the strange noises it was making yesterday might be the fan belt and intend using it as little as possible between now and whenever Mr Owen collects it. If I didn't have to shop in Devizes tomorrow I would even catch the bus in, but that would really be too inconvenient.

This wine is really agreeable.

Chadwick collared me after Communion—text was the Prodigal Son which made me maudlin as I recalled how long it's been since Gerald was in touch. I still can't speak to him as there's no signal for his portable telephone. There's a thought. I shall try to call him this afternoon. Or evening. What time is it in Sumatra? How does one even find out such a thing? I could ask Edith if she's heard anything new. Need to speak to her anyway as she wants to see where Boris is buried. Which reminds me; Angela Spendlove said she would telephone me once she had made arrangements with her friends, whoever they are. If I am to unbury poor Boris it will have to be after Edith has visited his grave. Otherwise matters will become uncommonly complicated. Speaking of the garden, Molly was right that something has been mucking about in it. Several shrubs are trampled and there are hoof prints in the flower beds. Doesn't look like faeries to me.

Where was I? Ah. Chadwick. He reminded me about Midsummer Eve on Thursday. Said I hadn't forgotten. Sid had a good laugh when I mentioned I would be covering the festivities.

"Turning you into one of 'em," he said. "What'll you be dressed as?"

I admitted I hadn't a clue. "Not as if I have a fancy-dress outfit. I'll just try to blend in best I can."

Sid didn't think I could blend in anywhere, which was harsh. But I could wear my kilt. Hardly pagan but it has a certain stylishness.

More happily KJU have invited me to give a second talk on MacGregor's library. This time at Arbinger, though it's not clear where exactly. The restored rooms I saw last month are far too small, unless it's a very select audience. Modest fee but again they're covering expenses.

It will give me a chance to revisit the new material at the KJU library. Wagner's letters were innocent enough and I can't imagine there was anything of thaumaturgical interest in Lady Helena's accounts book. Perhaps they were just being cautious. Hopefully, Solomon Drake can shed some light on it.

Lunch has arrived.

Postscriptum: half bottle of Pinot Grigio.

Evening; Avebury Trusloe

Good to have my feet back under my writing desk. O'Brien's visit is pencilled into my diary for Friday—must telephone Pea to confirm—and while there are only the last pages to finish it would be wise to go back over the work.

The last few chapters of editing have eased my mind regarding continuing with *Works of the Master* after I complete volume three of *Acts of the Servant*. There has been no repeat of the extraordinarily erotic element I found in the earlier chapters in the volume, though there's far more supernatural material than in the published text. I shall know rather more once I begin work on volume three, but for the moment I am at least open-minded about continuing.

Speaking of my diary, I am indeed free at the end of August and have inked in the dates for my talk at Arbinger. I shall write to them tomorrow and accept the invitation.

Spurred by this morning's sermon on The Prodigal Son I refreshed my memory: Sumatra is seven hours ahead by the sun and so it is presently four in the morning. I shall attempt to telephone Gerald first thing tomorrow and hope he is somewhere civilised with a connection.

Prodigal, or not, it wouldn't take much effort for Gerald to consider his parents' feelings.

Bed shortly. In view of the half-bottle at lunchtime and tomorrow's visit to Dr Saunders I am foregoing my usual nightcap.

PARIS

17 June; Market Street Tearooms, Devizes

The girl who is usually at the till was absent this morning and when I asked the proprietress if she was unwell I was answered with a curt, "And what concern is it of yours?"

I replied that I was only making a polite enquiry as I always thought the girl efficient and friendly.

"She's gone," the woman said.

"Oh dear. I hope without acrimony."

"Without what? Only we speak the King's English in here."

I did not think it worth explaining that 'acrimony' is a perfectly good, English word and replied indirectly.

"Without ill-feeling."

"Depends. She gave me a week's notice. A week! Said she was going to Paris to 'find herself.' I said I already knew where to find her, seven o'clock at my door."

"And she preferred Paris," I said demurely.

The woman glared at me.

"You wouldn't catch me living over there."

I doubt the French would want her. Instead of the girl there was a hollow-cheeked lad with a metal stud in his nose. He, too, I suspect will not be long for the tearoom, but he took my order efficiently and as I sat down by a window I was reminded that I would soon be in Rocamadour and, if all goes well, in Montmorillon interviewing Le Cocq a few weeks after. If it weren't for work and the lack of a decent pint of beer I could happily retire to France.

If you, which is to say my future self, detect a degree of bonhomie in these words then you are correct and while I would not say Dr Saunders and I are wholly *à l'unanimité*, she approved of the new slim-line (I am only using a trace of hyperbole) me. Admittedly, yesterday's half-bottle of Pinot

Grigio caught her eye, and she is convinced I could do more to reduce my drinking, but overall, she was pleased with my progress and believes I shall live to see my next birthday.

"That does not seem terribly reassuring," I said.

To my surprise, she laughed.

"I can't be too encouraging, or you might fall back into old habits."

I admitted it was a possibility.

"But I shall do my best to resist temptation. It has been an eventful few months, but rather encouraging."

Actually, I'm not sure why I said that. Since February there have been endless mishaps and disasters. But I have survived, body and soul intact, so that's something.

"It helps to stay positive," she said. "Your father had a more pessimistic view of life, or is that unfair?"

"No. I mean it isn't unfair at all. He did rather think the world was going to pot. I take more after my mother. Sunny disposition and all that. Have you been looking up my father?"

"It's my son," she said. "His English teacher was so impressed he had the signature of Thomas Warbrook's son in his text book he bought himself a collection of your father's poems. I hoped you might sign it. It's not the sort of thing doctors usually ask their patients, but he would be so proud."

It would have been ignorant to refuse, especially when she had been so encouraging, and she was all smiles after that.

In other news, I may have to buy another pair of trousers as these are a little baggy about the tummy.

Postscriptum: telephoned Gerald earlier but, inevitably, could not get through. I should try writing to him and reminding him his parents would like to hear from him once in a while.

Afternoon; Avebury Trusloe

Just as I was leaving the tearoom I caught a glimpse of that week's Messenger in the rack by the door. *Boat murder: woman, 36, questioned by police,* ran the headline above the now familiar picture of the girl murdered on her father's canal boat.

All the cheerfulness ran out of me and despite the June sunshine I was shivering as I returned to the Aller. They must be questioning the girl's mother. I mean, who else could it be?

I suppose there will be a court case and I'll be called as a witness. Wonder if I should telephone Inspector Donaldson and find out when it might be and what I'll be required to do. Is that even allowable under the law?

Put me in a bad mood all the way home.

Haven't begun to think about tidying the garden. The back is especially bad, and something has been trying to dig up poor Boris. That at least I have addressed and there is now a paving slab over him. Take something a good deal bigger than a deer to remove it. Though what a deer wants with a dead cat is anyone's guess. Assuming it *was* a deer.

It is all just the latest in a peculiar few months: my illness at Glastonbury; Nica having some sort of premonition at Malvern—not that one can put any faith in such things; bad dreams at Uffington, not to mention that nasty snow squall by the barrow; the horrid business with Merrowey in Edenborough, and that canary; and now the poor girl looking for her father.

Horrid, horrid, horrid.

And I nearly forgot falling into the pond. I really did see something peculiar in the water as I fell.

Shiver ran up my spine just then. I'll set aside time for a prayer tonight.

Meanwhile, I must complete the restoration of *This Iron Race, volume two.* I'm on the last chapter.

Postscriptum: feel much better after praying. Foregoing my usual nightcap. Trousers definitely too baggy, as is my shirt. Will have to rummage in the wardrobe to see if there's anything old that fits me again. Don't particularly want the expense of new things.

Paris, part deux

18 June; Avebury Trusloe

Barely finished my breakfast this morning when the telephone rang. It was Pea.

"Oh, hello, Pea. Any news on this French actor chappie?"

"News!" Pea squeaked. "Dessie's been expecting you to call all last week."

"Sorry, couldn't. I was in Wales."

There was a muffled noise on the line.

"Passing you to Dessie," Pea said. "Don't make him cross."

The line clicked as she transferred me.

"Wales! What the hell do you mean in Wales?"

"I was in Wales. Creative Havens. You know, they employ me."

"And do they not have 'phones in Taffyland?"

"I didn't think it was urgent. Besides, I was busy, earning a living."

"I know what they pay you and it's scarcely a living."

"It's regular. What can I do for *my* agent?"

"You can start by confirming you can fly out to see Le Cocq on the twenty-ninth. Given he has agreed to meet you in Paris and the flight's booked I suggest you say 'yes'."

"Paris?"

"He's filming there. It will be convenient for him. And for you. Damn sight easier to get to than darkest France."

At least he didn't say Frogland.

"Twenty-ninth. Twenty-ninth," I said as I thumbed my diary.

"Yes, the twenty-ninth. Have you any idea how much I do not want to send Dommy on this job?"

"Dommy? I thought—."

"Think again. Bloody good writer and I need some peace from my daughter. Can you do it or not?"

"Yes. Yes I am free that day and for a few days after."

"Good. Handing you back to Pea. Pea!"

I shielded my ear as he bellowed for Pea to reconnect her telephone. After a moment she came on the line.

"Nevil?"

"Still here. Have I made him happy? Rather hard to tell."

"He's not shouting and saying he'll have to let me go, so thank you."

"Good. So, I'm flying to Paris on the twenty-ninth. No idea who with or what time."

"It's with Aeronautique. Five o'clock flight from Staines. I'll post the tickets."

"Sensible hour for a change. Should arrive just in time for dinner. Assume I'll get expenses."

"Breakfast," she said. "And you can pay for that. Expenses are only for lunch with Le Cocq."

"You mean I have to be at Staines for five in the morning?"

"Sooner. Flight's at five. Need to check in an hour before. You're meeting him for lunch on the set where he's filming. Fly back Monday night. I'll send all the details."

"So even though Le Cocq is loaded Dessie is not splashing it about. Has it occurred to him that a degree of largesse impresses the client?"

"We haven't got any largesse."

"So, somehow I'm supposed to impress Le Cocq despite sleep deprivation. Not your fault, Pea. I await your letter, with interest."

I put the telephone down and stared blankly at the wall for half a minute. It really was too early in the day for that sort of thing. Five o'clock at Staines Aérodrome. I'll have to leave here at two in the morning at the latest and hope I can get some sleep after seeing Le Cocq for lunch; though snoozing in Paris is such a waste of the trip. Assuming I have somewhere to snooze as there's no mention of a hotel. Have to wait for Pea's communiqué.

Wonder what the film is? Just because it's Paris doesn't mean the film is set in Paris. Modern studios can conjure up anything.

Back to the real world. PCC meeting this evening so have to knuckle down to editing. Shame as it's warm and sunny.

LEMONADE

Later; Red Lion, Avebury

At one point this evening I felt like I was drowning. Desperately hot in the village hall after a day of full sun and the air was turgid. Flies buzzed incessantly and one trapped in a light fitting repeatedly crashed against the glass shade.

"Have you been in the pub?" asked Sid.

"I have not. Why, do I seem as though I have?"

"You look a bit queer."

"If you must know, I'm feeling rather faint."

"It's too hot in here," Prudence said.

"I love this weather," Lucy contradicted. She had arrived wearing a sleeveless dress and not much else. Hardly the image of the vicar's wife that Avebury is used to.

I excused myself and went outside for some air.

That blasted white van had turned up again outside the Henge Shop: the one with the hobgoblin on it. Why do people have to celebrate horrid things? The jackdaws were roosting and making an appalling din. I blew my nose and wondered if I was coming down with a summer cold. Head was all fuggy.

Looking on the bright side, Ruby Miller, our new Captain of the Tower, may prove something of a Godsend, and I do not write that lightly. She is as passionate about the bells as Fred ever was, but with far more vigour and a waspish way with words. She had done her homework as well and when Terry Woodson relayed the quotes he's had for the repair work—which are admittedly higher than we hoped—she put up a robust defence, citing a number of church and charitable bodies we can call on for funding. Ruby was instantly put in charge of raising funds for the work and will, I think, do very well.

Lucy reported that Peter has now spoken to the New Barn School about the proposed sharing of crèche facilities.

"They were very helpful; Peter explained our concerns, but they reassured him religious and spiritual issues are presented sensitively and without bias."

Prudence harrumphed.

"Surely, Peter understands that as Christians we expect children who come to church to become Christians, or at least that we should encourage them to become Christians."

"Of course," Lucy said. "Peter did not see anything at the New Barn School that might discourage their Christian growth. In fact, he was impressed with their holistic approach to faith and spirituality."

Sid, who may not know what holistic means, asked her to explain.

"They approach matters of faith without prejudice," Lucy explained. "He saw nothing wrong with their teaching of Christ and the church."

"But it's not that they don't teach about Christ," Prudence complained. "It's that they teach other beliefs as well. It will only confuse the children."

"If all you have are lemons, make lemonade," Terry said cryptically.

It was Prue's turn to not understand.

"I think what Terry means is that children are going to discover one way or another that the Bible and the church are not the only ways of living," Paul Durdle said.

"Just so," Terry agreed. "And I don't think we should pretend otherwise. If Peter thinks the New Barn School do a good job then that's good enough for me. Not all of us were raised in the church, but we came to it eventually and of our own accord. And I might say those who come late are often more sincere in their belief."

I wasn't clear whether Terry was referring to the congregation as a whole or just PCC members. I suppose either might be true, yours truly excepted.

Peter had recommended that we pass a motion to join our crèche with that at the New Barn School after consulting the families involved. Prue voted against, Paul abstained, but everyone else agreed, and the motion was carried.

We then turned to the solstice.

"We had hoped to keep the church open all night," Paul

said. "But we just haven't found the volunteers to keep a safe number of people on duty."

"There's no surprise," said Sid.

"Perhaps not, but it is disappointing," Paul said. "The church will be locked at seven and will open again at nine on Midsummer morning."

"I asked at The Red Lion and they're putting up security fencing, same as last year," Terry said.

"Makes the village look like it's under siege," Molly said. "It's awful."

"But don't worry," I said. "I'll be reporting from the Front Line."

"You will take care, won't you?" Molly said.

"I fully intend to blend in," I said. "No reason for anyone to notice me."

"That I should like to see," Sid said.

"You can, if you wish to." Paul said. "I'm sure Nevil won't mind some company."

"Indeed," I agreed. "But I can't see Sid blending in at all."

"I shall be safe at home," Sid said.

"The Linden Tree is full that night," Molly said. "But they seem awfully nice."

"Wicket people?" Sid asked.

"No. A film crew. All the way from Berlin."

"What do they want to see this for?"

"You must admit it can get exotic," Terry said. "It's not what you see anywhere else."

"No reason to make a fuss over it."

"We should be proud Avebury is so famous," Paul said.

Sid muttered something about happy obscurity, but I didn't catch his reply and decided it wasn't worth recording.

The meeting broke up soon after. The atmosphere was soporific, and I struggled not to yawn for the last hour. Popped in here for a pint as I had a raging thirst. Possibly more evidence of a pending cold. No sign of the security fencing just yet.

Still daylight. Sky is dark blue with hardly any clouds.

Rather beautiful, actually. Won't delay long as I don't fancy walking home in the twilight. Call me superstitious but it has been a queer month.

19 June; Avebury Trusloe

No mishaps on the walk back from the village last night. The meadow besides the Kennet was beautifully quiet and pleasantly cool after the heat of the village hall. Stood there filling my lungs for several minutes. The river was barely a murmur, and the loudest noise were the grasshoppers rasping away in the long grass. A bat swooped low, then spun about almost in its own length and fluttered away. Everything seemed at peace under a sky of lapis lazuli that only the brightest stars could pierce. Couldn't be certain but I think the brightest star of all was Venus, the evening star.

Just put the breakfast things away and am enjoying my second cup of tea. Tusker is sleeping peacefully. Odd how little he misses his brother. Still waiting to hear from Angela. There must be something I could write about letting sleeping cats lie, but of course Boris isn't sleeping. And may not even be dead.

'After I've seen O'Brien.' That is something of a mantra these last few days. Finish off editing volume two of *This Iron Race* and hand over the manuscript. Weight off me when it's done.

Can't avoid Mr Owen turning up, though. Delivering my Rover today and collecting his Aller. I shall miss it, though it's not practical for today's traffic. At least I'll have my motorcar back for this evening; taking Sid and Bert to Fyfield for dominoes. We usually do well against The Crooked Man but so much comes down to the luck of the bones, as Bert says.

Must stop and get on with the edits on *volume two.*

TIDE

Afternoon; Avebury Trusloe

Mr Owen telephoned about ten and said he was on his way.

He hoped to be with me by two. Knowing I had a good four hours while he was on the road I settled down to work and got a good deal done before breaking for lunch. I then prevaricated, thinking if I sat down again I was bound to be disturbed before I got back into the swing, but as it happened, Mr Owen didn't arrive until three, having been held up by roadworks.

He was rather keener to see I had taken care of the Aller than to show me the work on the Rover, but eventually he opened the bonnet.

"Replaced half the wiring, see. Most of the bulbs and new battery. Drained the fuel and flushed the tank. Time you might want to leave the windows open, let the damp out. Got in the upholstery, so it did."

"Thank you. That is excellent. Any trouble on the road?"

"None. It's a good motor."

"Good. Driving some friends out later. Dominoes match against a local pub. Glad to know it can be relied on."

"After dark, is it?"

"Leaving at eight. Journey back will be dark of course. Why do you ask?"

"Well, shouldn't be a trouble. On a short journey."

"The lights work, don't they?"

"To be sure, to be sure."

"Then what?"

"Only, they say..."

"If there is some fault I think I should know."

"Oh, it's not the car. The car's no trouble. It's the tide, see. Doesn't like to give up what it's claimed."

"Give up what?"

"Anything, so it is. But as I say, keep the windows open till the last of the damp's gone and if you're only going a few miles and with friends it should be well and good."

I offered Mr Owen a cup of tea, but he declined.

"Be home late enough as it is," he said.

"You might want to give the expressway a miss. Got a bit lively when a lorry overtook, which happened rather often.

I took the road through Aberdare."

"Long way round," he said. "No. She and I will be well. I know her ways and she knows mine."

I couldn't recall if Mr Owen has a wife but if he has I suspect she vies with the Aller for his affection. After exchanging keys and signing paperwork, he left for Wales, and I opened all the Rover's windows to let it air.

Occurs to me that Wiltshire is landlocked so the tide will have a job reclaiming anything this evening.

Nota bene; yes, that is meant to be facetious.

Later; Avebury Trusloe

Drove to Fyfield this evening with all the windows down. Sid and Bert complained, of course—especially Bert as he was in the back—but I explained that I needed to air the car thoroughly.

"Chap from the garage said it would take a while to properly dry out, so I need to keep it aired."

"What's that?" Bert asked.

I repeated, but louder so he could hear over the wind.

"You've got air enough back 'ere," he said.

"What I don't understand is why you left it on the beach in the first place," Sid said.

"It was only supposed to be for a few hours. They reckoned after my accident I had a bit of thermal shock. Coldness of the water, you see."

"We'll have the same, shouldn't wonder," Sid replied.

Bert leant forward so his mouth was at my ear.

"Won't have to do this on way back, will us?"

"I'll put the heater on."

"Fat lot of difference that'll make," he replied.

It had been a warm afternoon, so I don't know why they made a fuss. You would think they would be grateful given it is always me taking them to an away match. But no, it's either complaints about my driving or the condition of my motorcar. I shall have to put my foot down one night and insist they find their own way.

We arrived at The Crooked Man in good time and got our drinks in while we waited for the home team to arrive. Frank Gemmell, Jimmy O'Neil, and Jimmy's wife, Diane, are a good decade younger than us and frightfully keen. Nothing has been proven, but there's a rumour that Diane once played dominoes in the County League, and she has not lost her competitiveness.

I drew her in the first match and was soon struggling with a mediocre hand. I simply could not stop her scoring and only replied with miserable twos and threes. The match went to The Crooked Man and then we all swapped opponents. Bert had also lost his game while Sid had won convincingly against Jimmy.

In the end, Diane won all her games while The Red Lion managed three wins apiece and lost six-three.

One bit of news. Frank Gemmell was head of Fabric and Works at All Saints when they repaired the bell frame and is happy to come to the next PCC meeting and offer his experience.

The six of us sat around afterwards over a pint—Merit in my case as I was driving—but while Sid and Bert were in no hurry to leave, Jimmy and Diane were eager to get away as they had family staying. We all left at about half ten with the sky still carrying a faint trace of daylight in the west.

With a clear sky, the temperature had dropped, and the grass was dew-covered.

"Did y'see the way that Diane waves her bosoms at a man?" Sid protested.

"Puts him off his game," Bert said. "That husband of hers is in the wise of it."

"Not like she bothers to hide what she's doing."

"Or hide what she's doing it with."

"Now, now. We lost fair and square," I said.

"Trust you not to notice," Sid said.

"I did not say I hadn't. None of us had a good night."

"Reckon Jimmy will," Sid said.

The car was damp and cold, and the interior light was

dimmer than usual. Mr Owen mentioned replacing most of the wiring and some of the bulbs, but I can't imagine the tide reached the roof of the car.

"Get the heater on, will ye," Bert said. "Not that I'll feel it in the back."

"Swap with Sid," I said.

"No fear," Sid said. "Besides, I have to get out first."

The Rover has four doors so I'm not sure of his logic.

We hadn't gone far before the road dipped into a hollow near West Overton where it runs parallel with the river. At once the dashboard lights dimmed and the headlights failed completely. I could barely see the road and braked hard.

"Must be the battery," I said, but the words came out strange, as though from far away. Bert I think had dozed off and began making strange gargling noises. Sid coughed and had a hand at his throat. Whatever affected the lights did not trouble the engine and in another minute we climbed out of the hollow and the headlights flickered back on.

Bert woke up with a ferocious coughing fit. Sid heaved a great breath.

"Ruddy hell! What was that?"

"Probably the battery," I said.

"Battery my arse. I was bloody drowning!" Sid said.

Bert sneezed and said something about smelling salts.

"I think we must have hit a patch of mist," I said.

"Mist? Is that what you reckon?" Sid said. "Queerest mist I ever knew."

The lights held steady the rest of the way home and after dropping Sid in Beckhampton and Bert outside St James's, I drove home in silence. Took a risk and left the car on the driveway with the front windows wound down an inch to let the air in. Should be all right for one night.

Bloodline

20 June; Avebury Trusloe

The incompetence of some people defies belief. I came

downstairs this morning to find two letters on the doormat. One is from Desmond, or more exactly from Pea, with my airline ticket from Lunden, Staines, to Paris, Aéro du Nord, and instructions for meeting Jean-Maxim. All seems in order. The other was post-marked Rouen in France and had me perplexed until I opened it and found Rouen was the headquarters of the company doing the ancestry tests for Beavers. Somehow the blasted fools have got it all wrong or confused me with another chap for they declare I am thoroughly Scottish; being half Lowland Scot—presumably, Mummy's side of things—and half Highland Gael!

All nonsense, of course; Daddy could hardly have been more English if warm beer had run in his veins. Tempted to ignore the damn thing—it was free, after all—but if the idiots are giving out inaccurate information then I think they should be told before some poor chap questions whether he is the true father of his child and whole families are ruined.

The information pack from Bloodline came with a warning: *please use with discretion results from test as unforeseen circumstances regarding parentage and family history may occur.*

Discretion be damned: I know my own father, thank you very much! There's a telephone number to call but I'm not calling Rouen. Instead, I was straight on the telephone to Beavers. Seemed to be an age before someone picked up their end.

"Beavers of Edenborough speaking. How may I help?"

"Ah. Excellent." It was a pleasure to hear the Edenborough accent again. "I purchased a kilt and sporran from you a few weeks ago and wish to make a complaint."

"Certainly, sir. Can you tell me the name of the clan?"

"MacStrangie."

"Bear with me. I have you. Is that Mr Warbrook?"

"Indeed. You remember me."

"Your name is the only one listed against the MacStrangie tartan, sir. What is the problem?"

"This ancestry thingy. Spit in a pot, what have you."

"Beg pardon, sir?"

"That test. I gave you a sample of saliva and I have just received the results."

"The free offer. I understand. The testing is by a company called Bloodline. You might be better talking to them. They're in..."

"Rouen. Yes. I can read. Problem is they claim I am Scottish."

There was an extended pause.

"Sir, the vast majority of our clients are only too happy to learn they are Scottish. Being Scottish is a condition of wearing a registered tartan."

"Yes, yes. I appreciate that."

"I'm unconvinced you do, sir."

I appeared to be talking to an idiot.

"You might notice, given that you have my name in front of you, that Warbrook is not a Scottish name. I am a proud Scot on my mother's side, but my father was most definitely English. From Kent, which is about as far from Scotland as you can get and still be in England. The test claims that I am ninety-five percent Scots with a trace of Icelandic or Norwegian."

"Bloodline are very reliable, sir. You have read the warning that came with the results of the test?"

"I have indeed, and I assure you it does not apply in this case. I suggest they have confused my sample with that of someone who is even now dismayed to learn he is half-English."

I hoped the idea of one of their own receiving such appalling news might galvanise the fellow to do something. I was disappointed.

"Unfortunately, sir. If there has been any confusion you will have to resolve it with Bloodline. We are simply not able to deal with your complaint."

"Well, I think it is jolly unreasonable of you. Who knows what degree of upset you and this blasted company are causing. This sort of things leads to families breaking up. Questions of paternity. All sorts of accusations."

"But we only offer it as a reward for buying with us. Is the kilt satisfactory?"

"Perfectly so."

"Then I suggest you contact Bloodline. If there are no other matters I think you must allow me to see to a customer."

There was a hurried goodbye and he hung-up before I could say anything more. Hardly the way I expect to be treated after giving them three-hundred crowns of business.

It's hellishly expensive telephoning Rouen, and besides, I couldn't face going through it all again in French—Heaven only knows the translation for *genetic modelling*—so have put it off until after I have handed O'Brien the manuscript of *volume two*. Hopefully, all that's left is minor edits and presentation, but I must be at my desk, not blathering on the telephone. Need to think carefully about what I want to say vis-à-vis continuing work on *Works of the Master*, once volume three is out of the way. Still very much undecided. Either way, I do not need any distractions.

Nota bene; ran out of milk at breakfast. Will have to go to the village shop later.

MILK

Later; Avebury Trusloe

At least the revellers have a glorious day: sunshine since ten this morning and in the calm air the tribal drumming reaches even as far as Avebury Trusloe. Tonight's forecast is calm and mild, which is comforting as it is notoriously draughty in a kilt.

Wandered up to the village about lunchtime. Don't want to do a proper shop until Saturday, after O'Brien has paid his call. The editing is done but I find myself coming back to the text to confirm one or two details and always make some amendment. Happened three times today and each time I spotted something new. Bad habit, really. Going in to Devizes would cost me the best part of a day and I am reluctant to give up so much time this close to O'Brien's visit.

Of course, today was not the best day to call at the village shop, what with a few thousand hungry and thirsty revellers descending on us. Fortunately, the young are determined to be healthy and while the bottles of reduced milk had flown off the shelves the proper stuff with a head of cream had barely been touched and having taken a copy of the Devizes Messenger from the stand I joined the queue, which was about four deep.

Forward motion was slow, but I do not think the staff could be blamed. Doris at the till had to field a number of requests, though I couldn't quite tell what was passed in conversation. The chap in front of me had long curly hair tied in a ponytail and his calves were bare. There was also the distinct smell of something more exotic than tobacco, but I could not tell which body it emanated from.

I had determined to say nothing other than what politeness requires, but I was not allowed to keep my silence.

"Milk is murder," said a female voice behind me.

I did not respond as I didn't think it concerned me.

Then the speaker advanced to my side and pointed at the milk.

"That's murder."

My interrogator, if that's the right word, could have been barely out of school: she was tall and thin with her hair braided so tightly it pulled at the sides of her head and gave her face the appearance of having been stretched over the bone, rather like the photographs one sees of Egyptian mummies. Her eyes were blue and unblinking.

"I don't understand. I appreciate reduced milk is healthier, but this is hardly *murderous*, no matter how much the doctors..."

"For the cows," she said. "Not you. I don't care about you! They suck their breasts dry until the nipples bleed. Then they get disease and die."

"Ah, but this is local milk, and the cows are well cared for. Besides, they are called udders."

"What others?"

"Beg pardon?"

"Who are the others?"

"I haven't the faintest idea what you mean. Cows have udders. You have breasts. I mean women have breasts. Not cows."

"What about my breasts?"

Her arms had clasped over her bust, which was virtually non-existent.

"I am not referring to *your* breasts. I mean cows do not have breasts. They have udders. And teats. Women have nipples."

"Stop talking about my breasts!"

She had gone red, and her eyes were hard as opals.

"I am pointing out that cow and female, I mean human. I mean women's anatomy is different from cows. And I'm not talking about your breasts! It's not as if you have any to speak of."

"Monster!"

I admit I had been hasty. Despite her slenderness the girl possessed a mean right hand and it whipped across my face, knocking my spectacles across the shop counter. Then she stormed out having thrown aside whatever she was about to buy. A tall gangling man-child took her place. I don't think he approved of me but as I was rather lost without my spectacles I couldn't read his expression. After a moment, Doris retrieved my spectacles from the bag of bird seed where they had landed and passed them to me.

"Sorry about that, Doris. Bit of a misunderstanding. Just a pint and the Messenger, please."

"Sure you don't want two pints?" Doris asked and waggled her substantial bosom from side to side.

"Thank you, but no. This will suffice. I was hoping for a pack of flapjacks."

"Sold out. Reckon they're good for those with the munchies."

"Is that what they call them?"

Normally I'd have called at The Red Lion, but it was

surrounded by security fencing and two uniformed men guarded the entrance. It was as appealing as a border checkpoint, so I retraced my steps down the High Street and past the church.

Apart from Doris I didn't see one local person. They must be in hiding or gone away for the day. Don't blame them. It struck me after my scene with the young lady—for the benefit of my future self I am being sarcastic—that the mating rituals of these people must be extraordinary. I can hardly tell one sex from the other and assume they have a similar trouble. Though I believe that is less important than it once was and young people are inclined to be... what's the word they use in the newspapers (not the Messenger, I mean the national dailies) Flexy, something. That's it: Flexisexy, or flexibly-sexual. Reminds me of Lester Rookwood, who probably invented flexisexy, though he took it even further. Not even the cows would be safe from him.

Hopefully, he's now leaving Mummy in peace. Or do I mean that vice versa? Calling on her next week so shall find out.

After lunch I laid out my kilt, sporran, and white woollen socks on the bed upstairs. I have my usual jacket and a clean white shirt to finish it off. No hat though, which is disappointing. But what sort of hat? There's a poser. Can't be a bonnet as everyone will assume it's a beret and think you're French or a student plotting to overthrow capitalism. Though I suppose that's unlikely in a kilt as it's not the most practical garment. Had to use my sporran to conceal a notebook as I don't have a pocket large enough. Pen goes in my breast pocket and the camera will have to hang round my neck. Had bought a pork pie at the village shop intending to nibble on it tonight should I get hungry but I've nowhere to put it. All I've room for is an apple which just fits in my jacket pocket.

Anyway, that's all for later. Meantime I will distract myself with some Mahler. Hopefully, it will drown out the drumming.

MIDSUMMER'S EVE

Early evening; Avebury Trusloe

This, I believe, is the best I can do. I am ready in all but temperament. My camera is loaded with film and my shoes polished to an inch of their life. Ah. Must check my torch. Haven't used it since the vigil at Easter.

Had a bit of a moment in front of the bedroom mirror. I was adjusting my socks to reveal just the right amount of shinbone when a silly ditty came into my head, and I hummed into the glass like an idiot: "Hey diddly dee; A Scotsman's life for me; Hey diddly doo; a gay lassie I shall woo." I must have learned that at Mummy's knee and I'm quite certain I haven't sung it since I was seven, but suddenly the whole rotten thing with Bloodline seemed terribly disrespectful of poor Daddy and I began to blub. Utterly absurd and indecent for a man of my age, or any age after long trousers and hair on his chest.

Like the child I had been, when the urge came to pray it overtook me with fervour and I hitched up the kilt and dropped to my knees at the bedside.

"Dear Daddy, who art in Heaven. Please forgive my foolish ways. Of course, you are my father, English as toast and marmalade, and I want for no other."

I think I went on a bit beyond that, but I can't remember half of it and doubt I want to write it down if I did.

Afterwards I got up, dried my eyes, and brushed the carpet fluff off my knees before going downstairs. Wanted to make a cup of tea to steady myself but if I do I'll need the lavatory in half an hour, and I expect the queues will be horrendous. Too much of a strain on the bladder, so I had merely a sip of water from the tap.

Of course, one knows that far from being the garb of the ancient Scots, tartan is based on a few fragments of medieval cloth and a lot of wishful thinking and the MacStrangies, being lowlanders, never wore tartan of any description. What I am wearing is a nineteenth century invention of the Gaelic Society. Even the MacGregor tartan, allegedly rediscovered by Sir Tamburlaine himself, is certainly no older than the 1770s and may have been his own creation.

Even so, my kilt has more authenticity than anything else I will see this evening and I shall wear it with pride.

Sunset isn't far off and though it's all nonsense I thought I'd see it go down on Midsummer Eve. Gives a nice circularity to the night. Still undecided whether I'll stay out until dawn or sneak away after midnight for a few hours sleep before returning before sunrise. Rather depends how I fare.

Stand with me Daddy, tonight and always.